The

Retaking *of*

America

Richard B. Marrin

FIRESIDE FICTION
2008

FIRESIDE FICTION
AN IMPRINT OF HERITAGE BOOKS, INC.

Books, CDs, and more—Worldwide

For our listing of thousands of titles see our website
at
www.HeritageBooks.com

Published 2008 by
HERITAGE BOOKS, INC.
Publishing Division
100 Railroad Ave. #104
Westminster, Maryland 21157

International Standard Book Numbers
Paperbound: 978-0-7884-3378-8
Clothbound: 978-0-7884-7251-0

July 4, 2028

My Son:

Humor me one last time. When you read this, I will be dead and buried.

I need very much to tell someone the true story about the *coup* attempt on the Government back in 2008. I was involved. I know what happened. You can count on the fingers of one hand the people, still living, who can say that.

You must see it in perspective to understand. It had been building since the mid 1990's. Names differed, platforms changed but the underlying nature of the two sides in conflict remained the same.

On one side was the established, conservative citizens, hard working and proud of their American heritage. In the Congressional elections of 1994, they had approved "a Contract with America". It blamed runaway social programs like welfare and affirmative action on the Government. Washington had "usurped personal responsibility from families" and that had to end. No more free lunch. The Government was going out of the business of helping those who wouldn't help themselves. Multi-culturalism and pampered ethnic and cultural diversities threatened the American Way of Life. The doors of immigration were to be shut and kept closed. The nation needed to get back to its Western European, Greco/Roman, Judaic/Christian origin and the values prized by that culture. "If you do not fit in, then change or go back to where you came from" was the message, loud and clear.

On the other side of the conflict was a coalition of liberals who believed that compassion for the disadvantaged and tolerance to all views were more desirable characteristics for the community, than riches and self-righteousness. America was no longer a male dominated homogenous society. It was multi cultured. Diversity and immigration were to be applauded and encouraged. It was what built the Nation and still makes it work. Personal liberty in all things had to be preserved against attacks from the Government and the Christian Right.

These caring people – ordinary citizens who included intellectuals, feminists, gays, environmentalists, civil libertarians and anti war activists, banded together with minorities marching under other banners. United, they cursed the established and championed the rights of the disadvantaged and those discriminated against because they were not like the established folks.

The battle between the two ideologies was witnessed every four years in the Presidential elections. The coalition of the caring could not get the Office in 2000. The Presidential election that year, with the charges of a stolen election and a compliant conservative Supreme Court, enraged the caring people. The "us" against "them" sentiment smoldered the next four years .An intense effort to unseat the President in 2004 failed. Control of the White House and Congress fell to pro conservative forces.

Characterize the poles however you like – *Conservatives* against *Liberals, Right* against the *Left, Socialists* against *Capitalists, Rich* against the *Poor, Haves* against *Have Nots, Red States* against the *Green*, the enmity between them intensified. Battle was joined in the newspapers, on TV, at the ballot boxes, in the halls of Congress and, before the courts on dozens of issues: Should the United States be a Christian country any longer, a question which included abortion, gay marriages even the Pledge of Allegiance? Should taxes be increased and the affluent made to share their wealth with those in need? Should judicial appointments be quizzed as to how they would rule? Was the Media biased with a liberal agenda? Was it to be believed? Was the Mid East war legitimate or a pretense for an oil grab? Did the threat of terrorism justify becoming a police state? America was divided more in 2004 than any time since the Civil War.

Enter an ancient foe to ignite the tinderbox. The explosion that resulted led to the beginning of the New Order of the 21st

Century. How this was allowed to occur is important for Americans to know. Remember, I was there. The story is in the enclosed manuscript. It is not to be published, at least not in the traditional sense. No one else has seen it and, as will soon be obvious, you too must be very careful with it. If it were in the wrong hands, it would mean your life and those of my grand children.

Affectionately always

Your Father

Washington, D.C.

June 15, 2005

Senator Francis X. Moriarity, a tall, spare, gray haired man with a likable look of scholarly rectitude about him, was speaking with his aide, an attentive fellow half his age.

"The Battle of Monmouth Court House was fought on the outskirts of the town of Freehold. That's in central Jersey, you know, about 50 miles south of New York City, a little farther north of Philadelphia. It's a perfect, location" he went on. "Both cities have plenty of hotel space and we will need it. People will be coming from all over the U.S. and Europe too. It's about three or four hours from D.C. by car, an easy ride for the Senate and House members. Whoever would have guessed the attention this is getting?"

His aide shook his head as if in disbelief. He knew the Senator was asking a rhetorical question and that more was coming. He was not to be disappointed.

"But, I couldn't be happier about it" the Senator continued." Just imagine. Groups of all sorts want in on the act. This morning, a fellow named Joseph Brant, a Mohawk chief from Canada, called to say his people also want to be represented at the re-enactment."

The aide's reaction was real this time. Like many of his age, American history had only been a subject in class, not an obsession as it was with the Senator. "Indians fought in the American Revolution?"

He had asked the right person. In fact, it was the Senator's familiarity with the subject matter, together with his reputation for bipartisanship objectivity that had gotten him appointed as Chairman of the newly created Joint Senate and House Committee on the Renewal of American Values. It was to attempt to redefine Americanism, part of the effort to heal the growing rift in the 2004 election between the winners of the election and the minorities who feared practical disenfranchisement as the new Administration began to legislate its "mandate". The Committee's

4

task was to put back the "sizzle" in Americanism that all could identify with and support. Senator Moriarity believed that to understand America, a citizen had to know its history, especially the Colonial Period, those crucial years where American philosophy and values had been forged. The rights and duties of citizens come from the Revolution.

Answering his aide, the Senator took the chance to lecture: "Yes, actually, there were a number of Indians at the Battle of Monmouth. They were from Massachusetts. Native Americans were active elsewhere in the war but usually not on the American side. The Cherokee attacked the outlying white settlements in the Carolinas. There also were horrible massacres on the New Jersey frontier, in Pennsylvania and New York. Fact is that fellow I just mentioned, Joseph Brant, is the namesake of one of the worst, also a Mohawk chief. Undoubtedly, this Brant is kin to him. Check that out. That would be a nice touch. Burying the hatchet, so to speak." He chuckled at his own witticism.

Moriarity knew a lot about the Battle of Monmouth. Fought on June 28, 1778, it was the longest battle of the Revolution. Many considered it the turning point of the war for the Americans. The British army was marching across New Jersey en route from Philadelphia to New York City. General George Washington, his troops rested and now better trained, took the opportunity to attack the long British line of march. The battle was a draw. The Americans might well have routed the enemy, but an American general, Charles Lee, who was to engage the enemy first, fled the battlefield with his troops following him. Nevertheless, despite Lee's conduct, the day turned into a magnificent display of American bravery, a moral victory for the cause of Liberty.

The Battle of Monmouth raised General Washington even higher in the eyes of the patriots. Overrun by Lee's panicked, retreating troops, an heroic Washington, in the space of just a few moments, cursed down Lee, relieved him of his command, turned the soldiers around and personally led them and his own troops into the teeth of the pursuing British and Hessian troops.

At day's end, the Americans had stood their own against the cream of the British troops and fought them to a standstill. The

British declined to resume the fight the next day. Instead, in the dark of night, they retreated to the Jersey coast where they boarded transports back to the main camp at New York City.

Someone – no one remembers who --urged the Committee to use, among its tools, media to get its message across to a public accustomed to be entertained. The re-enactment of that battle might be a striking way of demonstrating to the American people the sacrifices that their ancestors had endured to achieve the rights that so many took for granted in modern times. Maybe, it would help to bring everyone together. That's why Moriarity's Joint Committee had been given overall charge of the event. Most of the battleground had been preserved as a park – nearly, two thousand acres. There was room for a good crowd of dignitaries and citizens to attend. It would also be televised around the world .The timing was good as well. The re-enactment was planned to take place just a few days before the 4th of July in the year 2008.

The re-enactment of the Battle of Monmouth had been conceived as a minor pageant with education its prime aim. But, to everyone's surprise, the idea caught on domestically and abroad. The Queen of England herself had telephoned the President and, without the usual hesitancy and obliqueness inherent in diplomacy, asked outright whether Britain would be invited to participate in the re-enactment. After all, she reminded him, Britain had been at the first one. The President, of course, immediately proffered an invitation to Her Highness, which she as promptly accepted. Later, a more official request to the same effect was received from Unified Germany on behalf of the many soldiers from the former independent German states of Hesse-Casel, Brunswick, Boos-Waldeck and Hanover, who had also fought and died that June day in 1778 in the wheat and corn fields near Monmouth Court House. A trio of Senators brought a request from the several African-American groups reminding the President of the role they had played in the history of America and asking how they could participate in the re-enactment. There were nearly a thousand black soldiers among the Continental soldiers at the Battle of Monmouth. Women's groups, citing to the role of the legendary Molly Pitcher who had taken over manning a cannon when her husband fell in the battle, demanded their equal opportunity to remind the American public of the contribution of women to American freedom. Now, the Chief of the Mohawk Indians!

Maybe, thought Senator Moriarity, the citizens were beginning to appreciate history, the process that would transform the children and grandchildren of newcomers into Americans, just as it always had. That was the answer. Make those who come to America into Americans, not make America a multi cultural bazaar.

"The more, the merrier!" the Senator said, seemingly to no one in particular.

*J*AMES RIVINGTON, BOOKSELLER, PRINTER and STATIONER, in New York, proposes to publish a weekly newspaper, every Thursday, differing materially in its plan from most others extant. He has been honored by encouragement from the first personages in this country and now begs leave to solicit the public patronage in behalf of RIVINGTON'S NEW YORK GAZETTEER, OR THE CONNECTICUT, NEW JERSEY, HUDSON'S RIVER AND QUEBEC WEEKLY ADVERTISER.

He will communicate the most important events, domestic and foreign. The mercantile interests in arrivals, departures and prices current, home and abroad, will be very vigilantly attended to. The state of learning shall be constantly reported. The best modern essays, and every laudable production from Helicon inserted. The new inventions in arts and sciences, mechanics and manufacturing, agriculture and natural history, together with a regular journal on the proceedings of the parliament and the speeches, which are frequently characteristic of the orator, in and out of administration, shall be constantly inserted. A review of new books will be included, with extracts from every deserving performance; each crafty attempt with cozening title, from the garrets of GRUB street, shall be proscribed. In short, every particular that may contribute to the improvement, information and entertainment of the public shall be constantly conveyed through the channel of the NEW YORK GAZETTEER.

From *The Pennsylvania Gazette*, February 24, 1773.

Monmouth Court House,
New Jersey
June 28, 1778

The lad could not have been more than 14 years of age. He had a fresh complexion with reddish brown hair and quick piercing hazel eyes. Well set and sturdy looking, he weighed almost 150 pounds and already stood a full five and a half foot tall – a remarkable accomplishment in a land torn by war, where nourishment was scarce. He had that look of one who could endure and even inch ahead in times of want. A slightly aquiline nose, protecting a firm mouth and steady chin, gave his face the appearance of a greater age than it was.

Despite their prisoner's youth, the Continental soldiers holding the boy prisoner were taking no chances. A soldier each held one of his arms, with two of their fellows and a sergeant standing by, if needed. The boy did not struggle. With his captors, he watched in awe at the scene unfolding before them. The commanding figure of General Washington himself – there was no mistaking who it was – was bending over the body of a wounded enemy soldier. They heard him ask the soldier the nature of his wound, but could not make out the man's response. The General nodded and commended the man for his gallant behavior, assuring him that he should want for nothing that his camp could furnish him. Then, he walked off in the direction of the boy and his guard.

"What have we here?" Washington asked.

The Sergeant answered, "General Clinton's servant boy, Your Excellency. He got separated from him. Colonel Dayton thought that you might like to question him." Washington did not answer. Out of the corner of his eye, he had seen an American soldier, a Valley Forge veteran, who thinking the wounded British soldier was dead, had come up to strip him of his valuable boots. The General took several steps in their direction and bid the soldier begone. Then, he ordered one of the soldiers, who was guarding the servant boy to stand sentry over the wounded prisoner instead, until he was carried to the field hospital to have his wounds dressed.

9

He returned his gaze to the boy: "Yes, I would like to examine him. Bring him to that farmhouse over there." As he pointed, he asked another soldier: "Please ask Colonel Dayton, if he would join us." As the boy and his attendants marched off in one direction and the messenger raced off in the other, the tall Virginia planter, on whose shoulders, history was to show, lay his country's fortunes, trod wearily by himself toward the farmhouse. The sun was not too long from setting, but the temperature still was in the upper 90's. His thoughts were on Lee. He had relieved him of his command almost a dozen hours earlier at the battle's start. The man was a coward. His panic had prevented the Americans from a victory they had deserved and needed badly.

Washington was an opportunist. His army was small, ill supplied and just beginning to be trained. Someone had described them as a force in which every man was his own company commander, if not his own colonel. It was true, they were an independent lot, but they knew what they wanted and would fight for it. They were not conscripts, but volunteers who had come forward to risk their lives to secure for themselves and their children those difficult to describe rights to liberty and independence. These were foreign words in a world where one was a master, a servant or a slave, but not a citizen.

As he walked to the farmhouse that was serving as his field headquarters, the General thought about the last three years of the war for independence and how this intangible concept of liberty had provided his troops with the strength and courage to go on in what appeared to many to be an attempt at suicide. It was a miracle and General Washington thought he could trace its birth to Christmas Eve, 1776. The date added to its awe. He had Tom Paine read a passage from his just written *Crisis* to his fellow soldiers.

> *These are the times that try men's souls.*
> *The summer soldier and the sunshine*
> *patriot will, in this crisis, shrink from*
> *the service of his country, but he that*
> *stands it now deserves the love and*
> *thanks of man and woman.*

Their courage led to the victories at Trenton and Princeton, erased the shame of his being chased out of New York City and across New Jersey and restored confidence among the troops in the Cause of Independence.

Since losing New York, Washington was determined not to risk his army in a major engagement. He abandoned the traditional European battle style in which the two armies met head to head, and fought like a prizefighter, throwing a quick punch and retreating. Washington though General Greene said it right: "We fight, get beat, rise and fight again."

For eighteen months, this strategy kept the British off their feet but it could not protect Philadelphia from an attack by sea. The British sailed up the Delaware captured the city but not before the Continental Congress could escape to the countryside. But, now the British were giving up Philadelphia and trying to march back across to New Jersey to New York City.

Washington smiled to himself as he recalled the loss of Philadelphia. It had turned out to be a blessing in disguise. America considered itself a land protected by the Almighty and it certainly seemed that He had been on their side, since that Christmas Eve, 1776. Howe's orders had not been to capture Philadelphia. An affair of the heart, Washington knew, had prompted that. Rather, he had been ordered to sail up the Hudson River from New York and to join General Burgoyne, who was marching south along the river from Canada. Together, they were to control the Hudson River, which would effectively cut the New England colonies and New York City from the rest of the rebellious provinces. By sending his forces to Philadelphia instead, Howe had doomed the plan as well as he had General Burgoyne. The undermanned Burgoyne's defeat at Saratoga, had given the French the confidence to join the war on America's side, a tremendous diplomatic victory engineered by Benjamin Franklin. Washington might have lost Philadelphia, but he knew it was a cheap cost for an alliance with France. The Lord, indeed, worked in mysterious ways.

Washington knew, although he expressed it to no one, that this new country was not likely to survive unless he took advantage of every opportunity and today had been an important

11

one missed. He could have matched the victories at Trenton and Princeton today. "Damn that Lee." Washington thought as he approached his field headquarters at Monmouth.

The smoke from several farmhouses that the British had put ablaze when they fell back was all about and their flames added to the heat of the evening. The residents of two of the homes and some helpful troops were trying to extinguish the fires that were consuming them. No one bothered to rush in and save the valuables. The British had already looted them. The General went to a door guarded by two soldiers, who immediately came to attention. The door was opened from within by a third sentinel. When Washington entered, a fourth man, the sergeant, said:

"We have put the lad in the parlor, Your Excellency."

Washington entered the room that once had been the pride of the lady of the house, now bare except for some furniture broken by the British and left behind. The boy and the three guards straightened up. Washington asked:

"Who are you, son?"

The boy responded: "Harmon Hays, Mr. Washington."

The soldiers saw Washington's face tighten. It was well known that, earlier in the war, Washington had returned, unopened, a peace proposal from the British because it had been addressed to Mr. Washington, not General Washington. He correctly recognized it as being a slap in the face then and knew the boy had repeated it in the same vein.

"You are a soldier?" Washington asked.

The boy replied: "No, I am this country born, but not a rebel. I am loyal to my Sovereign."

Washington did not miss the surly glare that accompanied the remark. He turned to the three soldiers who had witnessed this insubordination, and, with a grim look, instructed them: "Leave us." When the soldiers hesitated, Washington added: "He is but a boy who must be spoken to and taught some manners."

When the door closed, Washington approached young Hays. Shook his head, once or twice from side to side, as if sadly, and muttered "Master Hays, Master Hays." Then, he took the boy by the arm and pulled him unresisting to the middle of the room, as far from the door and the windows and as private as they could be. Then, for the first time, Washington's face softened and he shook the lad's hand with an obvious sincerity. "It is good to see you, Harmon. Well fed at Sir Henry's table, I see." The boy grinned back. "Yes, General, we do dine well, better than do your soldiers or you, I'd wager."

"Quickly, tell me what you have found out." For several minutes, the boy spoke without stop, Washington listening intently. Clinton's orders were to leave Philadelphia and to consolidate his forces in New York. That was why Howe had been removed as Commander in chief and Clinton appointed in his place. He was to return to the original plan to try to control, with part of his force, the Hudson River, thereby cutting the colonies in two like "you would do a snake." Clinton was to send other troops and his fleet to the Caribbean. Since France had entered the war, Britain rightfully feared that France's blow for American freedom would be to liberate for herself the valuable islands. Clinton also planned to send a force to the south. He thought the loyalists were strongest there. Suddenly, there was a knock on the door and Washington pushed the boy back to where they had been.

"Come in" he called. The door opened and Colonel Elias Dayton, followed by a guard, entered. He had a bandage on one hand and his face and uniform showed the rigors of the battle and the heat. Dayton was an able soldier whom the General relied upon greatly. From nearby Elizabeth Town, they had shared the same horribly cold summer the winter of 1777 at Morris town and last year's losses at Brandywine and Germantown.

"Colonel. I want you to try to get something out of this guttersnipe. You can take him away before I strike the insolent cur. But first, I want a word with you alone." He signaled the guard to remove the boy. The General's and the boy's eyes met once and, as the sergeant was to tell his messmates that night, "if looks could kill, they would have both been struck dead that night on the spot."

Alone with Dayton, Washington said, "Colonel, arrange for the boy to escape. First, have some of his hair burned off. I want Clinton to take him back so he must looked damaged. The lad is good, though. He will fool them." Dayton nodded knowingly and told the Commander. "Our scouts report that the British look as if they will march tonight. Should we attack again or pursue?" Washington shook his head "no." "The men are tired and we missed our chance. Lee is to be court martialed." He said no more. Colonel Dayton saluted, turned on his heel and left to execute his orders.

Washington walked to the windows and looked over the fields of wheat and oats of the plantations now in flames. Washington, the Spymaster. It was through his spy John Honeyman that he had learned of the Hessian strength at Trenton and it had been Honeyman, under personal instructions from the General himself, who had told the Hessians the false information about Washington's retiring for the winter that lulled them to sleep that fateful Christmas Eve. Some thought that Howe's affair of the heart that distracted him from his orders had been a stratagem of Washington's. Harmon Hays' information was every bit as important. An opportunity had been missed on the battlefield today but valuable intelligence learned on the British plans. If it were true, then Washington could adjust his thin forces accordingly. He needed every edge, every opportunity to accomplish the impossible.

Later that evening, Washington re-read the report he had just written to General Benedict Arnold, who had been assigned as military commander of Philadelphia, for him to deliver to the Continental Congress:

Fields near Monmouth Courthouse, June 28, 1778.

I have the honor to inform you that, at about seven o'clock yesterday this morning, both armies advanced on each other. About twelve, they met on the grounds near Monmouth Courthouse, where an action commenced. We forced the enemy from the field and encamped on the ground. They took a strong post in our front, secured on both flanks by morasses and thick woods, where they remain. I cannot at this time go into a detail of matters. When opportunity permits, I shall take the liberty of transmitting to Congress a more particular account of the day.

G. Washington

Giving the report to an aide to be delivered, after a hard night's ride, to the Congress in Philadelphia the next morning, Washington lay down. He had just turned 46 years of age. From his own inheritances and his wife's properties, he was one of the wealthiest men in America. His plantation in Virginia, at Mount Vernon, was a haven for body and soul for which he longed. What was he doing here in a ravaged farmhouse on a battlefield, where his life was as much at risk from a musket ball as it would be from a noose were he captured or the cause lost? For what did he risk all of this? Liberty? The right of men to be left alone, not to be bullied, to be allowed to govern themselves and live with the consequences of it? He had been active in the movement from the beginning, even before it began calling for independence. A member of the House of Burgess in Virginia he had been selected, virtually unanimously, by the Continental Congress to command the Continental forces in the conflict erupting that moment in Boston. Two and a half years later, the country's chances, he admitted to himself, had improved slightly. Today could have been a big step, had it not been for Lee, damn him. But the American soldiers had held their own and it was the British who were withdrawing at this moment under the cover of night. No matter. From the lad Hays, he has learned their plans. They were going to sit in New York and Washington determined to keep them pinned there and then starve them out. All in all it had not been such a bad day. Maybe, they were a little closer to independence.

As he drifted off to sleep, Washington's mind continued to work on the puzzle. How had it started? How had it progressed so far that Englishman was fighting Englishman, neighbor against neighbor, kin against kin?

British House of Commons

London, England

April 15, 1775

At five o'clock, the order of the day was moved for, for the third reading of the bill to restrain the trade and commerce of the Colonies and Provinces under certain conditions and limitations, and being read a third time, the question was put 'that the bill do pass' that produced a debate that continued within a few minutes of 8 o'clock, when, the question, being put, the House divided Yeas 192, Noes 46.

Mr. Hartley opposed the principle of the bill as beyond measure cruel and oppressive and observed with great concern that no power was vested anywhere to suspend the operation of the bill, or abate its rigor, in case America were willing to agree to certain temporary stipulations, till the claims of one country and the rights of the other could be fully ascertained and solidly established.

Lord North replied shortly, that it did not seem to him necessary that such a power should be vested in the King and Council, that the operation of the bill would cease, nay, the bill itself would exist or not exist at the option of the Americas, for if they had a mind to seek the friendship and protection of Great Britain, they would comply with the conditions of the bill.

Mr. Alderman Sawbridge spoke very strongly against the bill, observing as it originated in manifest injustice, so it inflicted a punishment to the last degree cruel and oppressive. He added that he hoped America would never tamely acquiesce to be being dragooned and compelled to terms as unjust as the power which dictated them was obnoxious to the natural rights of mankind in general and distinctive of those they were entitled to as freemen and British subjects.

Mr. Alderman Bull adopted the ideas of his worthy friend and dwelt very pathetically on the certain ruin that the present measures must inevitably be productive of, by their operation on our trade and manufactories. Though the rights were on our side, it would be folly to enforce it, but when it was evident to every impartial man that our claims were founded on principles diametrically opposite to those of the Constitution and to the established municipal rights and privileges of our colonies, it was at once uniting folly and wickedness in the extreme.

Buckingham House, London

December 1775

George William Frederick had ascended the throne of England in 1760, upon the death of his grandfather. History had a cruel fate ahead for him. King at 22, George III, would later lose the American colonies, suffer bouts of insanity due to the same rare genetic disease shared by many of his royal cousins throughout Europe, and spend his last ten years on earth blind, deaf and mad. With sufferings as those, longevity was not a blessing, but another curse. George III was England's longest living male monarch.

But, in December of 1775, not yet 40 years of age, the decline had not begun, while on the near horizon. George was still very much in command of himself and of England. Power was such a fragile thing. The Hanover line had come to England only sixty years before from the Electorate of Hanover in central north Germany, distant Protestant descendants of the predominantly Catholic Stuart heirs who would otherwise have taken the Crown. A distant stranger who did not speak English and who had never bothered to learn it was still preferable to a Catholic.

Gathered around him at Buckingham house were a handful of advisors. Reports had arrived from across the Atlantic Ocean that a number of American colonists – no one was sure how many – were in armed insurrection. It had begun in April in the Province of Massachusetts. Over a thousand British soldiers had been killed before the rest of them, and all residents loyal to the Crown, had to flee for their lives from Boston to Halifax, Nova Scotia. And Massachusetts was apparently not alone in the revolt. Supplies and men had come from other provinces to help in the rebellion. But there was no knowing yet how widespread the insurrection was.

Now seated at the slightly elevated head of a monstrous mahogany table, George III waited a moment to address those seated about him. At his coronation fifteen years before, Britain unquestionably had been the greatest empire since Rome. But, the possibility of not being able to disperse the mob and quell the insurrection in America could put it all in jeopardy. Yes, indeed, power is fragile. Order had to be maintained. A false step and ancient enemies, Catholic France and Spain, were ready to renew hostilities. The Empire could fall to the Catholic Stuarts who waited gleefully in the wings. Remember Guy Fawkes and his Jesuit priests who had tried to kill the King, his heir and Parliament in one great explosion in the beginning of the 1600's. The enemy was all about .This was a very serious thing that was happening in America.

The King cleared his throat and spoke: "You all know that the rebellion in America is spreading and will require my – and Parliament's – attention. I, for one, am not sorry that the line of conduct now seems chalked out. I know I am doing my duty and have no reason to retract. I wish nothing but good for England and her people. These rebels in Massachusetts must be punished and order and the proper balance restored. What say each of you?"

Lord North, seated closest to the King at his right. He was first to answer, as was his privilege given the seat he enjoyed: "I am satisfied, your Highness, that one active campaign, one smart action, and burning two or three of their towns will set everything aright." He had no reason to say more. North had been Prime Minister since 1770. It had been at his urging at both at King's elbow and before the House of Commons, that the Crown and Parliament had not backed down to the upstart Americans, now the cause of the crisis.

The Earl of Sandwich, head of the Admiralty, chimed in. "Aye, once the rebels have felt a smart blow or two they will submit quickly enough. They are raw, undisciplined, cowardly men. Indeed, I wish, Your Highness, that, instead of forty or fifty thousand of these *brave* fellows, the rebels produce in the field at least two hundred thousand; the more, the better and the easier will be the conquest. If they do not run away first, the Royal Navy will starve them to death." The Earl was almost 60 years old, during fifty of which, he had been an earl. He was a perfect example of how England of the time was a much corrupt place. Money purchased position and seats in Parliament, which then made a great deal more money for their owners. If one desired to maintain that revenue, then he complied with the requests of the King and his senior Ministers. Venal, corrupt and dissolute since his youth, all the Earl of Sandwich wanted to do was to get back to the gaming tables as soon as he could. He wondered why His Majesty had even wanted to see his Ministers about this. The reaction was obvious. One subdues a riot and punishes by execution its leaders. Mobs have always been handled in that fashion.

Lord Dartmouth, the Secretary of State for the American colonies, who, had the truth been known, did not favor the King's course of conduct but who nevertheless treasured his third seat at the Council Table, had a suggestion to make: "Sire, is not some reconciliation possible? Are we sending our soldiers to conquer the Americans or should our troops merely help assist the good Americans to subdue the bad ones? I understand that more than half the population – maybe many more than half – remains loyal to Your Highness and that many of the others are well intentioned, uneducated people with bad leaders. Are not the Howe brothers' orders to re-establish peace and our heretofore pleasant relationship? After all, the colonists are English men, our kin."

Lord North coughed a message to George and the King said nothing as he pondered the motivation in Dartmouth's repeating something that had been raised by a few in Parliament. It solidified the King's thinking in one respect. He would have Dartmouth removed from his council of advisors and replaced by Lord Germain as Secretary of State for the Americas. For the moment, however, he would answer Dartmouth. The possibility of reconciliation had been on the tips of many tongues.

"Were the American colonies to depart at will, why not the West Indies? Why not Ireland? The empire must be kept together or else it will perish. This island of Britain, reduced to itself, would be a very poor island indeed. If I must slay my own brother, I would do so to preserve England."

The lowest ranking of the King's advisors, at least judging by his second seat on the King's left hand, was also the most realistic. Lord Pitt, Earl of Chatham, was almost 70 years old, feeble and sometimes disoriented. He was known as the Great Commoner and, for three decades, had been George II's greatest advisor. George III was periodically attracted to Pitt for advice.

More often than not, George, not caring for the advice he received, banished him for a while from the inner circle. Now, he wanted to hear from him, even though he knew his views would not be favorable.

"Your Highness, you know that I have, without exception, disapproved of Lord North's repressive and coercive measures against the American colonists. They have been pushed to the position they have taken. You know also, Your Highness, that I, like the philosopher John Locke believe Parliament's taxes are contrary to the colonists' rights as Englishmen, that is, unless they are permitted a voice in Parliament. In the Magna Carta of 1215, the Monarch agreed to take no man's property without his consent. Pure and simple, taxes are money and money is property. Without being represented in the House of Commons, they simply have not given their consent." George III said nothing. Pitt sensed he had gone as far that way as he had dared.

"But, in this regard, I am only repeating what I have said before. There is another issue that should be touched upon. Since I was a soldier only briefly, I have sought the advice of several old military men who served under your grandfather in the conflicts with France and Spain, before Your highness ascended the throne and welcomed the era of peace we have had since. These old warriors ask me the same question that reasonable men ask before going to war "Can we win it? As veterans of many campaigns, Your Highness, they see many difficulties in going to war here.

The colonies are 3,000 miles away, a three-month voyage against the wind. Every soldier, every weapon, every horse, every musket ball, every article of clothing, food – everything – must be shipped there from here. So far, one in ten of our ships and troops has been lost on the crossing alone.

That to me, Your Worship, is the first difficulty, getting there. The second is at arrival. America is a vast country. Our soldiers have not been able to get more than a few miles inland before they are slaughtered from behind trees and rocks. The colonists all have rifles and spent – and saved – their lives learning how to kill with those weapons. Those, whose wisdom and experience I sought, believe America is unconquerable. The size of the country, the inhabitants familiarity with it and their access and precision at using firearms would make victory very questionable."

King George's face reddened with anger. He was prone to fits and one looked as if it were coming on. There was silence for well over two minutes. Finally, the King said quietly, but firmly to Pitt. "You may be correct, my Lord. America may be already lost for the present. But, England shall never abandon her rights to it. We are an island. We must have the Americas and the other parts of the empire we have discovered and fought so long to maintain. This I swear. The House of Hanover will never relinquish England's claim to America."

Congress of the Province of New Jersey

Burlington, New Jersey

June 17, 1776

An Address to the Inhabitants of New Jersey

Countrymen and Friends

This Province has been requested by the Continental Congress to send, without delay, from their Militia, Three Thousand Three Hundred Men to New York in consequence of authentic information that the grand attack of our common enemy this summer, which will probably prove the decisive campaign, is to be upon that city and that their force might be expected there in a few days. Your representatives in this Congress, with all the dispatch in their power, and with the utmost unanimity, prepared an ordinance for raising the number called for, as equally from the different parts of the province, as possible. They have determined to raise the men by voluntary enlistment in the several counties, in full confidence that, in this way, they will be raised most speedily, as well as consist of persons with the greatest spirit and alacrity for the important service. Filled with the same zeal for the defense of their country, they appeal to you by this short address to entreat you to give a new proof to the public of your courage and intrepidity as men, of your unalterable attachment to the liberties of America and the sincerity of your unanimous resolutions from the beginning of this contest.

The danger is not only certain but immediate and imminent. It does not admit of even a moment's delay, for our unjust and implacable enemy is at hand. The place where the attack is expected is of the last importance, not only a city of great extent, the interest of whose numerous inhabitants must be exceedingly dear to us, but situated in the middle of the Colonies and where the success of the enemy would separate the provinces and disunite their efforts by land, which are, of necessity, liable to interruption from the enemy's fleet by sea. It is scarce worth while to add that this Province, by its vicinity, would then be exposed to the cruel depredations of the enemy, who happily heretofore, have been able to do us little or no mischief but by theft and rapine.

We cannot help putting you in mind how significantly Almighty God has prospered us hitherto and crowned our virtuous efforts with success. The expulsion of the enemy from Boston, where they first took possession and their oppressive measures was an event as disgraceful to them as it was advantageous to the public cause and honorable to that brave and resolute army by which it was accomplished.

We must not forget the activity and success of the inhabitants of the southern colonies. They run to arms in the thousands the moment they hear of an attack, both in Virginia and in North Carolina. God was pleased in both instances to reward their alacrity, for they obtained a complete victory over their enemy with so little loss of blood as it was not barely wonderful, but scarcely incredible.

Everyone is now obliged to confess what many saw long ago, that entire and unconditional submission is the point to which our enemies are determined to bring us, if in their power, so that nothing remains for us but either the abject slavery of tributary slaves or to maintain our rights and liberties by force of arms and hand down the fair inheritance to our posterity, by a brave and determined defense.

We desire and expect that, in such a situation of things, all particular differences of small moment, arising from whatever the cause, whether religious denominations, rivalship of different classes of men, scarcity of some articles of commerce, or any other, may be entirely laid aside. The present danger requires the most perfect union.

That you may be under no apprehension, either of inequality of the burden or that of our coasts will be left unguarded by the destination of this brigade, we have thought it best to inform you that the Continental Congress have amply provided for the defense of this Province and that a flying camp of ten thousand men is now forming for the protection of the middle colonies, which we are credibly informed, is to have its chief station in this province. We add no more, but that we trust and *hope, that, while every province is making the most spirited efforts, New Jersey, in its place and duty, will be second to none.*

Signed in name and by appointment of Congress at Burlington

Samuel Tucker, President

Buckingham Palace
September 23, 2005

"Gentlemen, please sit."

The four men in the room took their seats at the scarred, old mahogany table where the Sovereigns of England had conducted their high matters of state for over two centuries.

"I have read your report and understand that you feel that the present is the most opportune time for us to try our fortune again. I need not remind you that the time is ripe here also. Soon we will be absorbed into the Common Market and our identity lost forever. My ancestor George III sat at this very table at the onset of the American Revolution and said the same thing to his advisors that I repeat here this afternoon. England cannot survive as an island.

"Operation Guy Fawkes has been set in motion and seems feasible. We will watch it for several more months. Any questions?"

No one had any. The Lady arose and the gentlemen jumped to their feet. Then, she was gone as if she were a spirit.

St. John's, New Brunswick

Canada

June 25, 2005

John Agnew stood before the podium, surrounded by men with cameras on their shoulders, all pointed at him. Others held racks of lights aloft, like banners, to bathe the speaker in sunshine. Only the flourish of a trumpet was lacking. Perhaps, that would be more than the announcement deserved. The gray haired, bespectacled Agnew, clad in a dark business suit and looking more like a clergyman, than the college professor he was, began:

"Representatives of the Media, thank you for attending this press conference. I have prepared a statement that I shall read to you. You need not take notes as a printed version of it will be available to you at the conference's conclusion. Please hold any questions until the end."

Agnew looked around, as he was accustomed to in the lecture halls of the university, to see if any one were paying attention. The red lights of the several cameras confirmed he had an audience.

"The United Empire Loyalists of Canada have determined to accept the invitation of the President of the United States to participate in the 230th anniversary re-enactment of the Battle of Monmouth Court House on June 28, 2008. We believe this an historic moment in the relationship between the people of the United States today and the descendants of another forgotten people who struggled and suffered during those same hostilities, but did not prevail. Their principles were as lofty and idealistic as were those of the American patriots, but instead of liberty, they believed in loyalty, instead of independence, they cherished their tradition of the rights and obligations of the English system from the Magna Carta through the common law.

By way of background, those of you who are not from New Brunswick or Canada may not be overly familiar with the United Empire Loyalists. If so, let me introduce ourselves to you.

We are a hereditary organization that was created by England in 1789 to honor those who rallied to the defense of the Crown during the American Revolution. For those of you from the States, it is something like your Sons and Daughters of the American Revolution.

The Loyalists, or Tories as they were sometimes called, consider what began in America in 1776 to have been a civil war, not one for independence. Our ancestors refused to renounce their allegiance to the British Crown. We estimate that almost half a million – 20 percent of the white population of the American colonies – were open in their opposition to independence and that a like number pretended allegiance to the American states because they were powerless to do anything else.

Many Loyalists had enlisted in the British army .The largest unit was Cortlandt Skinner's New Jersey Volunteers and it is that unit – or rather their Canadian descendants – that will be engaged in the military part of the re-enactment of the Battle of Monmouth.

Once again, I apologize for those of you who already know about this, but the study of history being so rare these days and our American audience not quite so schooled about the other side of the Revolution, not everyone knows what happened to all those colonists who had remained loyal. They went into exile. Some refugees returned to England, others tried the Caribbean, but the majority came here to Canada to the Province of New Brunswick.

You can well imagine how many in this province today are descended from the thousands of exiled Loyalists that came here over two centuries ago. It has not always been an easy life but we persevered without compromising our loyalty to our sovereign or other values we held and continue to hold dear. We, the descendants of those Loyalists, are especially happy to have the opportunity to represent our country Canada and to be able to proudly display our Loyalist ancestry to the watching world at Monmouth." Agnew's voice broke toward the end, his thoughts about his own ancestors overwhelming him.

Finally, the London Chapter of the United Empire

Loyalists and we Canadian Loyalists' will work together in the overall planning necessary for an event of this historic magnitude. We had hoped its President, Harry Clinton could have been here today, but he seems to have been delayed."

There had been a few questions from the audience and some individual interviews with different TV and news reporters. Agnew was enjoying the limelight, not for himself so much as for his family name. Agnew was possessed by his ancestors. His *great, great, great, great grandfather*, also named John Agnew, had been an Anglican minister in Suffolk Parish, Virginia. He could not compromise his values. He not only condemned the rebels and praised the King, but he banned all who believed otherwise from his church as sinners. When the Revolution broke out, he was forced to flee and became Chaplain to the Queen's Rangers, a Loyalist corp. There, at least, he had the satisfaction of witnessing the British troops raiding and burning the town that had turned him out. The Reverend's son had been a captain in the Queens Rangers with his father, until wounded and imprisoned. The Past remained real for each succeeding generation of Agnews down to the present.

Agnew left the hotel where the news conference had been held and walked the ten blocks to the older part of St. John's where he was to have lunch at an old inn with Harry Clinton, Chairman of the Board of the Associated Loyalists. As he had mentioned to the press, he had hoped Clinton could have arrived in time for the press conference, but he had mentioned he had earlier meetings of some urgency in the province to which he must attend first.

Agnew had no idea if Clinton had any life beyond the Board. He was devoted to it more than anyone was to any career or profession. His family had been on the London side of the Loyalist cause as long as Agnew's family had been in New Brunswick – that is, from the beginning. He was a direct descendant of Sir Henry Clinton, through a relationship, which the Loyalist community charitably called "a late life love interest," with a mistress, Mary Blundell. She had been the daughter of Sir Henry Clinton's butler at his headquarters in New York City during the war. Mary had fled New York and returned to England with Sir Henry, a widower, as part of his household/family, when he was relieved of the American command in 1781. A sister, Helen, was produced by the union, which, although open, had never been legitimized by the parents' marriage.

Harry Clinton was already seated when Agnew arrived. The table was in the corner of the original part of the inn, near the great fireplace that had warmed the room for more than two centuries. A window, added to the structure after a furnace had been installed, faced a bay of the cold Atlantic and beyond that, England.

The two chatted amiably about a number of subjects. They had a wide selection of topics to choose among as each had known the other since his youth. Their fathers, grandfathers and generations past had enjoyed a similar relationship. It had been stressed to Agnew that he too must foster and preserve that relationship. On the boy's 18th birthday, the senior Agnew repeated once more the sad history of the Loyalists, but this time in a most moving and unforgettable way. Then, he had given his son John a sealed portfolio which he said contained messages from each Agnew in the first-born male line since they had fled to Canada after the American Revolution. He handed him also a separate envelope, the handwriting on which he recognized to be his father's. He was told to read the last one only upon his father's death. Finally, the elder Agnew enjoined the younger to keep alive the tradition, and that, on both sides of the Atlantic, there were others – the Clintons being among a half dozen he named – that were making the same covenants, promises that spanned oceans, generations and centuries.

After they had dined, the dishes taken away and the coffee cups filled a second time, Harry Clinton said to his friend:

"John, you have read the letter your father left to read upon his death?"

Agnew's eyes grew wide. It was a topic he had never before discussed with anyone. Sometimes he doubted it was even real, more a product of filial imagination. Speechless, he nodded a "yes."

"The time has come for you to go somewhere to read the

letters that accompanied your father's. Go somewhere far enough away so as not to be intruded upon until you have absorbed their messages, which I assure you will take some hours. Be distant enough from your fellows so that you can read them and re-read them, the dozen times you will need. The letters will explain everything. However, the oldest and the most important message will be in cipher so you will need to know the code." Clinton reached into his breast pocket and removed an envelope. Handing it over to him. "Here, it is. These are the keys to the Kingdom. You cannot doubt the authenticity of the message from your ancestors or their intentions for you. That envelope has been in your family's possession for more than two centuries, passed from father to son. Without the cipher, I am giving you, there is no meaning in the message. With it, it will all make sense. Read it and if you want to go forward, send me your assent in the same cipher. Any questions?"

Agnew still had nothing to say. He was dumbfounded. He stood up when Clinton did, shook his hand and watched him leave for a taxi to the airport to begin the long journey home to London.

Agnew sank back into his seat and looked at the envelope he had been given. Tomorrow, he would go out to New Suffolk, the land awarded the Agnew family by the Crown in compensation of their losses and preserved by the family as part of its Loyalist legacy. No one had attempted agriculture there in the last century and the timbering was limited to preserving the plantation's history. Mostly, it now served John Agnew as a place to be alone. Tomorrow, he would take the envelopes out there and open them.

New York City

June 30, 1778

Clinton's carriage had worked its way as far on Old Slip as it could. Sir Henry had returned to New York City. A sleek 30-foot long canoe like perriauger had sped the British Commander in Chief of His Majesty's Forces in America the twenty miles from the Highlands of Middletown in New Jersey. It had sailed across Sandy Hook Bay, through the Narrows and into New York harbor to this dock at the foot of the Island of Manhattan. Clinton had waited until he had been certain there would be no follow up assault by the rebels upon his troops as they were being loaded on transports for the sail to their camps on Staten and Manhattan Islands. Everyone was weary from the march, much of it forced, from Philadelphia across New Jersey and the battle that had been fought midway, at Monmouth Court House.

The carriage waiting at the boat had not been necessary. The distance from the pier to Clinton's Headquarters at the Kennedy House at the foot of Broadway was no more than a few hundred yards. It was one of the few buildings still standing after the fires of 1776. Yet, the carriage afforded him privacy and Clinton wanted to be left alone.

He had half hoped to see the old New York of his youth, the 1740's when the American colonists had been proud to be English. But, the New York that he saw now, as he looked out the curtained window of the carriage, was a far different sight. In September of 1776, when the rebels were fleeing New York City, the Sons of Liberty burned as much of the town as they could so as to provide no sustenance to the approaching British. The fires were set simultaneously, all in the same lower, older part of the City, where the Dutch had begun their settlement more than a century before. The first blaze spotted was in a sailor's brothel near Whitehall Slip, also at the foot of Broadway, near the tip of the island. Still another conflagration had broken out at *The Fighting Cocks Tavern* at the Battery, close by. A third began at the *White Hall Inn*, on Broadway near the Bowling Green. The fires then spread to what was known as the Mall, a grove of ancient elms planted by Peter Stuyvesant one hundred years before. Soon, all the lower city was aflame. There had been a drought for many weeks, one of the worst of the century. The wells had all gone dry and brackish river water was being hawked in the streets at high prices. Those who had started the fires also had been careful to sabotage all the fire fighting equipment so that, even had there been sufficient water, nothing could be done to prevent the spread of the blazes.

The cedar shaked wooden buildings were tinder dry and the fire quickly leapt from building to building, from street to street up the island, across and north of Wall Street, burning down thousands of residences and shops in the mercantile area of the city. Another branch of the fire headed west toward the Hudson, destroying in its path the venerable Trinity Church and the river homes of the wealthy .

Clinton had been a first hand witness to the fires. He had fought in the Battle of Long Island in August of 1776, where the British almost had trapped Washington and his army. That probably would have ended the war right there. But Washington and his troops cleverly had escaped, evacuated across the East River by a flotilla of small craft, navigated by a company of soldier/boatmen from Martha's Vineyard in Massachusetts. Making matters worse, when the disappointed British reached New York, they found it ablaze. Some of those setting the fires were caught red handed, with bundles of sticks wrapped in resin and brimstone. They were strung up by the heels and hung from tavern signs or bayoneted and cast into the fires they had themselves created.

No, quite definitely, the quaint seaport town of New York of Clinton's youth was far different from the one he saw through the carriage window tonight. It had been replaced by burned out buildings, sheltering British soldiers and camp followers. Any trees still standing had been chopped down and used to barricade positions against an enemy attack. Trenches were dug as part of the defense along Broad and Wall Streets and bulwarks thrown up behind the burned out hulk of Trinity Church and north near Chatham Square.

Clinton had been born in North America and was still a

youth when his father became the Royal Governor of New York. He lived there until he was 21 years old. Indeed, he considered New York City to be his boyhood home.

But do not fool yourself. He may have been born on this western side of the Atlantic but Clinton did not think of himself as either an American or even as a colonial. He was British, from an honorable and well-connected family. His military record was impressive, dating back to the mid century wars with Germany and the Seven Years War against France and her colonies. He left soldiering in 1772 as a Major General to join the House of Commons.

Clinton smiled to himself, as the carriage door was opened for him and an outstretched arm of anonymous assistance offered him. How curious it was to find himself here, in the burned out city of his youth, battling what he had thought were kinsmen, rather than the more hospitable, genteel halls of Parliament. The outbreak of hostilities in America had brought him back into the military. He led the last, valiant charge at Bunker Hill in Boston at the War's start in 1775. Promoted to second in command of the British army in America, he lost an attack on Charleston, South Carolina but was victorious at the Battle of Long Island and, at year's end, at Newport, Rhode Island. He returned to England in 1777 where a knighthood awaited him. Later that year, When Lord Howe was removed for failure to follow his orders, Sir Henry replaced him and was ordered to evacuate Philadelphia and return his forces to New York. It had been that order that Clinton had been attempting to obey when Washington and his forces interfered at Monmouth Court House.

Mounting the front stairs of the Kennedy House, Clinton's mind was on the next day and the days after. He had completed half his task. His troops were safely back in New York as ordered. He knew he had been fortunate. He had nearly lost many of them. Had the Americans pressed their original attack on his rear, they could have gobbled him up. His line of march was almost a dozen miles long and his best troops, were far ahead. But, by some miracle, the first Americans had fled the field of battle and, in the meanwhile, Clinton was able to rally his troops and bring in reinforcements to face the second assault. But Clinton knew it had almost been a disaster and that he had been very fortunate. Washington was a worthy foe, for a colonial.

France had just joined the war on the American side and Clinton knew that support for the American cause would only grow stronger as time went on. Parliament had mis-estimated the Loyalist support in America, at least in New England.

His orders were clear, the same ones his predecessor Howe had ignored. Divide the colonies into two. Then, put all his pressure to bear on the northern provinces. Once he had disciplined the New Englanders and those in the Middle Atlantic region, then he could turn his attention to the South, if the Loyalists there had not sued already for peace by then, as Clinton thought likely. The Hudson River was the key to that. If he could control the river all the way up to still loyal Canada, then the colonies would be divided. To control the Hudson, he needed to take the key Hudson fort of West Point.

An eager faced lieutenant, who had remained at headquarters during Clinton's trip south to retrieve his army, stood erect at attention. Clinton barely looked at him as he climbed the staircase to the second floor where his living quarters were located, but said:

"When Major Andre returns, I want to see him."

Lake Tahoe, California

July 1, 2005

Chic, *old money* Lake Tahoe is a sandy fringe of people that the fir forests permit to dwell alongside a deep mountain lake. There is a certain snobbery to the place, that one might expect of a spot so divine. Closer to the heavens, more than 9,000 feet above the commoner who lives at sea level along the coast, Tahoe is a blessed, distant place, often mantled in light white clouds, like a gossamer garment, and, in some years, even wearing a tiara of snow throughout the summer. A single street that follows the contours of the lake serves as fashionable Tahoe City's main avenue, lined with shops that sold the necessities of life, as well as its luxuries, to the affluent.

If one looked closely, outside one collage of stores, he could see representatives of two of Tahoe's old line families engaged in light conversation regarding that evening's Independence Day concert. The San Francisco Symphony dutifully performs one each summer, during the first week of July, for its wealthy patrons at their summer cottages at the Lake. One of the pair in conversation was a patrician looking gray haired lady who had been coming to Tahoe, ever since she had been a girl during the Depression. What terrible years they were that had afflicted so many. Thank God, not her family. She had been waiting outside a gift store, where she had been browsing for something to cheer a few of her contemporaries, whose healths, not unexpectedly, were beginning to fail. Her companion in chatting was a pleasant looking man in his mid to late 30's. He had a boyish, shy smile and twinkling eyes that made him instantaneously attractive to the ladies, even this maiden of more than 65 Tahoe summers. Men, however, tended to view him differently, with a degree of trepidation, seeing the power behind his build of six foot two inches, two hundred pounds and the strength of character chiseled in his face. But, soon, even they too were drawn to him and his sincerity. He seemed too good to be real but, in no one's memory – and Tahoe's had a long one – had he ever betrayed the community by acting dishonorably.

Everyone at Tahoe City called him Jackie. And, although, at his age, he was getting too old for such a youthful appellation, the practice was not likely to change. He has spent all his summers in this alpine retreat in the Sierra Madre Mountains between California and Nevada. His neighbors and friends – that may well be redundant – and all the trades people in town, could not comprehend calling him anything else. The engraved stationary at the distinguished law firm in San Francisco, where he was a partner listed him as he had been christened "John Coffee Hays, IV," but, as in Tahoe, none of his colleagues called him that. He was Jackie to one and all.

Finishing his shopping for the evening meal and tomorrow's breakfast, Jackie remounted his bicycle for the four-mile trip around the perimeter of Lake Tahoe back to his family's *cottage*. He had the place to himself for the next few days. His sister and her children were back in San Francisco and his mother rarely ever came to the Lake since Jackie's father had passed away a couple of years before.

Jackie's great, great grandfather, the first John Coffee Hays, had purchased thousands and thousands of acres of California land in the years following the Civil War. He knew California well. He had been its Surveyor General during its days as a Territory, before statehood. Among his purchases had been much of the forest engulfing the Lake Tahoe waterfront. Some of it had been transferred over the decades but the family hung on to forty acres of the best part. Although, like Jackie, it never could shake its first name, the original *cottage*, had grown over time to become a three storied, 10 bed roomed mansion with turrets, a few guest cottages, servants quarters, play houses for the children, boat houses and a long dock that stretched fifty yards from the shoreline into the cool solitude of the lake. Huge pines, straight as an arrow and reaching up hundreds of feet to the wispy clouds hurrying across the lake, shielded the cottage from the eyes and ears of other men.

It was good that the cottage was so secluded. Jackie wanted no company for the next couple of days. He had an important task ahead of him.

Putting away the groceries, Jackie thought about how he

37

was going to approach what he had to do. First, he needed to verbalize the issues, if only to himself sitting at the end of that dock sticking so far into the lake as to be private. This was the way he practiced law. First, the facts had to be discovered, then assembled. The ones not relevant were excluded and those remaining put into some intelligible order. Only then, when all that could be verified was in fact verified and all that was only speculation at that time was recognized as such and put aside, then, and only then, could an issue be properly addressed and a reliable solution ultimately found. This evening – there would be only a few more hours of sunlight – he would devote to collecting all the information he had on the issue. Tomorrow, he would try to come up with a way to begin resolving it.

Jackie Hays had grown up with the proverbial silver spoon in his mouth. Yet, he was not the spoiled, weak product one would expect from generations of such coddling. His father and grandfather had seen to that. With both of them, he had spent many hours on this same dock over the course of a third of a century, looking at stars, and trying, as most humbled men do, to understand their places in the larger universe. Each had used these opportunities to train young Jackie's mind and character for some role they anticipated his playing in the future. Each told him, from his own perspective – and equally precious in Jackie's memory – essentially the same thing.

A man must be strong and tough because in life most others leave strong and tough people alone. They told him that strong and tough meant both physical and spiritual fortitude. The football star who has the inner toughness to study, the stunning blonde who has the moral convictions of a nun. Jackie's father and grandfather told him also how, in addition to being tough and strong, a man had to be smart – book smart and street smart, a student of literature and history as well as a shrewd judge of man's lesser qualities. The football player who was a pre-med student; the blonde who was a Latin major. People avoided confronting others who were smarter than they. And, his father and grandfather told him, if Jackie were both stronger and smarter, then most everyone would defer to him. When that happened, then he could step up and become their leader ."A leader, Jackie, is the person to whom others turn in times of trouble."

But being a tough and smart man, able to command the respect of comrades, was empty unless he was also *good*, morally aware of all his blessings and wealth. The Hays family had enjoyed both to unimaginable degrees .All of it was unearned by him. It had value, only if he could lead others in the same way that all great leaders did, that is, as a servant, not as a war load. They also warned him in allegories that a true leader must expect to someday suffer and die for those he leads and that, if he were to lead, then death might well be his fate.

Jackie remembered the last time he and his father had sat out on the dock and watched the stars. It had been fewer than three years ago, only four months before his father succumbed to the cancer he had been so valiantly fighting. His father did not speak in allegories and parables then. He had not the time, nor literally, the breath. Instead he spoke his mind directly. Jackie was spell bound as the old trial lawyer father told his story. It went back to the first John Coffee Hays. Jackie knew all about him – or thought he had. Books had been written about the man, but, as he was to learn from his father, there was one chapter they all had missed.

Sitting at the end of the dock, fifty yards into the lake, Jackie began to talk aloud, even though he was by himself. His only audience was a spider laboring away to build a web between the railings of the dock, a trap to snare some insect that had thought itself safe from predators this far from land. Had the spider been listening to Jackie's presentation of the facts, he would have learned the Hays family pedigree. It dated back to America before the Revolution. His great, great grandfather, Harmon Hays had been a boy in the War. His great-grandfather, had been the famed Jack Coffee Hays who fought in the Texas War of Independence as part of a spy force that scouted desolate south Texas against the advance of the Mexicans.

Here, Jackie paused a bit to refill his glass of wine and to glance over to the spider to see if it had stopped weaving its web to listen to Jackie's recitation about Jack Hay's and Texas in 1835. The spider seemed interested – at least, it hadn't left – so Jackie resumed.

"After Texas got its freedom, my soon to be famous forebear tried his hand at surveying but found it dull. His niche lay with the Texas Rangers who were just forming .Rangers were something of a cross between the local peace officer and the military – with a little bit of judge and executioner in times of unavoidable necessity. The ranger's first duty was to restore or maintain order in situations that get beyond the control of the local authorities."

"He became a legend," bragged Jackie to the spider "I was taught all about him. He became a captain of his own Ranger Company at the age of twenty-three, he fought the Indians at Plum Creek, Enchanted Rock and Bandera Pass. They say he never fought fewer than ten, and sometimes forty times his own number and never was beat!" The Spider did not seem convinced and Jackie continued.

"You don't believe, me? Too bad we don' let spiders indoors because I can prove it. We got the newspaper articles up in the cottage."

Jackie paused and grinned. Here he was, a grown man, playacting with a spider. But the news clippings on the cottage wall were fascinating. One of them was an interview with Captain Jack Hays after a battle between him and fifteen of his men and a large Indian force high up on the Perdenales. Growing up, Jackie had recreated the battle a thousand times, sometimes with friends, sometimes alone. Always, he was Captain Jack and he practiced the coolness and detachment with which his ancestor had fought. He tried to imitate the modesty of his great grandfather. Somehow, it fit into his scheme of being a leader that his father and grandfather had been teaching him.

"Anyway, turning his attention back to the Spider, he concluded his family's history. "Gold took Captain Jack from Texas to California. He led a party of Texans, eager to strike it rich, on the dangerous trek across Texas and the Southwest to California. He became sheriff of San Francisco during the wild Gold Rush days."

Jackie stopped his summary of his great, great grandfather's life to take another glass of wine. He thought he knew a lot about his illustrious forebears, but apparently he had not known it all. As dusk grew closer, he resumed his soliloquy on his stage sticking into Lake Tahoe.

"So my father tells me, virtually on his death bed, that not only was my great, grandfather a spy, so was his father before him. Then, he tells me that he himself has been a spy all his adult life and so was his father. Then, the crusher. It was now my turn to be a spy!"

Hays tried to make his speech sound humorous to his audience of the spider and the corpses it had collected, but it fell flat. Truth was that it was not funny. His father had entrusted – burdened? – him with some vague duty that had been passed down father to son in his family for five generations. He might never be called to perform. His father and grandfather had never been summoned, so it all might amount to nothing. His father had told him that, in a safe deposit box in the main Wells Fargo Bank office in San Francisco that belonged to the Hays Family Trust, was an envelope with his name on it. He was to remove it and review its contents, if and when he received a communication from or on behalf of someone named Elias Dayton .

Just yesterday, Jackie received a call from a fellow by that name, a lawyer from New York. He introduced himself as a friend of Jackie's father. After a few moments of chatting about the great respect with which the late John Coffee Hays III had been viewed by the New York legal community, Dayton asked Jackie whether his father had ever mentioned his name to him. When Hays said "yes" and that he been told to someday he be contacted by him, Dayton merely said "Fine. Then, we should meet." Jackie had planned to be on the east coast the third week of July. A luncheon date was set for Dayton's luncheon club, the India House in Hanover Square, near the southern tip of the isle of Manhattan.

Yesterday, Jackie had gone to Wells Fargo and had collected the envelope of materials from the Trust's safety deposit box. He had taken it with him to Tahoe. Tomorrow, he would devote the day to studying it and finally learn what this silly spy talk was all about. Later, he would fly to New York to meet with Dayton.

John Agnew did not have to re-read his father's letter. He could recite it from memory, so many times had he tried to decipher some meaning beyond its words:

Dear John:

I will be laid to rest by the time you read this and, I hope, at peace, but, most certainly, earning whatever rewards or punishments that are my due. Live your life well and I will re-live mine in my grandson John.

You have one duty that is as dear to me as is my grandson. One day you may be approached by someone known to you, as his father was known to me and our grandfathers were to each other going back to the American War. He will ask your aid. You cannot refuse him under any circumstance. It is the demand of all your forebears.

This message was given to me by my father and he said he had received it from his father, and his from his, all the way to the time of our seeking refuge in dear Canada. My father also gave me a sealed envelope to be opened when the request for assistance is received. But, no one has come to me with any such plea, unless it was during the War when I was away. Thus, the envelope is still sealed and, together with my father's letter to me and his to him, I now entrust them to you.

Prepare your son as I did you. He is to know the sons of the families you know. And he is to be given the envelope, upon your death, even as you receive it now.

Farewell. Take care of my grandson.

Affectionately,

Father

Agnew remembered Clinton's telling him to pick a spot to read the letters where he would have the solitude needed to absorb the instructions he was to receive. Even without his friend's advice, Agnew would shave chosen New Suffolk. It was the land that the Crown had given the Agnew family in recognition of the Reverend John Agnew's and his son's loyalty to the King in the American War and to compensate the family for the loss of its properties in America. They had thought the name symbolic, Suffolk having been the name of the community in Virginia from which they had been banished by the American rebels and which they burned to the ground as avenging Loyalists.

The Agnews had attempted to farm New Suffolk for several generations with freed slaves and indentured servants but, as their interests turned more toward trade and commerce (and, in John Agnew's case, education and scholarship), they gave up the effort and New Suffolk became a rustic retreat for those of the family who sought it. Not an acre of it had ever been transferred out of the family. It would be selling a part of the Agnew heritage.

New Suffolk was nearly three thousand acres of timber, some of it ancient, if not primeval, forest. There were hundreds of acres more of fruit and nut orchards, the progeny of the first years of colonization, and as many acres of meadows, where Agnew's ancestors had ranged cattle, horses and hogs. Most of the crops had been grown along the robust stream that ran through the valley, dividing the plantation in two.

No one lived in the 215-year-old farmhouse, except the spirits of his ancestors and Agnew would have welcomed their appearance. Although the main house was still quite habitable, Agnew preferred a two room lodge he had built for his own sole use, along the stream amid the ruins of an iron works on the one side and a saw mill and corn mill, a fewer hundred yards further downstream, on the other. It was there, among these skeletons, he brought to read the materials given him by his father.

There were two envelopes,

The seal of the first was signed on its flap by John Agnew. Everyone in the Agnew family knew who John Agnew was .He was a legend in the often-recited family history. He enjoyed both a

Black Sheep and Prodigal Son reputation. They called him "Cowboy John". Only months after his father passed away, young John suddenly upped, turned over the operation of New Suffolk to his younger brother and left Canada. And after a year in England and another in Germany visiting friends of his father's, he showed up in Texas. There, he began a trading company representing British and Prussian interests and prospered, especially during the American Civil War. The Confederacy needed provisions and the Union's embargo gave the chance for a smart trader to do business, first from Texas, then from New Orleans and Charleston and finally from all over the South.

Despite Cowboy John's being a non-combatant, he must have witnessed many battles, or he knew men who did who had described the fights to him. In later years, when he returned to New Suffolk, he would tell wide eyed grandsons tales of cavalry charges and men bayoneting one another, with all the credibility of a man who had been there.

John Agnew's hands trembled as he tried to unfold the letter. The paper was thicker than modern paper and noticeably aging, but the black ink jumped out as boldly as the day it was written. The author's script, perfect and confident in its strokes, bespoke of a man in command. Addressed to his son, it told that he had been visited by a family friend with a request that his father had told him could not be refused by an Agnew.

"I regret to tell you, my son, that, although I did not soil the Agnew name by refusing the charge when it came and devoted half a dozen years to its success, our effort failed. Therefore you and succeeding generations must continue to be alert to the call.

I cannot reveal what happened. History is not to know of it, if it has any chance of succeeding in the future. But we failed in our attempt. The noble farmers of the South could not defeat an industrial North with its inexhaustible supply of emigrants and conscripts.

Take care of your son as I will live in him."

This left a single envelope that showed evidences of having been opened and resealed .Agnew opened it again and removed the parchment within. In communion with his ancestors, he read the text:

Seed of our seed:

We do not know your name, you, our descendant, who reads this note. We do not know your century or your time's customs. But, it matters little for the duty we give you is universal, not dependent on time or circumstances. It is the duty of a son to his fathers in time and it cannot be altered or refused.

Someday, your aid will be asked by someone known to you and us. He will give you the key to know your duty. Give that aid and be certain that your sons and grandsons, our sons and grandsons, are like instructed and will obey. Your family honor requires it.

Mr. Reverend John Agnew

Had any one been present, he would have been astounded to see the change that had overcome Agnew as he stared at the letter in his hands. He was in communication with his ancestors. Their collective spirit had rushed into him, possessing him, like on Pentecost, and securing for itself every part of his body and mind. Slowly, almost mechanically, under the control of a new brain, Agnew removed a pamphlet from the envelope. It was old and yellow, more fragile by far than the letters he had been reading. It was an old print script where, amid other differences, "f"'s and "s"'s were interchanged. It had been entitled *Narrative of an Abused Loyalist in the Rebellion in Americas*, authored by Judge Thomas Jones .Then Agnew removed the envelope which Clinton had given him at the inn at St. John's and opened it. There was nothing but rows of numbers, always in ascending order: "12, 23, 33, 78, 81, 105..." He thought for a few minutes, realizing he would be furnished with no further clues. When he was a boy, he and his father had played a game (which he played with his own son) that used a simple code. His father would give him a book in which random words were circled in pencil and young John had to collect them and arrange their meaning, which always revealed the location of some treat his father had purchased for him. Nothing was circled in the pamphlet but perhaps the numbers on Clinton's sheet referred to word positions - the 12th word, the 23rd, the 78th etc." It was a start and very slowly, to be certain of his count, he hunted out the first few words "your ... fealty ... until ... death ..." Agnew knew that this was more than coincidence that the first four words fell in a readable sequence. The cipher was easy, if you had the ancient pamphlet, the random numbers which Clinton had given him, and the simple scheme that had been passed from father to son for two centuries in the form of a child's game. Agnew, again exhibiting remarkable restraint in waiting to extract all the words from the pamphlet before reading the entire message:

Your fealty until death has been pledged by your fathers to me, George III of the House of Hanover, King of Britain and all her provinces, and to my successors in our restoration to England of her lost North American colonies. The time will come in the future – a month, a year, a decade, a century away – for you to leave your manor, instruct your sons and servants in your duties and obey the commands you shall receive. America must be returned to England, her sovereignty of the planet rests upon it. Those who refuse will live but briefly before they meet their ancestors in shame. Heed my messenger when he comes.

Lake Tahoe, California

July 2, 2005

Lake Tahoe is just about the whole North American continent away from Agnew's New Suffolk plantation in the Canadian province of New Brunswick. Yet, whether out of coincidence, fate or some other design, at each place, at relatively the same hour of the same day, a man was opening a door to the past and communicating with his revered forebears. It was not an everyday thing.

A choice room in a Tahoe cottage on the California side of the lake faces east. Its sleepers are awakened at first light by that same first light. Those who like to sleep later take a back bedroom but most Californians do not like to waste the day with sleeping. Too many better things to do. Jackie Hays opened his eyes fully to the sun. He paused a moment to determine if he had a headache. At the symphony concert last night, sipping each clan's favorite white or red Californian wine was mandatory. Being relatively young, charming, wealthy and still eligible, Jackie was the subject of the offers to sip from many such clans and their guests, none declined.

But, he felt fine, clear headed and ready to dive into reading the materials that his father had left for him at the Trust's safe deposit box. A half hour saw him shower, shave, make up his room and breakfast. He chose a portion of the dining room table as his desk. Slowly, but without undue ritual or caution, he unsealed the outer envelope and removed from it a single sheet of paper and a second sealed envelope. The note was in his father's handwriting, which was shaky with illness, written probably not too long before his death. Its thinking was not shaky, retaining the crispness of a keen intellect and lawyer's setting the background .Jackie read it slowly, word by word, as if savoring of this communication with his idol:

Son:

Remember how we talked many times about your being tough, strong, smart and morally sound enough as to have others turn to you in times of crisis as their leader. Remember also, we spoke about how being so blessed, you had an obligation to lead those who sought your leadership, but to lead them as a servant. Remember finally that the price you pay to serve other men may mean your life. As you will be unable to dispute when you read this, death comes earlier to some than to others. That being so, then death might as well be in sacrifice for others than wasted at the hands of painful diseases. Dulce et decorum est, pro patria mori. It is sweet and fitting to die for one's fatherland .

It is possible that there will be a request made to you for assistance. To serve and render that assistance is the reason I taught you in the way my father had taught me and his father had taught him, all the way to Texas and earlier. All that was done to help you in carrying out this mission. The report from your great grandfather will describe it for you.

Don't worry. You'll do fine.

Love

Dad

There was a second envelope in the redwell and, in it, several folded sheets of paper. One was a list of some vaguely familiar names, like Moon, Walker, Gillespie, Moore, Erath and others which, although familiar. Jackie could not readily identify, as he quickly scanned the list. His attention was on the other document, a letter from his famed great grandfather, John Coffee Hays:

Dear Son:

I am writing this at the Cottage. Your mother has gone home to Texas to visit her kin and, I expect, bury some of them. It is the season. I shall spend September here by myself. Don't pity me. I am happy to ride the mountains alone, thinking, like all old men, of past adventures. It is a good way to spend one's final years.

In the evening, I have been writing out some instructions for you and young John, when he comes of age. These are not requests, but, as I said, instructions, orders you do not have the discretion to refuse. Your country's independence is, once again, at stake.

You may think what I tell you is unbelievable. I can see in my mind's eye your half baffled, half skeptical – but still, I am sure, respectful – expression, wondering if I were playing with you or whether my mind had gone, never considering the possibility that what I was saying was accurate, so outlandish is the tale. But it is true and much depends upon your acting upon it.

It did not seem so incredible when my father told me, but he was a witness to the events. Later, I learned first hand for myself that what I tell you is true and terrible.

My father Harmon as a youth came to New York City in a ship full of Loyalists fleeing Charleston, South Carolina. There, he becomes indentured to a book and newspaper publisher in New York City. The man was a great Loyalist who, for a while, when the Americans held New York, had to flee to England for his very safety. He sold the indenture for my father's bondage to another man, his friend, who later conveyed him to the British general, Sir Henry Clinton when he returned with the army to New York in 1776. My father was valuable to Clinton. He knew New York City like a guttersnipe; he could procure anything asked of him and Clinton would often send him on missions of assorted natures around the burned buildings of lower New York.

My father had not come to New York City by chance. He had been recruited to the American Cause and agreed to act as a spy for the benefit of General Washington in the War for Independence. Clinton was a widower and his household a small one. Trusted for the errands he ran and, like any good servant, invisible, although always at hand, my father blended into the background. His boy's countenance masked his eager eyes and ears. During the first years, Clinton was second in command to General Howe. Then, he became the commander in chief in Howe's stead. There was much to be picked up and passed on

49

through a network of fellow agents.

One snatch of conversation overheard and reported to General Washington led to my fathers, almost 17 years of age, being asked by the General himself – it was a request, not an order, but equally not to be refused – to return to England with Clinton, near the war's end, and to continue his role as an agent for several years longer. He did it and confirmed the British secret stratagem, an ongoing plan by Britain to recapture the United States at some uncertain time in the future.

This bit of intelligence that Britain was plotting a long range hostility against the United States led General Washington, by then a private citizen once again, it being prior to the enactment of the Constitution and his election as president, to re-establish the network of spies that had served him so well in the war and to entrust to them – and, if necessary, to their children and their children's children – the charge to stay awake, while awaiting the British return .

The British did try several times to re-attach America to the Empire – only once by force of arms in 1812. Each time, alert to Britain's intent, my father and his allies were able to scout the British advance, discover their plan, rally America and frustrate their efforts.

Elias Dayton, General Washington's aide had helped establish the spy network in 1776 and reactivated it in 1783, when, your grandfather, returning from England, confirmed the English plot. Elias Dayton's son, Jonathan, contacted me just after my father had died. I was 18 and he told me it was time that I replace my father in the defense network.

You see England, with the assistance of the people of the German states, who were kin of the English king and descendants of the Hessians, Waldeckers and other mercenaries of the Revolution, were planning to seize Texas from Mexico and to set up an independent nation. The new nation, under the influence of the British, would immediately ally itself with the Canadian provinces and then make overtures to the American agricultural South, which daily was growing further away in sentiment from the industrialized dominated New England. The plan then was to *either purchase or conquer the Mexican interests in the southwest and California – the English were already eyeing Oregon – to create one North American colony to loom over then much smaller United States. Thusly, England and our Nation's positions would have changed. New England would become the island and Old England, the continent.*

It was a bold plan and Britain was given her chance to execute it due to the abolitionists in America – mostly New Englanders. They did not want Texas to join the Union because it would add another slave state. During the decade of her independence, thousands of immigrants were sent to Texas by British interests, Englishmen, Welsh, Scotch, Northern Irish and Germans. The last came in great numbers, their princes employing Texas as colonies for their large populations at home.

Besides helping to people it, England and the German states also offered the new Republic of Texas the financial assistance it needed. Texas was land rich but poor in bullion. The costs of the Revolution and beginning a new nation were huge and the offers from Europe for large tracts of land onto which to settle their excess population could not be resisted. However, among the immigrants came soldiers disguised as farmers and tradesmen. Some were the peasant children of Hessian mercenaries, others the sons of true Englishmen or still others adventurers, well paid and well equipped. They were led by Sir Henry Clinton – or at least by his spirit embodied in the seed of his bastard son. His aides were the sons of Clinton allies from the days of the American Revolution, come to have their honor's revenge .They formed militias and ranger companies. There was need for that too. Texas could not afford an army to protect its settlers. The Indians and Mexicans were always threats on the frontier and virtually all of Texas that was not unexplored wilderness, was frontier. But these militias had other purposes, including seizing the government of the Republic, if necessary, in a Revolution staged by England.

We formed Ranger units of our own – we called them the Texas Rangers and they were to become quite well known. We also fought the Indians and Mexicans as well as watching closely the Dutch Rangers, as they had begun calling themselves. We recognized each other as enemies and, more than once, far out on the Plains away from witnessing civilization, we skirmished with them, in preparation for the day we would battle on Texas soil to preserve American independence. The day never came .At the end, while the slave issue gave Britain the opportunity to control the orphan Texas, it also thwarted it. The British had condemned the practice of slavery throughout the Empire, well before their pious New Englander cousins in America had objected to it. To embrace Texas and permit her to keep her slaves would not sit well at home. But, it was equally clear that neither the Texans nor the southerners would agree to abolishing slavery, even were Britain to pay them top price for their slaves, as they offered to do. But, maybe, even if a solution to the slavery obstacle had been found, it might not have been enough to convince Texans to repudiate the United States and join the British Empire. A decade in America, surviving and thriving on their own, against Indians and sometimes a harsh nature had lessened the serf like allegiances they had held to some distant Prince Frederick or Sir Henry. The American colonist sixty years before had reached his maturity on his own with little help from the faraway motherland. So too did the English and German seedlings in Texas grow to be American, not European, oaks. They were Texans and, by assimilation, devotees to the concepts of liberty and independence and they would not take up arms against the land that had given birth to Liberty.

England tried again, of course, during the Civil War when it and its Canadian provinces supported the South against the North, hoping that, when it was all over, England would again replace New England as what they described to be the brain of America. We were able to beat them back again. I was out here then but was able to be of some assistance in the effort.

It has been quiet since and, if there is another call to arms, then my son it is you or your son who must fall in. Amid these papers, there is a list of those who rode in my company in the Rangers. They and their descendants stayed in Texas, many in our own Hays County. Go to them for help. They know to keep watch also. Your commander will be of the Dayton line.

I know you will not fail your country. The peril for your person is great but the peril for the country greater. Be ready when the call comes.

Affectionately,

Your Father

Jackie Hays read the letter over at least a score of times and, slowly, some feeling returned to his brain as it does to a frozen extremity reunited with warmth. He was sitting in the same house – at the same table, most likely, – as had his great grandfather, John Coffee Hays, when he had written that message to his descendants. This voice from the dead was telling him two things. First, England was trying to take back America and, secondly, he and some Texans whom he had never met were supposed to stop them. Yet, his ancestor's prediction of his reader's incredibility reaction kept forcing itself into Jackie's thoughts. He had insisted that the story was true, and, if it were, wow!

Putting the papers aside, Jackie rose from the table and went out into the sunshine as if a change of locale would bring his thoughts into better focus. He had grown up with the image of his great grandfather always looming over him. The books that had been written about him, the newspaper accounts, lining the cottage walls, of his celebrated battles with the Mexicans and Indians and, most of all, his family's devotion to the gentle, sensitive side of Captain Jack, all influenced young Jackie in ways no longer even traceable. Certainly, the boy had patterned his conduct on how Captain Jack would have acted. He had even centered his fantasies around the exploits of his famous forebear. Thus, it was not totally unexpected that, at times, Jackie thought himself possessed by the benign spirit of this man. Perhaps, that spirit was the inspiration for Jackie's initial plans. The words *"have to round up the boys"* inexplicably kept buzzing around Jackie's brain until he could corner the phrase and identify it. It was a reference to the members of Captain Jack's Ranger Company. Should he gather up the members – their great grand children more accurately, of the Texas Ranger band that had helped save America once before?

In the early days of the Republic of Texas, when a military was unaffordable and the region too big and sparsely settled for local authorities to be of much help, the most effective and economic force was to have small well mounted squads that could travel a great distance, grapple with Indians and bandits, a force that could repel any enemy that threatened the security of the citizens. Sometimes, they were the captors, judges and executioners of the threatening forces. A ranger like squad was what he needed now - some comrades, together with whom, Jackie could execute the orders from the past. Today was Monday. He was to be in New York in two weeks time to meet with Dayton. In between, he would go back to Hays County, Texas. Large tracts of the county had been given by a grateful Republic to the riders from Captain Jack's Ranger Company. These first settlers petitioned that the county be named in honor of their leader Jack Hays and the legislature quickly bestowed the honor. Chances are some of their descendants still lived there. The letter had said they also had been told to stay alert to repulse the next enemy assault. He would go "round up the boys."

New York City
September 28, 1778

James Rivington, editor, publisher and owner of *The Royal Gazette* waited patiently for his cup of cider to be refilled by one of the lasses who waited on guests at the British Coffee House. Despite its name and the prevailing practice in London, this establishment sold beverages of all kinds. Rivington was in no hurry, the first mug having satisfied his thirst – for the moment, at least. The first one would soon become lonesome for a companion. His printing press was only a few hundred feet away on the other side of Hanover Square. His apprentices had just begun to set type for this week's edition and, so, he had no need to be there any time soon. Anyway, the British Coffee House was where he gathered many of his news items. It was frequented by the senior officers of the British army in New York, many of whom lived in the adjoining boarding house. When full of drink, they were remarkably full of newsworthy information as well about the war and, especially, regarding what was going to happen next.

Rivington had begun his newspaper more than five years before. Stridently pro British, Rivington taunted the rebels unmercifully in his press. He printed accounts, often made out of whole cloth that ridiculed the Americans and their sacred cause. The Patriots first tried to silence him by a boycott, then The Sons of Liberty of New York burned his printing office, destroyed his press and carried away a large quantity of type to be melted and made into patriot bullets .Rivington left New York, returned to London and purchased a new press. Appointed the "King's Printer" in New York, he returned when Howe captured the city in August of 1776. He rebuilt his printing house on the lower part of the island of Manhattan and, now with the British army as his protector, Rivington resumed publishing his newspaper critical of the Rebels.

He could see the Coffee House's owner, Robert Townsend on the other side of the room, sitting with a tall, slender, thin faced, man with sandy straight hair and a dueling scar on one cheek. The man's dress was meticulous – an immaculate uniform, high riding boots, leather breeches and a heavy cavalry saber. Rivington knew who he was: Fredrich Baum, an officer among the German mercenaries hired by George III to fill out his army.

Baum had a reputation for complaining. Some of it was justified. His was a cavalry troop of 336 men but he had no horses, a dispute having arisen between his Hessian Prince and the British employer as to whether the price paid was to include horses. But, Baum stubbornly refused to surrender his company's elaborate and cumbersome cavalry gear. As a result, they made for peculiar looking and acting foot soldiers. He became one of the more vocal critics with how the war was being waged. And there was much to criticize. The war was being prosecuted in a most peculiar fashion.

The Howe brothers, William and Richard, one the Commander in Chief of British forces in America and the other Admiral of the fleet, had been given the dual tasks of suppressing the rebellion and, at the same time, of negotiating a peace that kept the American colonies productive and happy. It was a delicate, perhaps impossible, assignment. If the British crushed the Americans, as the Romans had suppressed the rebellious Jews, seventeen centuries before, leaving "not a stone left upon a stone", then the prospect of a peace that would bring kinsmen – and that was what they were – back together again afterwards would be impossible. On the other hand, a failure to display dominance would permit the rebellion to grow in size and would encourage the rebels' confidence. Even worse, it would encourage other colonies of England to do the same and then where would that tiny island be?

Townsend had been glancing around the room at the same time as Rivington had been. They caught each other's eye and Townsend gestured Rivington to join them. Rivington rose from his seat and joined them. With a bluntness characteristic of the German, Baum, in broken English, asked Rivington:

"Editor Rivington, you write news papers, but you never have – uh – amusing items, like poetry or clever sayings, in your paper .Do you think these items are amusing?" With that, he removed from his uniform breast pocket, two folded newspaper pages. He unfolded the first and handed it to Rivington:

(A Poem on General Howe's late expedition

to attack the army of the United States)

Threat'ning to drive us from the hill,

Sir William march'd t' attack our men;

But finding that we all stood still,

Sir William, he marched back again.

Rivington read the poem quickly. He had seen it before, of course. It was from *The New Jersey Gazette*, the rebel newspaper across the Hudson .He lifted his head to look at Baum who took that as a sign to give Rivington a second newspaper clipping, from the same paper but of a slightly later date. The item was based upon the coincidence that both the British and the American armies had senior officers with the same surname as senior officers in the American army. The British had General William Howe and his brother Admiral Richard Howe; the Americans had Robert Howe, a general. William Howe was replaced by Sir Henry Clinton, no relation to Generals George Clinton and James Clinton on the American side.

BON MOT

A British officer in New York, being in company with a lady whose sentiments were favorable to the cause of liberty, was making some severe remarks upon the American troops.

"However, Madam" said he, "I think you have a Howe and a Clinton in your Army."

"We have, Sir," replied the Lady, "but you have not a 'Washington' in yours."

"Sir, what is your purpose in showing me theses libelous, rebel lies? If I interpret them correctly, you should be hung." Rivington said in a voice seemingly barely under control.

Baum's reaction was as if he had been slapped. He had not expected Rivington's acid response. He had imagined the press items would precipitate a discussion of British policy and the competence of its generals, not be challenged as conduct for which he could be executed. Baum blustered back: "Sir, I simply showed you items your rival uses to make fun of us and the British in order to ask you why you do not do likewise to them."

"You doubt my loyalty, do you Major? I do not carry scandalous seditious documents with me to show around to loyal Britishers to raise trouble." Rivington said, his voice growing louder and attracting the attention of several around him .Townsend stood up and restrained his friend by the arm.

"James, James, control your temper .The Major does not question your loyalty to the Crown any more than we question his. Is not that true, Major?" Townsend asked with an innocent look on his face, giving the Hessian a face saving route out of his blunder, which he eagerly accepted.

"I am loyal to my Commander in America, Sir Henry Clinton and to King George in Britain. I will remain so if this war lasts another year, decade or century. That is my oath to my Prince, the Duke of Brunswick."

Townsend ordered a drink for all in the housing in the name of victory over the rebels. Then resuming his seat, Townsend remarked to Major Baum:

"Surely, the war will not take another year, much less a decade. It certainly will not last take a century, I hope."

The major, draining half his cup in one swallow of relief, sought to ingratiate himself with those who had, a moment earlier, been prepared to denounce him as a traitor. "No, it will not last so long, but if it did, I would be prepared to serve for the length of it. Our leader, Col. von Knyphausen, told me personally that Sir Henry's orders last year from the King himself, when he was told he would replace General Howe as commander, was that England would never give up the colonies even if victory would take a century. They would honor no peace. Were they expelled, they would return a second and a third time, if necessary to secure what was theirs. That is what I mean. I would be loyal for a century."

Rivington broke in belligerently as if anxious to resume the hostilities just averted: "The King did not have a audience with General Clinton about the war. Preposterous! Sir Henry receives his orders from Lord North and Lord Germain, not the monarch.

You have made that up."

This time the figurative slap across the face was one of a challenge. The Major had to give some credibility to his statement, but he found himself in a difficult situation. He had not been told of this meeting, as he had claimed, by von Knyphausen, but he had read it, without authorization, in a dispatch, with which he had been briefly entrusted, from von Knyphausen to the Prince. It had reported a statement made by Clinton to von Knyphausen, upon Clinton's return from England and receiving his knighthood. He could not reveal that source; nor could he afford to be in a duel about the subject at all as von Knyphausen would know immediately that Baum had been spying on him, however harmless his motive of curiosity had been.

"Sir, there are matters that are not for civilian ears and already I have said more than prudence should have permitted. I assure you, on my honor as an officer, that my representations to you that the King of England will never relax his claim upon these colonies, if it were to take a century of several efforts, that he has given this very instruction to Sir Henry and that I and my troops will obey our orders from him for as long as it takes, are all truthful. Beyond that, I can say no more and must take my leave." He finished his cup in a second gulp, raised up from his chair, bowed slightly, shook the proffered hands of both Rivington and Townsend and went out to the late afternoon sunshine of Hanover Square, eager to get as far away as possible from such conspiring.

After Baum had left, the two friends looked at each other without any comment at first. They believed the Major and his claim that King George was of the mind set of victory, however long it took and that there would be no peace in the offering.

Rivington was the first to speak: "A century?" He got up and threw into the fire the two news clippings that Baum had left behind. Could it be possible?

British Airways Flight # 1044

En route to London

July 17, 2005

Harry Clinton did not bear much resemblance to his great, great, great-grandfather. Sir Henry had been a pasty faced, long nosed, weak chinned man, described, by a contemporary, as remarkably ugly in both his countenance and personality. The younger Clinton was considerably more personable and better looking. A middle sized slender man with delicate features, fair skin and light hair, Clinton would be thought by many to be handsome and elegant. While never known as a cheerful chap, he had learned to display a natural enough looking, engaging smile, not the scowl that had been his ancestor's hallmark.

The flight home across the Atlantic would take five hours and Clinton used the chance to review the events of his trip to America. Accepting a glass of scotch from the stewardess, he leaned back in his comfortable first cabin seat, loosened his tie, and slipped off his shoes – for stiff Harry, acts bordering on public indecency. But British Airways was not his London club and his fellow first class passengers, while undoubtedly very nice people, were not his peers. It had been a busy trip, his meeting with Agnew being the final of four meetings he had in New Brunswick and Nova Scotia with similar "old" family friends. As in the case of Agnew, Clinton had known each of these men since they had been boys. Their fathers, grandfathers and farther back had been friends and this generation had been no exception, as it was hoped the next would not be. Each of them also had an ancestor who had been an ally of Sir Henry Clinton more than two centuries ago.

The first meeting had been with the Butler brothers, twins in their late thirties who lived above the famous fall, on the Canadian side of the Niagara River that divides northern New York from Canada. . Butler Trading Ltd., the family's business, for the prior two centuries, had begun in trading, with the Indians and, later with the white settlements that began to spring up throughout Canada. That network was expanded by the grandfather of the boys to include public and merchant banking and other finance. Today, it was the premier channel into Canada's old-line powerful families and interests.

For the first time since the obligation to assist Britain in retaking America had been passed down from generation to generation in certain families, twins had been "the eldest son" to whom the secret – and the duty which followed it – had been bequeathed. Harry's father, as leader of the United Loyalists at the time, had reasoned, that, since the boys were identical, not fraternal, twins, – that is, from the same egg and conceived at the same instant, they should equally represent the next Butler generation. It had been a wise resolution. Each brother was smart and capable of fulfilling his role in the recapture of America. But, at times – most times – they acted as a single person in two bodies.

Harry knew the Butler family history. It had been intertwined with the American War, the Loyalist Cause and their Indian allies .The first Butler, John, a trader among the Indians, had recruited and commanded a unit of Indian auxiliaries in the French and Indian War. When the revolution erupted, Butler and his son Walter, unquestionably Loyalists, fled north to Fort Niagara in Canada and recruited Indian allies and began to organize raids by mixed loyalist and Indian forces into the upper New York valleys.

Known as Butler's Rangers, they terrorized the American settlers on the frontiers of western New Jersey, eastern Pennsylvania and the lower Hudson River. They had several major victories, which the Americans called "massacres" where the captured were tortured and killed by Butler's Indian allies.

After the war, John Butler was awarded extensive holdings in Canada in recognition of his services. He became a trader and Indian agent to the many Indians who had aided the British and who themselves had to flee to Canada.

Butler had lost his son Walter, in the War but he had Walter's only son, named John after his grandfather, to raise in his stead. It was to his grandson that he revealed the obligation he had accepted for the family from Sir Henry Clinton to stand ready for the next assault upon America. Young John complied, when called in the War of 1812, and he passed on the obligation, all the way to the twin boys, with whom it now rested. Harry had been confident of their assistance and was not disappointed. They knew their obligations. They had written instructions from their ancestors as well as to heed Clinton's summons. And they were important to Clinton's plan. Their trading empire spread throughout Canada, to the oldest families in the regions, Indian and white. They were known and trusted and, all in all, Harry mused, should be perfect for the role he had planned for them.

Harry's recollection of his meeting with the Butler brothers was interrupted by the attractive stewardess, asking him his choice of an entree that evening. Clinton selected the trout and was pleasantly surprised at its fresh flavor and the light sauce that accompanied it. It was, after all, still airline fare. The wine was French and adequate. He detested the California wines – referring to them as colonial wines – and, consequently was happy to be going home to his own well-stocked cellar.

Clinton's thoughts shifted from the Butler brothers to their allies, the Mohawks and other members of the Iroquois Confederation. He had met this trip with one of their descendants, a Joseph Brant. He knew his story well also. The adopted son of Sir William Johnson, an American colonial fur trader, land speculator, soldier and Indian agent in the lower Mohawk Valley, Johnson saw to it that the Indian lad Joseph was raised alongside his own son, John. He provided for his education, both at school and on the battlefield during the French and Indian War.

Converted to Anglicanism in 1765, Joseph Brant became personal secretary and interpreter to the Johnson family. A decade later, when the American Revolution broke out, Brant allied the Iroquois with the English, was made a captain in the British army and assigned a special military unit of Indians that he was to form and command. He personally led them throughout the war in their savage attacks upon the American settlers.

At the war's end, Brant's leadership shifted from the battlefield to being chief of the Mohawks and Rector at St. Paul's, Her Majesty's Chapel of the Mohawks in Brantford. There, he translated The Anglican Book of Common Prayer and the Gospel of Mark into the Mohawk language.

It had been in Brantford where Harry Clinton had met with Joseph Brant's great, great, great grandson, who too bore his ancestors name. He also was an ordained minister in the Church of England in Canada. Clinton suspected that, despite the family's long association with the white settlers, Brant was still a full-blooded Mohawk. This Chief Brant, like his forebears, displayed the classic copper skin tones, high cheekbones and jet-black hair of the North American Indian. He was slim, an inch or so short of being six foot. Despite his being nearly 50 years of age, it was obvious why he had been as celebrated a lacrosse player in Canada as his great ancestor had been a warrior and leader. His speech, of course, was indistinguishable from that of his fellow Canadians, and his education undoubtedly superior, especially from his days abroad as a Rhodes Scholar.

"Joseph Brant was one of Sir Henry Clinton's first allies, when he had received his orders from King George, Lord North and the others, to prepare for the day of England's re-unification with its American colonies. My ancestors always kept their covenants to help and we shall do so now. You need only tell us what you want my people to do and it shall be done". The present chief said to Clinton as they walked together along a forest trail, far from any others who might listen in on the two old friends.

"Indeed, we shall do so gladly. When the Americans destroyed our villages and torched our lands, they destroyed our hunting grounds and the place where our ancestors sleep. We are Christians, of course, now but we still see the Great Spirit in the God of Abraham and the risen Christ. That Spirit has been offended. We shall do what you ask."

The woman across the aisle from him was already napping, the cabin's lights turned down, when Clinton turned his attention to, perhaps, the most unusual of his four meeting this trip. It had taken place on Cape Breton Island, off the Atlantic coast. The weather had been pleasant, if somewhat crisp, and Clinton knew he had come in the best season. Summer was not very long this far north. Although the ocean and the meandering Gulf Stream kept the winters from being arctic like, it was still on the edge of being inhabitable.

It was the last place one would expect to meet a Black

63

man, much less a community of them that had resided there for more than two centuries. Clinton knew their story also, although few did.

From the war's inception, the British promised freedom to all slaves who were willing to desert their American masters. "Every Negro who shall desert the rebel standard ... full security to follow within the British] lines any occupation which he shall think proper." The effects of the appeal, advertised to the slaves under the banner of "freedom and a farm" were formidable. While 5,000 slaves had thrown their lot in with the rebels, accepting their offers of manumission in exchange for joining the American cause, twenty times as many – 100,000 slaves, one fifth of the slave population in America, preferred the British offer of freedom.

At war's end, the British, before leaving New York, kept Sir Henry's pledge. From May, 1782 to November, 1783, on every Wednesday morning, Negroes came to the *Queens Head* Tavern (now Fraunces) still standing on the same corner of Pearl Street and Broad at the foot of Manhattan Island. Maintained there by a joint commission of Americans and British was the *"Book Of Negroes"* .It determined which Negroes were eligible to be evacuated and which had to be returned to slavery with their American masters. In it was logged details of each black's enslavement, escape and military service. If their stories checked out, the former slave would be given a pass that read:

New York

This is to certify to whomever it may concern that the bearer hereof

[name],

a Negro, reported to the British Lines in consequence of the Proclamations of Sir William Howe and Sir Henry Clinton, late Commanders in Chief in America, and that the said Negro hereby has his Excellency Sir Guy Carleton's permission to go to Nova Scotia or where else [he or she] thinks proper.

[Samuel] Birch]

Most former slaves elected to sail north to Canada and Nova Scotia. It was the northernmost frontier of European settlement in the New World and among the least desirable because of the cold and thin rocky soil. One group, led by a Thomas Brownspriggs, went even further north to Chedabucto Bay and Cape Breton Island. It is there where one still can find the descendants of the group. And it was to a cottage there that Harry Clinton went. The Thomas Brownspriggs Clinton knew was a fisherman. His father before him and his father before him, all the way to their coming here. Inside the comfortable cottage, as tucked away as one can get on the rugged coast, Harry immediately looked for what he knew to be the Brownspriggs family most prized possession. It still hung on the wall as it had in prior visits – the pass signed by General Birch, the proof that Thomas Brownspriggs, late a Carolina slave, was a free man as was all of his descendants. Clinton moved to it immediately upon entering and reread it. It was a ritual he performed every visit. His ancestor had been the man who freed Tom's ancestor and, from their exile at the war's end, they had become related in some mystical manner.

Tom's accent was of a Cape Bretoner, the shade of skin meaningless in such things. Speaking with a brogue of sorts in an island dialect stuck in the 1700's, Tom could at times be difficult to follow. The pipe that never left his mouth did not help, nor the moments of silence into which fishermen, accustomed to solitude, sometimes lapse. But, on the whole, they spent a wonderful day out in Tom's boat and he checked his string of lobster pots. They talked on many things, but principally of sons, fishing and "duty." At day's end, with a tank full of plugged, brown green lobsters climbing over themselves on their first leg to market, Harry asked his friend whether he had been told to expect a request from him someday. Tom looked at him, as if he had been expecting the question, nodded a yes but said nothing.

Harry spoke again. "It is time."

Tom nodded once more and despite his accent, the pipe clenched in his mouth and the groans of the boat's engine as it struggled to bring them back to shore, there was no mistaken his answer. "Tell me want you want me to do."

Harry Clinton must have dozed off for a moment .The dinner dishes had been cleared away long before but he still had a firm hold on his coffee cup. Perhaps, it had been thinking about the roll of Brownspriggs boat that had put Harry to sleep. More likely, it had been the last several days of traveling and meetings. It had gone well he thought. He could report to Mother favorably and he thought that would trigger Phase Two of the plan.

Clinton knew he had also to report – in general terms, she did not need more than that – to Pamela about his trip to Canada. No one knew about Pamela, not even Mother. Sir Henry had insisted there be a failsafe mechanism in the event he did not have a male descendant or, if something happened to the male during the exercise, that someone of Clinton's line could replace him. As Sir Henry had only a daughter besides his son Henry, the task of being the insurance policy fell to her and her line. Sir Harry and his American mistress of many years, the girl's mother, had instructed their daughter of her responsibility as a back up in the plot. Thereafter, it would be her duty to insure that her oldest daughter was similarly instructed and that the tradition be passed down for as long as it would take to recapture America. The present occupant of that seat as Sir Henry's first-born great, great, great, granddaughter was Pamela, a stunning 30-year-old London barrister.

Since, six generations back, their ancestors had shared the same parents – Sir Henry and Mistress Blundell – Harry and Pamela were cousins of some degree. But it was far enough removed to permit Harry to think of her as a woman as well as co-conspirator. She was a very intelligent girl, and aggressive as a man in some things. But she was also very much a woman, earthy, lusty in her full figure and long blond hair. Harry would ring Pamela tomorrow and have lunch with her so she could be up to date on every thing. He would also see if Mother needed to see him. Confident he had thought out as much as he could at present,

Harry asked the stewardess for a glass of port, but was asleep by the time she brought it.

New York City

July 6, 1778

Sir Henry Clinton, for the past few months, the Commander in Chief of His Majesty King George's Army in America had had a busy beginning. He had relieved Sir William Howe of the command in May, immediately prepared to evacuate Philadelphia and, by the end of June, had marched his army across New Jersey to consolidate it with his other forces in the occupied City of New York. En route he had encountered General Washington at Monmouth Court House and had barely escaped, having left some of the British pride on the fled battlefield. Now, less than a week later, he had called his adjutant, Major John Andre, into the room at the Kennedy House that he had converted into his sitting room. The Kennedy House was one of only a few buildings remaining in downtown Manhattan after the fleeing Americans had torched it.

Andre had been Clinton's second in command only since Howe had left and that had not been enough time for Clinton to fully evaluate him as an officer. So far, however, he was pleased with the young man's abilities and loyalties. Andre was a romantic enough figure to be sure. Not English, but of French Huguenot parentage, he had come to England, via Geneva and joined British army.

Andre had little battle experience. In fact, he had been captured in his first battle in America. Exchanged, he was later to serve at German Town and Brandywine, but he was never in the thick of the fighting. Clinton knew all of this, of course, but considered Andre's possible service to be of a different nature than martial. Andre was his spymaster. It was he who was putting together an intelligence gathering apparatus for Clinton that purchased traitors for gold.

Andre had a second value to Clinton, as a liaison with the Loyalist community. Clinton was acutely aware that the Loyalists in New York did not like him. In fact, Judge Thomas Jones, the spokesman for the Loyalist in New York City had gone so far as to describe Clinton, as being "haughty, morose, churlish, stupid and scarcely ever to be spoken with." Major Andre, on the other hand, had been at the center of the loyalist social set in Philadelphia. The handsome dark Andre proved very popular especially among the female loyalists. He had organized an extravagant ball, known as the Mischanzia, in honor of General Howe, given a few months before, he returned to England. One of Andre's special friends in Philadelphia had been Peggy Shippen, attractive young women who was passionately pro English .Peggy was soon to begin dating, and then would marry, the new American military commander of the British evacuated Philadelphia, Benedict Arnold. It would lead to a connection that almost allowed Clinton to win the war in a single stroke.

"Major," Clinton said, "I want to split the American colonies in half and I want to cut it along the Hudson River. If we can control the river and prevent the rebels from the south from sending reinforcements and supplies across, then we can concentrate our forces on the traitors in New England and exterminate them first. After that, we can turn our attention on those in the south who still have any stomach to fight. Do you understand what I am saying, Major?"

Major Andre, eyes aglow with excitement, snapped back "yes Sir" and Clinton continued.

"We tried to do that militarily but Sir William for reasons of his own condemned that effort to failure by heading to Philadelphia rather than up the Hudson to meet General Burgoyne. The key to suppressing this insurrection is the Hudson River and the key to the river is the rebel fort at West Point. If we can take West Point, then the Hudson can be lined with the ships of our fleet, its banks with our artillery and soldiers. We can seal off New England and scour it, hanging every rebel we find. Understand?"

"Yes sir."

"I want you to form a plan to take West Point, preferably by stealth and surprise but by force if required."

Major Andre acknowledged that he had understood his orders and was dismissed.

"Boy!" Clinton shouted. From nowhere it seemed,

Harmon Hays appeared. "Boy, I want to go riding. Lay out what I need and have them bring my horse around. And advise Mistress Blundell of my plans and tell her we shall lunch afterwards."

Clinton watched his servant boy leave, as quietly and unobtrusively as he had appeared. He was a good lad. His short hair, necessitated by its having caught on fire at Monmouth, was proof of his loyalty .He could have easily runaway during the confusion of the evacuation and have melted among the Americans, thus achieving his freedom three years before his indenture terminated. But he had not. That was loyalty and that was a sign of a good servant, thought Clinton. The decision to acquire the boy had turned out nicely. He had been Robert Townsend's servant lad.

Townsend had also sent over Oliver Blundell, a Falstaff looking fellow to be Sir Henry's Butler and head of household staff. However, it was not Townsend's recommendation that secured this chap the job but his very attractive daughter Mary. Clinton had been a widower since 1772, childless and lonely. The 48-year-old general had been smitten immediately by this lusty 19 year old.

Clinton paused in his preparations to think about Mary Blundell for a moment. He liked doing that, as if it were an elixir that gave him energy. She was quite a beauty, full faced, round figured and always laughing and smiling. She seemed, Clinton thought, genuinely fond of him, despite their differences in age and station. The truth was that, oddly enough, Mary Blundell did not find Sir Henry as offensive as many others did. Indeed, over the past 18 months, she had grown attracted to the point of being in love with him. She had become his mistress, in the parlance of the times, and they were both made happy by it.

The Kennedy Mansion was located at the foot of Broadway, near the burned Mall and New York Bay. It had become a custom for Clinton and his entourage to "take a ride" on the mornings that Clinton proclaimed. They would mount their horses and then race at full speed up Broadway, past the burned out hulk of Trinity Church, pass St. Paul's Church that had escaped the American blazes (and still stands) and further north to one of the two public houses that were left standing. It had been the site of an orchard but now was a notorious part of town. Not far from the cluster of courthouses that are there now, Clinton and his aides would gamble, drink, bet on cockfights and gray crew cut, but he was not completely sure. Many clever people flitted from topic to topic that way, peppering the air with questions and comments but never answers. Hays, who was adept at banter himself and could return a barb or volley any subject, was at a loss to even get in the conversation play at billiards and ten pins, until such time as Sir Henry grew tried of the sports. Then, at his command, they would remount and dash back downtown "like a sportsman at a fox chase."

Clinton knew that this was not much of a way to fight a war. He had all his forces back in New York now – Washington was over in New Jersey, half pinning the British in New York City, ready to shadow the British troops if they moved from their camp in the city. The harbor was full of His Majesty's Fleet. Thousands and thousands of troops were encamped over, across the harbor, on Staten Island, awaiting Clinton's command to move. But where should he go? His recent encounter with Washington at Monmouth had frightened him. He should go north and take West Point and the Hudson River. He had the forces to do it. But what about the West Indies? France was in the war now and could be expected to aid the American cause by seizing the rich Caribbean trade for herself. Clinton had to consider that also. There were so many options and Clinton had to wade through them. He knew some claimed he was indecisive and he resented it. Some things just had to be thought through and that was what he was doing .

New York City

July 6, 1778

Back at his printing office on Hanover Square, James Rivington hovered over the first newssheet from his press as it dried on a rack. He tried not to touch anything. The ink stained and stunk. The item that commanded his attention was one written by himself, reporting on a recent birthday celebration held for King George at the British Coffee House, next door. All the military and civilian dignitaries in New York City had been there, including the Royal Governors of New York, New Jersey and North Carolina, all now in exile, the civil administrators, the British and Hessian senior officers, the more important Loyalist civilians who had come to New York as refugees of the war, and, of course, amidst them all, drinking, laughing and shouting comments, was James Rivington himself. It had been a long boisterous night with the increasingly drunker participants searching for names or ideals to which to toast: Rivington reported on them all:

Yesterday being HIS MAJESTY'S BIRTHDAY, and an elegant Entertainment was given by his Excellency General Tyron, at which were present the Governors of New Jersey and North Carolina and members of his Majesty's Council for the Province of New York, the Judges and other Officers of Government. The following toasts were drank on the Occasion:

1. The KING

2. The QUEEN and Royal Family

3. The LANDGRAVE of Hesse

4. The Foreign Powers in amity with Great Britain.

5. The Army and Navy

6. The Commander in Chief and Success to his Majesty's Arms.

7. His Majesty's Ministers

8. Governor Tyron and the speedy Restoration of Government to New York

9. *Governor Franklin and the speedy Restoration of Government to New Jersey*

10. *Governor Martin and the speedy Restoration of Government to North Carolina*

11. *Unanimity and Firmness to Great Britain*

12. *General Haldimand and our Friends in Canada*

14. *General Knyphausen and the Hessian Corps under his Command*

15. *The COMMANDANT of New York*

16. *Mr. MATTHEWS, the Mayor and LOYAL CITIZENS OF NEW YORK*

17. *The LOYALISTS of the Continent of America*

18. *Success to the Exertions of the Refugees*

19. *a speedy suppression to rebellion*

20. *a happy restoration of Civil Government in his Majesty's Colonies*

21. *CHURCH AND STATE*

Rivington recalled the optimism that liquor had brought to the evening. But, he also knew that, as much as he ridiculed it in his press, that liberty and independence were much more intoxicating than rum or brandy and that it had been of the first two spirits that the rebels had been imbibing. He read this week's issue of *The New Jersey Gazette*, a rebel paper in Trenton that had sprung up a year before. It contained a report on another birthday being celebrated, this one, across the Hudson River at Princeton:

Last Saturday, the Anniversary of the Declaration of our Independence was commemorated at Princeton with the greatest demonstration of joy for our happy deliverance from tyranny and arbitrary power and the glorious prospect of transmitting freedom and happiness to our latest posterity. At six o'clock in the afternoon (a signal gun having been previously fired to collect the inhabitants) the solemnity commenced by the discharge of thirteen rounds of cannon, being some of the brass fieldpieces having been previously taken from General Burgoyne, one of the three so called conquerors of America. The discharge of the cannon was preceded by three huzzas from a large concourse of people, all exulting in the opportunity of expressing their gratulations in being delivered from the yoke of a merciless tyranny and his execrable minions. After this, His Excellency the Governor, with such of the Members of the Legislative Council and General Assembly as were in Town, with the Officers of the Army and Militia, repaired to the Governor's Quarters, where they passed the rest of the day with great festivity and decorum and drank the following toasts:

1. The Honorable Congress

2. The Free and Independent States of America

3. His Excellency General Washington

4. The American Army and Navy

5. May our Independence endure while the sun shall shine or the rivers flow

6. His Most Christian Majesty of France, our illustrious Ally and the magnanimous Protector of the rights of mankind

7. May the Confederated States of America be ever supported by the same public virtue and patriotism by which they were established

8. Benjamin Franklin, our Ambassador at the Court of Versailles

9. The State of New Jersey

10. Our brave and patriotic Militia

11. House in which we obtained a complete victory over the choicest and most veteran of the enemy's troops

12. The memory of all the heroes who have fallen in defense of American liberty during the war

13 May our example excite the oppressed in every part of the world to resist the outrages of tyranny and may they be equally as successful in asserting the natural and unalienable rights of mankind.

In the evening the inhabitants testified their joy by a general illumination of the village.

Rivington paused after reading the report from Princeton,

wondering whether, the editor of *The New Jersey Gazette*, like Rivington himself, invented the news more than he reported it. Could the rebels be so sincere and virtuous in their sentiments? Rivington shook his head. He did not know the answer.

In south central Texas, Hays County is almost 700 square miles in size and has a population of about 65,000. The upper three-quarters of the county are rolling hills, with a lot of ranching, mostly beef, but some sheep and goats. The southeastern part of the county, originally prairie, is now farmland, producing crops of cotton, hay, wheat, corn and sorghum.

The county had been named in 1848 in honor of the famous Captain Jack Hays, Texas Ranger and Indian fighter. The first settlers had insisted upon that name for the county. They had all rode with Captain Jack Hays as members of his Ranger Company. They were brave, tough men who shared an almost religious respect and devotion for their slim, smooth faced, young captain. He could outride his fellows as well and outfight them, either with his fists, a Colt 45 or the infamous Bowie knife.

The region soon began to draw more of Hays' comrades from the Rangers as they left the risks of fighting Indians, Mexican bandits and American desperados, for ranching. Captain Jack has listed their names in the materials, passed down from generation to generation, that Jackie had opened that day in Tahoe. These had been the fellows with whom Hays had rode during the years of the Texas Republic and helped to prevent the British takeover of Texas as part of its plan to recapture America.

Jackie Hays understood the instructions he had received from the grave to round up the descendants of Hays' comrades of a century and a half before. But where to start? He had their names but did any of them still live in Hays County. Probably not. These kind of men kept moving west. They were men who could only thrive on the frontier borders where courage and self-reliance were needed most. With civilization came the meddling of a smug government and its bureaucracy and those things smothered this type of man.

He looked in the telephone book and found several of those surnames on the list, a cluster of them, up north by Dripping Springs, a town of about a thousand. Hays thought that the local library there might be an appropriate place to ask some questions. It was a tiny place and the attractive blonde behind the desk gave a big smile as he walked in. Whether it was because Jackie had been the first person to come by since noontime or whether it was his handsome, boyish look that triggered it is any one's guess. But the greeting was genuine.

"Good afternoon, stranger. New in town?" she asked in such a becoming way that Jackie, even with all his Tahoe *savoir-faire* and California aplomb, was nevertheless taken aback. He stuttered an unintelligible response. This embarrassed him and made him blush. This, in turn, caused her to laugh, which made him blush all the more. Regaining his composure, Jackie finally answered:

"Unfortunately, I am just passing through because this certainly seems to be a most attractive town." There was a twinkle in his eye and an emphasis on the word "attractive" that made it the librarian's turn to blush .Seeing how friendly she was, Jackie opted to drop the line of questioning he had planned in favor of a simple statement as to what he needed.

"I am certain librarians are asked to help on the strangest of topics. I have an odd one. Do you have a minute?"

She smiled. She had plenty of time and, even if she had not, she would have found some. "Depends on what kind of help you're looking for, stranger. I had one request that made me get this pistol out of the drawer" she replied, reaching down and taking out a revolver.

Jackie did not change his expression and, lawyer like asked: "And then what happened?

She threw back her head and howled, "That fellow tore out of here as if Jack Hays himself were after him".

"What did you say?" he asked, wondering if he had heard her correctly. She repeated the phrase and he exclaimed, "That's amazing. That's the very subject I needed your help on – Jack Hays. He is my ancestor and I want to locate the descendants of some of the men who rode with him in the Texas Rangers. A lot settled hereabouts, I'm told. I have a list of their names. I just do not know how to go about tracing them for four or five generations. I came here to try. Quite a coincidence, your mentioning Jack Hays. Any ideas?" As he spoke, he retrieved a copy of the list from his bag and handed it to her. It had a half dozen or so names circled, those whom Jackie had been able to find in the telephone book.

The girl's expression changed. A serious, studious face replaced the pretty farm girl look, as she put on her glasses. She had been a history minor at Abilene Christian University. She, of course, knew about Captain Jack Hays. Everyone in Hays County knew about Captain Jack Hays and she had been born and bred in the county. Fact is many people in the county, including her own poppa, claimed descent from one or another of Hays Rangers. Yup, there was the name Moon on the list. Should she tell him her name was Debbie Jean Moon. She knew that, after he left Texas, Hays had gone to California and died an extremely wealthy man. Here before her was this good looking man and, without a wedding ring on, as she had noticed immediately upon his entry.

Yet, something held her back from blurting that information. It could all be some kind of trick. This fellow had a clever look about him and who says that this is really why he wanted to find certain people. She was the one who had first mentioned Jack Hays, not he. He just followed up on it. And what would he want with her Poppa, anyway? He ain't done nothing wrong. The wrestling within her mind must have revealed itself on her face because Jackie asked whether anything were wrong.

She smiled and said, "I'm thinking, I'm thinking. It's not an everyday question you know. Everyone's in a hurry. You wouldn't be a Yankee from New York, would you?" she asked with a mock squint, as if that accounted for his rushing her.

As they had first traded blushes, they now traded smiles.

"No, California. San Francisco area actually."

"I've never been to San Francisco. I'd love to someday," she said wistfully. "Dripping Springs is a pretty small place, you know. Let me get you started with the Civil War rolls from the county and see if anybody of these names were residents of Hays County then. I'll look for some other stuff in the meanwhile." She went off and came back with several books that contained records from the Civil War era and then she went into the back.

Jackie first inventoried what he had before him. In skimming through it, he had seen many of the names from the list. Just as he was going to go through it a second time, taking notes, a very firm, no nonsense voice behind him, said:

"Son, you just get up real slowly, now. I want your hands above you, where I can see them. O.K. That's good. Now, I'm going to reach into your back pocket and remove your wallet because I want to see who you are. Do you understand that?"

Jackie nodded his yes with the back of his head, not trusting his voice.

He felt a hand go into his right rear pocket and remove the wallet. There was silence for about sixty seconds, as the man was obviously searching through the wallet. Then, the voice said

"Please turn around, Mr. Hays."

Jackie did, but slowly as if anticipating a blow or some other attack. There was none. There was only a large man, maybe 300 pounds over his 6 foot two inch frame and approaching 60 years of age. He wore a khaki uniform, with a big Texas star dominant on his chest. He was returning his gun it its holster, after which, he handed Jackie back his wallet.

"Mr. Hays, it is a genuine pleasure to meet kin of John Coffee Hays. To us, he's more than a legend. Our fathers held him up to us an example when we were growing up. We played all his battles, each of us played our ancestors part."

Hays cut in, his confidence immediately returning. He had seen his opening. "Sheriff, I know what you mean. My father reared me the same way, as his father had reared him and Captain Jack was in the center. My favorite battle was Emerald Rock. What was yours?"

The Sheriff answered without a moment's delay. "Plum Creek Fight. My grand daddy was a scout for Captain Jack in that one."

Your last name doesn't happen to be McCullough, does it, Sheriff?"

The sheriff broke in to a broad grin. "Yes sir, Ben McCullough was his name."

Hays continued. "I know. And you carried on the law business too, haven't you, Sheriff. As I recall Ben went with Captain Jack out to California for a while and he became Sheriff of Sacramento about the same time that Jack was Sheriff of San Francisco."

"That's right", the sheriff replied. "Then, Ben come back to Texas and became a lawman here."

"Didn't Ben have a brother who fought with Captain Jack too at Plum Creek and later in the Mexican War?"

"Sure did, by the name of Henry. He kept fighting Indians when the others went off to California. He became a federal lawman too, like Ben, until the Civil War, of course. Got killed there."

"Do you ever keep in touch with Henry's side of the family?"

"Like brothers, we are, even though that side went east to New York, after Ben got killed. Many of the families of the men who rode with Captain Jack have remained in touch over the generations."

"Really" said Jackie. "If some one were to want to get in touch with them, Sheriff, how would you suggest his going about that? Is there someone in particular to contact?"

"You are looking at him Mr. Hays. I am in touch with the boys."

"Well" continued Hays in almost a casual way, as if the favor to be sought were a small one "I do believe I would like to visit with the boys for awhile."

"What should I tell them it's about?"

While Hays did not hesitate in his answer, it was not rushed either. "Your ancestors and mine had a pact to which their sons forever are bound. I am to call on you for help. Our nation is in danger. We must ride together."

Sheriff McCollough got up and, as he was leaving, said, "I'll be in touch, Captain." Each man realized at the same time the title that the Sheriff had unconsciously given Hays but neither corrected it. It looked as if Captain Jack Hays were back.

San Antonio is among the most picturesque cities in America and Jackie Hays quickly had accepted Sheriff McCollough's suggestion that he go there and await a meeting that McCollough would set up among Hays and the boys. The San Antonio River, fed by artesian springs, meanders through the old part of town. There was much there to trigger Hays' thoughts about the task he had before him.

San Antonio de Bexar was central to the history of Texas. Founded as a Spanish garrison in 1718, it was intended to protect the several Indian missions, which lay nearby.

Of course, Hays, like all Americans, best knew San Antonio for its being the stage for the most courageous act of the Texas War of Independence from Mexico, the valiant defense of the Alamo.

Hays went over, first thing, to see the fort where 190 Texans had held out for a dozen days before being massacred to a man by bloody Mexican dictator, Santa Anna. The Alamo is more a shrine than a museum – "Gentlemen are requested to remove their hats before entering"! Hays could not stay away from it. He found himself drawn to it a half dozen times at least in his two-day visit. He studied all he could about this symbol of the sacrifices that men will endure to insure freedom and liberty for their progeny. As he walked within the Alamo, reading about the acts of heroism of its defenders and martyrs, Travis, Bowie, Crockett and Bonham, Hays began to visualize the role ahead for him. It, too, was heroic. It, too, was to insure liberty and independence. He, too, was prepared to die. His father and grandfather had prepared him for that. He had been warned that being a leader and a servant to others might require suffering, even the supreme sacrifice of his life. He was prepared to join the heroes of the Alamo, if his duty demanded it.

Across the plaza from the Alamo is the Menger Hotel,

where Hays was staying as he waited to hear from Sheriff McCollough. After Texas had secured its independence from Mexico, thousands of immigrants had swarmed into Texas. Many were directly from Europe. The German independent states like Hesse and Prussia, claiming overpopulation at home, had set up German colonies in central Texas, including San Antonio. One of them, William Menger, had a brewery right on the square near the Alamo. Before the Civil War he built a hotel next to it, which, expanded and modernized several times in the decades since, since stands on the Square. A lot of Texas history is attached to the place. It was on its front porch and taproom that Teddy Roosevelt had returned to recruit some of his Texas cowboys chums to join his Rough Riders in the Spanish American War of 1898.

At around 4:30, on the afternoon of his second day at the hotel, Hays answered the telephone to hear Sheriff McCollough invite him down to the bar tap room in the hotel to meet some of the fellows. When Hays got there, however, he saw a handwritten sign on its door that stated that it was closed for a private party. Hays turned to go. Maybe, there was another bar at the hotel. But, at that moment, the door opened from within and a grinning Sheriff McCollough waved Hays in with a cheerful:

"In here, Captain Hays."

This time the term "captain" had not been used by accident. To McCollough, he was Captain Jack, reincarnated. The taproom had been installed in the 1880's and was a replica, oddly enough, of the taproom in the House of Lords Club in London. The solid cherry bar with paneling of the same wood, French mirrors and gold plated bar railing and spittoons must have been quite a contrast to the dusty, frontier life outside a hundred years ago.

The room was full of men, at least 30 of them. Some were sitting; some were lounging about. Their dress was as varied as their ages – the full spectrum from ranchers in jeans and ostrich skin boots, farmers in overalls, to businessmen in thousand dollar suits, 18 year olders and septuagenarians. None was drinking. They had come to a meeting .A church would have been more appropriate than a taproom.

"Captain Hays, let me introduce you to the descendants of some of the Texas Rangers the men who rode with your great, great grand pappy, Captain John Coffee Hays". Then, like a roll call, he introduced each and briefly informed Hays about both the ancestor and the descendant.

Each stood erect, as if at attention, while McCollough spoke about him and his ancestor. When he had finished, each acknowledged the attention with a slight nod of his head in the direction of McCollough and Hays, a nod which Hays returned with just the faintest trace of a smile.

After he had finished going around the room in like fashion, McCollough concluded:

"Captain, except for Henry McCullough's descendant, whose plane from New York last night was canceled, everyone is present."

Hays waited a moment to collect his thoughts before beginning. It was a self-discipline he had learned in court, to wait until everyone was ready to listen and, at the same time, reviewing what he was about to say one final time.

"Thank you, Lieutenant McCullough," a battlefield promotion of the Sheriff to second in command. "Is there any one in this room, Lieutenant, in front of whom we cannot speak with absolute candor?"

McCullough replied without any hesitation. "Each of us is secure, sir, and we have taken precautions to be certain that our perimeter is free of eavesdroppers."

"Very good." then, turning his attention to the others in the room, Hays began. "Gentlemen. I have received orders from beyond the grave to undertake an important task. I was advised that you, the descendants of Captain Jack Hays' closest comrades, would again help a Hays. The assignment is incredible but I suspect, no more incredible than the one that your ancestors and mine rendered our country 160 years ago. Do any of you know more about Captain Jack Hays and his Rangers from 1836 through the Mexican War, other than what the history books say about it?

McCullough answered for the group;

"Sir, the reason why we were able to organize as quickly as we did to meet with you was that our fathers all taught us, as their fathers had taught them, to await a call from Captain Jack's descendant and, when it comes, to follow his orders without hesitation. As to why, we know little from our forebears beyond the fact that the history books do not tell the whole story, but what is omitted we do not know" – and, he added, "and, as good soldiers, we do not need to know."

Hays nodded and said: "Those under me will always know as much as I do, if at all practical. But right now, I know only a little more than you. I expect to learn more in New York later next week. After that, we will meet again for several days – some place isolated – and make our plans.

But for now, I can give you only an outline but, perhaps, that will be enough to digest at one time, it being, as I said an incredible story – but, let me assure you, a true one. Your own ancestors' instructions to you bear that out.

It seems that the Texas Rangers, under Captain Hays, played a greater role than fighting Indians, capturing bandits and keeping back the Mexicans. They were agents for the United States, charged with foiling a plan by Great Britain to first annex Texas, then the American south and, finally, to use those territories and Canada to the north as a vise in which to squeeze what would be left of the United States into an economic island. The plot had been formulated in British Royal Court back in 1783, when England supposedly agreed to a peace treaty with its former colonies. But, Britain had really continued to view America as her own and had waited for its chance to re-assert its rights to it.

All your ancestors knew that this was their role. They also knew that, even when they succeeded in thwarting the English plan, that it was not over – that the British would try again when the next opportunity presented itself. That is why Captain Jack never disbanded his company and why your ancestors still considered themselves and their issue bound to their duty to repel the next attempt.

This next attempt, if not imminent, is on the horizon. I will learn further details about what our role is, but I am certain that it will involve great risk, perhaps death. If any of you wish to withdraw from the Company at this time, you may do so without any dishonor in my eyes. I would charge you to be silent about any of this, but, of course, no one would believe you anyway."

Hays waited to see if any one wished to withdraw. The image of William Travis at the Alamo giving a similar chance to the defenders crossed Hay's mind, as it must have every other Texan there. However, here, in the taproom of the Menger House, there was not even one to leave.

"Very well," Hays said. "I do believe that the subject is closed until we learn some more information. In the meanwhile, I will stand drinks for any man that will join me. I'd like to meet the men with whom I am going to ride."

New York City

July 14, 2005

Jack Hays had been coming to New York City with his father on business trips east, since he had been a boy. He knew the city just enough not to be either lured, bullied or lulled by it. He stayed at the Waldorf, again his father's favorite. As Jackie himself grew older, he seemed to better appreciate his father's tastes in things.

Sheriff McCollough had suggested that, on his visit to New York, Hays speak with a distant cousin of his, Jim McCullough, who lived in the city. Jim, who had missed the meeting in San Antonio, was the descendant of another Ranger, Henry McCollough, whose family had returned east after the Civil War. The Sheriff arranged for the two of them to meet at The Bull and The Bear, the more manly of the Waldorf's bars.

But, McCollough was late – 15 minutes and Hays found himself divided between excusing the man or finding fault with his tardiness. He lived way up in the Bronx, where he was a schoolteacher, and was probably coming by subway. You would not drive in midtown New York City, even if you could afford the parking, which a schoolteacher normally could not. On the other hand, Hays reasoned, we had an appointment and timing, especially for an outfit like the Rangers, was critical. He should have left earlier or, like the canceled flight from New York, made other arrangements to insure his performance.

There were at least two dozen people along the dark wooded, scalloped bar. Elevated at its center was a bronzed bull and bear. Hays did not know the significance of the statutes, unless they had something to do with the markets named after them on Wall Street. He had asked the bar boy about it but received a pleasant enough *non comprende* shrug of ignorance in reply.

Most of the bar's patrons were in groups of twos and threes, excluding any of them as candidates for being

87

McCollough. The few that were alone were obviously not the missing Ranger – a Japanese businessman, glancing at his watch impatiently; a portly priest in his mid fifties, devouring a bowl of complimentary cashews; a shaky octogenarian, a regular on his way home leaning against the bar for support as he sipped from his second martini; an athletic looking Black man who had signed some autographs for a group seated at one of the tables that surround the standing bar. Hays looked at his own watch again and was startled to hear someone ask:

"Captain Hays, I presume."

Hays turned his head. It was the priest. He had come around on Hays backside and surprised him.

"Yes" was all Hays could utter.

"Thought so. You looked as if you were waiting for someone and I thought I would see how observant you were. Cousin Ben did not tell you I was a priest, I gather? The Texas side of the family hasn't accepted it yet" he grinned"

Hays' smile was spontaneous and genuine. It was also disarming and sometimes, like here, that was very useful, allowing him the moment necessary to collect his thoughts and arm his wit. "No, no one did or else, even a hayseed like me would have been able to pick you out of a crowd. Sheriff McCollough said you were a teacher and I guess I had another image in mind." Hays confessed as he shook the priest's proffered hand.

"Well, I hope this teaches you not to jump to unsupported conclusions the next time. Yes, I am a teacher. Philosophy. In fact, I am head of the Department, up at Fordham University in the Bronx. Do you teach?"

"No, I am a lawyer. In San Francisco."

Oh, pity. Oh, not about San Francisco. I like San Francisco well enough – taught at the University of San Francisco. I meant about lawyers. A lot of our graduates become lawyers. Fact is we have a whole school of them. Pity."

Hays did not how to respond. He believed he was having his leg pulled by this chunky man with the. Father McCollough was the teacher, lecturing in the Socratic method, using questions as his way to start the student's mind working. Sometimes, he waited for an answer, most times not. The questions were rhetorical and the philosophy professor was already racing off on a new line of inquiry.

After a while - and several drinks each – Hays began to understand and like the flow. They stood at the bar for well more than half an hour, the priest raising non stop a string of interesting provocative matters that Hays tried to tuck away in his mind to contemplate some day sitting on the dock at Lake Tahoe .

Finally, Hays suggested that they have dinner. He had asked the priest where he would like to eat, thinking it would be a treat for him, a change from the diet a cleric usually suffers. "Captain, I am a Jesuit priest. My mind and my stomach are always filled with the finest ideas and foods. Because of my concupiscence, I was never drawn toward mysticism, the missions or being a hermit. Indeed, my palate and my pride vie to be my greatest failure." He then asked Hays his preferences for dinner and, finally, at that point in polite conversation when each has sufficiently asked the other "to chose" a place or food, Father McCollough suggested a favorite spot of his nearby. He even knew its address. Hays elected that one.

They had no reservations but that did not seem to cause any problem, despite there being a number of people at the bar, waiting for a table. The owner left the elegant woman to whom he had been speaking and came right over to Father McCollough and hugged him. The priest returned the embrace with as much gusto as it had been given. He turned to introduce Jackie to the owner of the restaurant, Joe D'Allasandro, explaining, at the same time, that this had been one of his most promising students two decades before until he had discovered the world of business and women.

"Is the room available?" Father McCollough asked, knowing that it was because he had called that afternoon, confident in an omniscient way that this was where they were going to dine.

"Of course, Father. Please follow me"

They walked across the restaurant floor and up a small staircase on the far side of the room, through a single door and into a private dining room, hidden from the rest of the restaurant. A door across the room led to a separate private passage out of the restaurant.

"Some notable people from mobsters to presidents, movie starlets and movie moguls alike, have dined at this table. It is quiet and you need not be afraid of being overheard or disturbed." D'Allasandro explained as he handed each a menu and took a drink order from them.

"Margaret will bring you your drinks. Then buzz when you want Emilio to take your order. The owner smiled at his former teacher and bowed slightly at Hays and left.

Within a few moments, a striking blonde brought in their drinks. She and Father McCollough obviously knew each other also as there was no hesitancy in the kisses on the cheek they exchanged. "Margaret, Margaret, how pretty you always are. But still not on the stage?"

"Not yet, Father, but soon, I'm sure. I am having a lot of auditions and callbacks. You told me. If it were easy, every one would be doing it."

"Margaret, a teacher so loves to hear a favorite student remember her lessons. God bless you."

After the girl had left, Father McCollough explained: "I taught her father as well as her. She was an English major. Top of her class. Could have had a fellowship most places. But she wanted to be an actress. She's done well, but it is a slow process. I got Joe to give her this job so she could have the flexibility for auditions and the like. She will make it. Neither she nor I have the slightest doubt as to that."

Picking up his glass, Father McCollough said. "I am a happy man, although sometimes a weak one. I have no needs. The community of fellow Jesuits with whom I live are my family and all that we do, we do for the common purpose: *ad majoram gloriam Dei* – for the greater glory of God. You see I have many friends, like those you met just now, all over New York and elsewhere .I work with young minds to teach them to think clearly and communicate effectively, so as to be leaders. I also teach them in the Jesuit tradition that they are men and women for other men and women. They are to serve others, while yet leading them. *Amare et servare.* To love and serve. A paradox. I don't think so. I am a happy man."

"Captain Hays, my father told me many years ago to expect you. You see our side of the McCollough family is a little bit different from my cousin, Ben's. Henry had come east during the days of the Texas Republic and, by fate, met Eugenie, the pretty daughter of a French family of minor nobility that had fled the French Revolution some decades before. They fell in love and she returned with him to Texas. Their marriage had been happy and blessed one, despite her not being an enthusiastic frontier wife. Moreover, her family was Catholic and she had abolitionist views. Henry was Texan and a southerner. When he was killed in the Civil War, Eugenie came back east to her family with their teenage children. Henry, aware he might not return from the War, had spoken to his son about his obligations to Captain Hays and left full written instructions with Eugenie to hold for the boy, which she dutifully did, until he was settled. Uncle Ben McCollough, who survived the Civil War, also made certain that the New York branch knew their duty. But we have been New Yorkers ever since. I have never been on a horse. We have a great many squirrels on our lovely campus but I am afraid those creatures are the extent of my knowledge of the natural world. I have never shot a gun, although I firmly believe in the right of every citizen to have one in the event their duty to their God and fellow beings require them to revolt against the existing order. I am not spry nor well conditioned. I am not the stuff of which they make Texas Rangers. Compare me to those you met at the Menger Hotel. I fall far short of their physical attributes. In short, whatever aid it was that your great, great grandfather had sought from mine, I wonder if either contemplated that I would be the deliverer."

Hays smiled. That had been his immediate reaction also. Of what help could this man be? Yet, when he heard him talk about creating leaders who unselfishly serve those they lead, he remembered the identical thrust of his own father's and grandfather's lessons. They, too, had said it was his duty to lead, but as a servant not a warlord. That altruism and his obedience to the will of his ancestors to honor their word, given to a man dead over a hundred years, also sounded like the type of man with whom he wanted to serve.

"You could always be Chaplain."

"Captain, I'm a Yankee and a Catholic. I'd wager everyone else in your company is Presbyterian, Baptist, Church of Christ, not exactly staunch supporters of the Pope."

Hays chuckled, at first to himself, then out loud. "Not true, we got some Mexicans," he replied with a grin.

"Seriously, Father, we are all Christians. Besides, I'm the Captain and they will comply with my orders. Henry McCullough was one of Captain Jack's most trusted lieutenants. You are his heir. The Lord moves in strange ways. But, do me a favor, don't mention the Pope too much to the fellows."

Father McCollough roared with laughter that, were it not for the soundproofed walls, would have been heard by the diners in the main room.

"Can do. To be honest, sometimes, he's not among our greatest supporters either."

Standing up, he put out his hand towards Hays.

"Sir, I'd like to sign up with your Rangers."

Hays stood also, took the priest's extended hand, shook it and said."Padre, its already been arranged by forces greater than we."

They sat down in silence, which Father McCollough broke after some seconds: "Captain, you must try the mussels. The chef is from Marseilles and the white wine sauce is exquisite.

New York City

September 28, 1778

"You are fortunate, my friend", James Rivington said to his friend Robert Townsend as the two were seated, early in the afternoon, in the nearly empty British Coffee House next to Hanover Square "that you do live across the North river in New Jersey. There, your loyalist sentiments would penalize you with the fairer sex. Read this."

Rivington handed him a copy of the rebel paper, rival to his own *New York Royal Loyal Gazette*:

Mr. Isaac Collins

Editor of the New Jersey Gazette

Trenton, New Jersey

Dear Mr. Collins,

I do not remember whether your Gazette has hitherto given us the production of any woman correspondent. Indeed, nothing but the most pressing call of my country could have induced me to appear in print. But rather than suffer your sex to be caught by the bait of that archfoe to American Liberty, Lord North, I think that our's ought, to a woman, to draw their pens and enter our solemn protest against it. Nay, the fair ones in our neighborhood have already entered into a resolve for every mother to disown her son and refuse the caresses of her husband and for every maiden to reject the advances of her gallant, where such husband, son or gallant, shows the least symptoms of being imposed upon by this flimsy subterfuge, which, I call, the dying speech, and last groans of Great Britain, pronounced and grunted out by her great oracle, and little politician, who now appears ready to hang himself, for having brought the nation to the brink

93

of that ruin from which he can not deliver her. You will be kind enough to correct my spelling, a part of my education in which I have been much neglected.

I am your sincere friend

BELINDA

"Hardly original" Townsend said after a belly laugh at the image of the Amazon patriot women, who forced their men to war. Is it not a variation of Aristophanie's theme in *Lysistrada* – the women refusing relations until the Peloponnesian war had stopped? Who is Belinda, do you know?

"Ann Stockton, Elias Boudinot's sister. They are rebels through and through. I swear sometimes these rebels act as giddy, infatuated youths."

"An apt analogy, my friend, because they do act as those in love, in love with what they see as liberty."

"Watch your tongue, Robert, this is a British tavern in a British city and some have been hung for even more cryptic statements.

Townshend replied: "Would it not be nice to know the future, James? How all this will turn out?

Harry Clinton confessed to being nervous around Pamela, normally not a reaction of his. Indeed, he had not been this uncomfortable in the several meetings on this affair that he had had with the highest-ranking woman in the Kingdom. Clinton had handled himself then with infinitely more finesse and aplomb than he was now acting with this lady of no rank. Clinton was more than nervous. He was intimidated by her. Not that Pamela had displayed any aggressiveness. Quite the contrary. She was always the lady, feminine, interested, and deferential, at least until it was her turn to participate. Then, she was well spoken, direct, witty and, all in all, quite a pleasant person to be around. This was the effect Pamela always had on him. Clinton had long since concluded it was her formidable appearance that silenced him into ceding dominance in their relationship. The way she wore her blonde hair up, which accentuated her high cheek bones. Her blue eyes that always looked as if they had just figured Clinton out. There was a perfection about her face, features flawlessly sculptured and freshly colored. If it were not her appearance that intimidated Clinton so, then it must have been her intellect that frightened him into submission. Only in her early thirties, she already enjoyed a reputation as a barrister with an equally sharp mind, tongue and wit. Pamela was Clinton's equal, despite the difference in sex. He knew it and accepted it, as a gentleman does when bested in a fair competition by another. He only wished he could be at ease with her, as he could with his other peers. But, then again, his other peers were men.

Although no legal relationship between Sir Henry Clinton and Mary Blundell had ever been documented, the British General's American born, commoner companion for life had been accepted by most, over time, as his wife. Sir Henry certainly had given her all the trappings and authority of the position, including having commissioned an oil portrait of her. It now hung at Clinton's manor in Shropshire, Clinton's ancestral home in the English countryside. Harry Clinton studied it each time he was off to meet Pamela, as if to gain some clue of their common ancestor,

95

which he could use to understand her better.

Sir Henry Clinton and Mistress Blundell, married or not, had had two children. The elder, a boy, became his father's heir, inherited the estate which, over several succeeding generations, had been passed to its current holder, great, great grandson Harry Clinton. The younger child, a daughter, upon reaching the proper age, was given a dowry by Sir Henry which assured a very comfortable and happy match with an impoverished member of the gentry of good blood lines – and, with Clinton's assistance, a better future. Pamela was a direct descendant, through the maternal line of that daughter.

The law of primogeniture in England meant the oldest son inherited almost everything. Sir Henry bequeathed obligations in almost the same proportion. As with his assets, he gave the male line significantly more of the duties than he did the female. However, when he passed on to his son the obligation that he and all his succeeding generations must be ready to assist the Crown in the recapture of the American colonies, he purposely had his daughter present. Sir Henry instructed her and, through her, all her succeeding generations, to stand ready to assist in, or even take over, the responsibilities of her brother and his line, if that were to become necessary. It was an act by Clinton that was beyond his authority. He had been instructed by Lord North and King George that the network he was to form that crossed oceans and generations was to be according to the workings of the same law of primogeniture, passed along only to the first born son. Yet, Sir Henry had been the commander of the British forces in America in a great defeat. He felt a frustration and personal guilt because of it, and wanted to insure that the Clinton name was present at the glorious victory, whenever that would be. A second son would have been preferable, but a daughter would have to do.

"Everything went quite well across the ocean. Agnew will do his part I am sure. Brant, the Butler brothers and Brownspriggs theirs. They were the final ones. Now, we have all our troops enlisted. Over the next two years, we will position them for the Battle." Harry Clinton reported to Pamela in their private dining room in The House of Lords Club in London.

Pamela nodded an acknowledgment of having both heard

and understood. "What about the fifth columnists?" she asked.

"We have identified the most likely. Contacts are being made with them now. Over the next 18 months, I'll meet with them and arrange how many pieces of silver they want to betray their land." He answered matter of factly .

"Mother is fully informed?" Pamela asked

Clinton replied, "Yes, in the usual channels. She even made a telephone call for us to the White House. She was much amused by being, as she said, *part of the plot.*"

"Well, thank God, she could use the amusement, I would wager, with some of the other problems she has in that family of hers these days." replied Pamela. Then, she changed gears. "But, what about me? Cannot I play a better role, be part of the plot too? I am capable you know. I want to be in on the kill as well!" Pamela pled, the last bit with an overly dramatic look, almost a pout, followed by a coy look that betrayed that what she asked for was a request, not a demand.

"It was not Sir Henry's intent. You are to be in reserve, if some thing happens to me. You cannot be risked near the action. I wish it were otherwise but your role is not to be known to anyone but me." Harry answered sternly and seemingly inflexibly.

Pamela's face fell enough for Harry to know it was genuine disappointment and, then, he made the mistake most men make. "But, maybe I can figure a way to have you there as you put it, *at the kill.*" He was rewarded by a smile from her and such a delightful rush within himself that he sought to trigger another smile by a second promise. "Yes, Pamela, you will be at the Battle too. That means you have a little less than two years to find something appropriate to wear for the victory gala that will follow at the White House."

Pamela held out her champagne glass in toast: "To the restoration of British rule."

New York City
July 18, 2005

Jack Hays walked from the Waldorf down Park Avenue to Grand Central. From there, he took a subway to Wall Street, at the foot of Manhattan Island. He was an hour early for his lunch with Elias Dayton at the India House on Hanover Square. He figured to use the time to walk around a part of the city that seems never fully appreciated by either the millions that flow into it each morning to work in its financial markets, departing at night to their homes elsewhere, or even to the tourists from around the world that flock to see the shrine to the World Trade Center attack, fabled Wall Street and The New York Stock Exchange.

But there was a lot of history to the area besides the Stock Exchange. This was the oldest part of the city of New York, as attested by its narrow cobblestone streets, built for wagons long before the auto was ever conceived and now the only thoroughfares through the maze canyons of office buildings. Broadway runs the length of the island from south to north along a ridge that forms its spine. At its southern end is a small park encircled by an iron, spiked fence, painted black. Jack's father had pointed it out to him, over thirty years before, when they had first visited New York City together. He told young Jack that a careful observer could see that every twelfth spike of the fence was rounder and thicker than its companions on either side. In addition, something noticeably had been twisted off the top of each. At one time, there had been a Crown on every twelfth spike, symbol of the British Empire. A much larger statute of King George III on horseback sat in the middle of the park. These monuments had been ripped down by the Sons of Liberty in September, 1776 as the Americans abandoned the City to the British. The statutes were carted off and melted down at a Connecticut foundry, recast as bullets for patriot rifles, and gladly returned to George III and his troops in that altered form .

On the west side of the park, across a street a dozen feet wide, would have been where the Kennedy House stood. Sir

Henry Clinton, for almost half a dozen years, had made it his headquarters in New York. Young Harmon Hays, Washington's spy in the British camp, had lived there, right where his descendant, Jack Hays, was now standing. Like any boy, Harmon Hays had probably run his hand across the same spikes of the same fence as he walked past. Jack glanced about to see if any one were paying any particular attention to him. No one was. For all purposes, he was as alone as if he were at the end of a dock into Lake Tahoe. About him, New Yorkers hurried from place to place, like drivers on a freeway, watching only those in front of them and keeping an eye out for a chance to dart ahead. Jack ran his hand across several of the spikes as he imagined his ancestor Harmon would have. Then, he repeated silently to himself the line from the poet Wadsworth: "the son is father to the man". In a vow, that was part prayer, part a mystic utterance from the soul, Jack Hays promised to keep his duty to his forefathers, even if he were to die in the effort.

Then, he walked east, a short block or two from the Park. On the corner of Broad and Pearl Streets, was a two storied yellow brick building, where his father had also brought him thirty years before - Fraunces tavern. During the British occupation, it was the public house that served as the nearest competition to Rivington and Townsend's British Coffee House. It was called The Queens Head Tavern after Queen Charlotte. It operated under the same name, near the end of war when it was the site selected for the ex-slaves, who had fled to the British lines, to register and to receive the certificate from General Birch that proved that they and their families were free people. But, when the British withdrew and New York became the seat of American government, its owner cast off its old name and it became known by the same name as it is today, Fraunces Tavern. There, George Washington had most of his meals. It was at Fraunces Tavern that General Washington had bid his officers farewell at the War's end, warning them and all Americans of the dangers of foreign entanglements in the future that would slow our nation's own growth.

Jackie walked two blocks from Fraunces Tavern, north on Broad Street, to where it meets Wall. There General Washington was sworn in as the first President of the United States.

As he walked from site to site on the lower tip of Manhattan, Jackie began to experience a similar sense of reverence as he had a few days earlier at the Alamo. Despite the traffic of a million feet a day, this was nevertheless sacred ground.

As he walked amid the puzzle of short streets that veer off, like New York walkers themselves, in whatever direction they choose, Hays thought about the man he was to meet, Elias Dayton, the descendant of Elias Dayton, Washington's trusted aide. He had done some research on young Elias. Oddly enough, Dayton appeared to be a mirror image of Hays, merely an East Coast version. Relatively close in age, – Dayton was a dozen years older – they had both come from prominent families, well educated, athletic, and more or less a leader by acclaim among their peers. Both followed the law as had their father and grandfather, joining the old-line family firm. Both were able, conscientious men, so accustomed already to the status for which the ambitious aspire as not to be tempted or distracted by it as might men of lesser stations.

But, Elias Dayton, the elder, had a secret life that was not revealed until many years later. From 1777 onward, he had also been General Washington's spymaster, responsible for recruiting agents like young Harmon Hays through a spy ring he had set up on Manhattan and Staten Island. As with Harmon Hay's own obligations to be ready for another British plot, so too had the spy master put a similar obligation upon his progeny.

Hays thought how ironic it was that the great, great, grandsons of two of Washington's spies would be meeting at Hanover Square, so near the spot where Harmon Hays had followed the orders of Elias Dayton two hundred and twenty years before.

Hays mounted the flight of stone stairs leading to the India House. Entering the Club through the large outside doors, Hays faced another short flight of steps and a door, guarded by a Buddha like statute. A man climbing the steps just before Hays, rubbed the Buddha's belly making Hays believe it was some sort of boys' club ritual that members retained among themselves, like a secret handshake. The door on top of the stairs was opened for Hays from within. He was ushered into an entranceway, complete with a concierge to greet members and assist guests. Hays turned to him promptly. He knew he was an intruder in a private club and that he must be the submissive one.

"Good afternoon, I am a moment or two early to lunch with Mr. Elias Dayton. My name is Hays, John Hays, from San Francisco."

"Of course, Mr. Hays. Colonel Dayton has not arrived yet but his office is nearby and I am sure he will be here in a moment. Please make yourself comfortable in our reading room, unless there is something else with which I may assist you?"

"Please, no", responded Hays, his eyes looking around the Club and its centuries old decor, evidencing the days of New York dominance in world commerce. "If you do not mind, I can occupy myself nicely looking at these splendid items you have all about."

"We would be delighted," replied the concierge, disappearing. Hays walked around the entry, figureheads from sailing ships of bygone days; ten foot long models of clipper ships, detailed down to miniature marlinespikes; old photographs, maps and memorabilia of a time when the harbor was full of sailing ships from around the world. As he studied the decor, Jackie wondered. The concierge had called Dayton, "Colonel", a title that Hays' research of Dayton in the professional directories, had not revealed.

Hays followed his curiosity into the reading room, lined with oil paintings of ships long dead in some watery graveyards. Despite giving the appearance of being deep in the study of the items on the wall, Hays was aware of a man's entering the club and speaking to the concierge who then nodded in Hays' direction. He had let a priest sneak up on him the night before and he was more alert this afternoon. This, Hays thought, must be Dayton, and so he was not really startled, when a few seconds later, his study was interrupted with the question "Excuse me. John Hays?"

Jack gave one of the smiles that he was famous for in Tahoe and, apparently, it had the same salutary effect in New York as it did high amid the Sierra Madre Mountains. "Yes, Elias Dayton?"

They shook hands, Dayton apologizing for being late –

even though he was not, being exactly on time as he was – and Hays stating that he had welcomed the chance to view such a wonderful room. Talking, they walked back to the entranceway, nodding an acknowledgment to the concierge as they passed that he needn't worry about them any longer, they had found each other. They climbed a wooded stairway lined with painted wooden maidens, figureheads saved from favorite ships.

"Excuse me." Hays asked as they stood at the top of the stairs waiting for the maitre de. "I do not mean to pry but the concierge referred to you as colonel and I did want to be disrespectful in failing to do so."

"Oh, please don't bother" Dayton laughed. "I am a Colonel in the Reserves but no one call me that except Paul, downstairs. He had served under me in Vietnam, back in 1968. I was a captain, he a sergeant. We became friends. In fact, I recommended him for the position here. So he calls me, Colonel, but no body else does, at least not Monday to Friday.

Dayton had a private room reserved and, after a drink order was taken - both men electing a glass of beer - they shifted the talk from the Club, to Hays' flight into New York, to the practice of law and mutual friends in each other's firms. Then, having their beer in front of them and their lunches ordered, the waiter closed the door and the two of them settled down to business, with Dayton beginning:

"Let me see if I can tell you where we are now, how we got here and where I think we are going." It was one lawyer presenting facts and conclusions to another and, if the waiter happened back, he would think it was just one more conversation of a kind he had interrupted countless times without ever understanding or caring about a word of it.

"The Revolutionary War did not end when everyone else thought it did. England merely suspended hostilities until she felt confident to try to win back as much of North America as she could. A German mercenary unknowingly discovered the plot. Harmon Hays confirmed its existence. He reported it to Elias Dayton, who reported it General Washington. A spy network to be on the look out for the British second coming was designed by the

General that would span future generations. He used his trusted operatives, like your ancestors and mine, to insure it by passing the obligation to us and by assuring that we are prepared for the day, should it come during our watch.

"You know from your letter from Captain Jack Hays – your great grandfather – that the British have tried several times already to recapture America. Captain Jack prevented them in Texas. Elias Dayton's son Jonathan thwarted them when they corrupted Burr into trying to raise an insurrection in the western territories."

Hays had read about Jonathan Dayton. He had graduated from Princeton at the age of 16 and joined his father's regiment, fought with General Sullivan against the Indians, was captured and exchanged and rejoined his father, fighting with him and Washington at the Battle of Yorktown. After the War, he practiced law in New Jersey, served in Congress and became the Speaker of the House in 1799 and then served in the United States Senate on behalf of New Jersey. Then, it all had come crashing down. He was indicted in 1807 with Aaron Burr for treason against the United States, arising out of a land speculation out west in which they were partners. He was never tried and the indictment later was dismissed but his reputation was ruined and he retired from public service. It was an uncharacteristic blot on the Dayton name and never seems to have been repeated.

"The reason we have been so successful in blocking their attempts is that they have never discovered that we are on to their plot. My ancestor Jonathan Dayton had to be disgraced or else the British would have known we had infiltrated their plot. They think individual heroics or bad fortune have prevented their other attempts. They do not know that we watch them; Harry Clinton, the current manifestation of old Sir Henry Clinton, has been in Canada and met with a lot of his allies. Something is up. We are not certain yet exactly what their plan is. Truth is, at present, we are in the dark on it, but we will keep watching and trailing them. Meanwhile, organize your boys, like the Rangers of old, and be ready to fly at any time, I call. We will have to react quickly and bravely, those were the specialties, you know, of Captain Jack Hay and his Company of Rangers – speed and courage."

The rest of the lunch was spent in details. They seemed to work well together. Hays told him of his meeting at the Menger Hotel and his favorable impression of this generation of Hay's Rangers. Dayton, in turn, told him about the people Clinton had been contacting in Canada and, together, they speculated as to what the British plot could be. But, they both came to the same conclusion – there were not enough facts at hand yet to conclude anything. They would just have to maintain their advantage – the British not knowing they had been uncovered --- and wait to see what developed and then respond immediately.

They departed the club together and Hays watched Dayton perform the same ritual with the Buddha as had the fellow on the stairs ahead of Hays earlier. He asked Dayton about it. Dayton explained it was a club superstition that patting the Buddha's belly brought good luck.

"Mind, if I try it?" Hays asked.

"Not all, we can use all the luck we can get. Try saying a prayer too."

Buckingham Palace
November 11, 2005

Clinton looked on occasion in the direction of the two men who sat across the magnificent mahogany table from him, but his focus and attention, as he spoke, were on the older woman who sat at the table's far end in a seat slightly elevated above the others.

"The line of persuasion, would be the same essentially to all the American minorities, even though the specific proposal will differ for each group.

Look what the new regime in America is doing to you. They are taking away all the rights of the minorities and banishing them to a second-class citizenship. It is only a question of time before they will extinguish all minority rights, and begin herding any one who is not an Old Time American into concentration camps for the different. You will not be able to rebel because your good intentioned gun control, when it took away all the guns of the citizens, also took away the weapons of revolt. You will boil a generation or two longer in the Melting Pot of America to determine whether you develop that taste that only Old Time Americans have. We offer you an opportunity to avoid becoming second-class citizens and to rejoin the British Empire on negotiated terms. We will agree in advance on the conditions under which become part of the British Commonwealth."

Then, I will modify the proposal to include protections for that specific minority with which I am dealing."

One of the men nodded and, after being certain that the lady did not want to speak first, asked Clinton: "I understand but do you not anticipate that some of these people might question how you are going to bring about the opportunity for them to join the Empire?"

"Yes, my Lord, we do expect such a question and we shall assure them that it will happen quickly, without bloodshed, without gun fire. It will be complete. All they must do, when the announcement is made of the change, is to immediately support it.

Each of our ally groups must be vocal and unanimous that joining the British Commonwealth will save its members from extinction, which is true. There can be no indecisiveness, no debates, referendums, public opinion polls of that type of tripe."

The second gentleman, also after being certain not to interfere with the lady's opportunity to ask a question and being assured by her nod to go ahead, asked, "And just what, Sir, do you propose to give these . . ." An older man, he had some difficulty finding the right word and finally settled on something from his colonial experience in South Africa, "these tribes. What do you give these tribes in exchange for their support?"

"A homeland, Your Worship. At least a homeland of sorts where they can live according to those particular customs or mores that make them distinctive. If the gays want a Gay State, they can have one. We'll move everyone around to make everyone who supported us happy. The properties of the so called Old Time Americans will be divided and redistributed on some equitable basis to our allies for their help. We will give back to the Loyalists their properties that were taken from them in the American War for Independence. The rest will belong to the Crown."

"And you think you can accomplish all of this?

Clinton did not hesitate. "Theoretically, yes. The next 18 months or so should tell, if it is practical as well. Our lieutenants – all of them, like us, sworn by blood oaths across the generations – and I will begin meeting in earnest. We have, of course, done extensive research as to the highest members of each group in America most likely to see the opportunity we represent to them and to take advantage of it. We will begin approaching them within a fortnight."

Clinton waited. There were no more questions. He summed it up simply. "Each of us has promised his or her ancestors to do whatever is necessary to accomplish the re-unification of America to the Empire and to reestablish the authority of the Crown there. I and my lads shall do their duty. We shall make captive the American nation and deliver it to Her Majesty in chains."

There were several moments of silence as all three men

looked up at the woman. She returned their looks and merely said:

"Splendid. We would like that. Proceed with the next phase. Good day, gentlemen."

New York City

October 30, 1778

Sir Henry Clinton sat at his desk on the second floor of the Kennedy House on lower Broadway in New York City and re-reading a final time the intelligence he had received from Major Andre.

Clinton shouted for his servant boy Hays. "Boy, where ..." and before he could finish, young Harmon Hays appeared at his elbow, as if from nowhere.

"Oh, there you are. I was about to call for you. Run downstairs and ask Major Andre to come up here for a moment, will you?"

As Clinton waited for Andre's knock on the door, he thought about the portion of his orders, to divide the American colonies by controlling the Hudson River. To accomplish that, the British had to capture the rebel Fort West Point on the Hudson. Clinton had been thinking about it for several months now and the mild winter they were having was making him restless to begin and do it. When Andre came in, Clinton revealed to him his plan to build a British fort across from West Point, at a place called Stoney Point by the locals, to use as the British base for attack and order Andre to begin preparations.

"Sir" Andre replied, nodding. "If an assault is not successful against the fort, I have another plan. At this moment, it is in a very early stage, but it has great potential. Only one agent and I know about it. I am disturbed over how the rebels learned our secrets. May, I tell you about it?"

Clinton replied. "Yes, good idea. Come around here and whisper it in my good ear. This way only you and I know of it."

Andre was not certain that this was not more Clinton sarcasm, but he was not going to test it by disobedience to an order. He walked around to Clinton's good ear and Clinton cocked his head in cooperation. He was serious and for thirty seconds or so Andre whispered his plan.

Harmon Hays was behind a curtain only a few yards a way, but could nothing of what Andre whispered. At one point, he made out Clinton's astonished question to something Andre had told him. It was sinister sounding phrase but not very revealing. Hays noted it to pass along to General Washington. The question the startled Clinton had asked Major Andre was "What does this general want in return?"

West Texas

February 12, 2006

Captain Jack Hays IV had accepted the offer of one of the Rangers, Sam Luckie, to make his *Lucky Linda* ranch in West Texas available for a training session for the newly formed Ranger Company .He had sold off most of the herd that he had ranged here, the remainder trucked off to another ranch, the *Lucky Laura*, that Luckie owned further west. Come spring, he would restock the place, but the price of beef this autumn had been so tempting – and Luckie's anticipation of a cold winter with higher prices for feeding and keeping a herd, so keen --- that he had decided to follow his hunch, take his profit and sell them off.

The cattle and the cowboys' departure had provided the Rangers with a bunkhouse for the men and the main house for Hays and his officers. There was not another ranch for some miles in any direction, no distractions, no interferences. Hays had some 32 men with him, about the size of a Ranger company in the beginning .All were the sons of the sons of his great, great grandfathers' comrades in the days of the Texas Republic. All had sworn allegiances that crossed generations. Each, as his forebears before him had been, was prepared to die in order to thwart a 230 year old English plot to deprive Americans of their Liberty.

Hays had learned enough from Colonel Dayton to form a preliminary plan of action and to begin instructing his men as to what would be expected of them. They were all assembled before him in the bunkhouse, some sitting on beds and chairs, others leaning against the wall and a couple squatting on the floor .The members of this Ranger Company were certainly a mixed lot. Among them were a former pro football player, several ranchers and farmers, two lawmen, a newspaperman, three oil men, a half dozen of businessmen of differing sorts, a doctor, and even a priest/professor in sneakers with a sweat shirt with the university name Fordham emblazoned across its front. Men of differing ages, occupations and education, yet all united in performing a mission and each, Hays was confident, competent and disciplined to perform what would be demanded of them. From what Hays knew from his research on the members of his great, great grandfather's company, they also had been from many different backgrounds, drawn to the frontier by inexplicable forces within them.

"Is everyone comfortable?" Hays asked

Hearing no objection and seeing a few nods in the affirmative, Hays went on: "I hope you all had a good trip in and are prepared to give us your full uninterrupted attention for the next couple of weeks." Hays felt as if he were addressing an intra company-marketing meeting, not a platoon of irregular troops.

"As I told you in San Antonio, I have met with my commanding officer and have learned some little more of what our orders are. I shall share them with you completely. I shall always share what I know with you. Rank is necessary for the chain of command so that the unit can act as if with one brain .We all understand that without any further need for explanation. But each of us is an American, born without rank, and, when this mission is over, any of you can come and try to punch me in the nose, wrestle me or tell me off with impunity." He smiled, and most everyone in the room returned it in varying degrees. "I hope that soon we will be the comrades that our ancestors had been. What I know, you will know. Our great grandfathers worked that way and so shall we."

Hays waited a full half-minute before resuming. "I realize that the tale that I will tell you is incredible. But the way we were all summoned here by our great grandfathers to complete a mission begun a century and a half ago is unbelievable itself. Don't doubt for a moment the truth of what I am going to tell you."

Again, Hays waited a few seconds for dramatic effect. "Great Britain is plotting this very moment to take over the United States – and it has been ever since the American Revolution was over! Its aim is to reduce the U.S. to again being a part of the British Empire. This is not its first attempt. I gather there have been several in the last two hundred years. In fact, Britain and their Hessians were the real enemy that our great, great grandfathers were guarding against in the days of the Republic.

The Indians, bandits and Mexicans were their cover, if you will. The Civil War was also something the British had put in motion to try to get back a large part of the U.S., again unsuccessfully.

Now, they're back, but we don't know what their strategy is this time. We know that England cannot accomplish a takeover of America by force. We are more powerful and better armed. So, it must be by some kind of stealth, we figure, likely with the assistance of some of their traditional allies, the Canadians and the Indians. Probably, there will be some traitors among the American people. When, from what direction and in what manner, the coup attempt will be made, is unknown. Nor, obviously, do we know who the traitors will be in America. We must discover these things. Those are our orders for the moment. To learn Britain's plan and stop it.

We are fortunate that we have a great advantage over them. While we know little of their plans, they know absolutely nothing about us. They never have. Even when our ancestors frustrated their attempt to use the Republic of Texas as the means of recapturing America, they never knew that it was we who had checkmated them at every turn."

"Fact is, no one knows about us, except us. Our government doesn't know. When the British plot was first discovered, the United States did not yet even exist. I am told by my commanding officer, whose kin was General Washington's right hand, that the General viewed America's best response to this threat was fashioning a citizen militia, men like ourselves, who would come out to protect their fellow citizens when the attack seemed likely. General Washington contemplated the obligation that we all share being passed down, generation by generation. Some have been detailed to shadow the enemy over the centuries to discover its next attempt and then to call out us and other militiamen out to repel the attack. Supposedly, there is a method to alert the President and to prove to him beyond doubt as to the danger – it has been done before, when absolutely necessary – but it is too dangerous now. We do not know Britain's plot and we do not know whom here they have bought with their gold. We cannot risk their learning about us. Our invisibility is our greatest advantage."

Hays looked at the spell bound faces watching him. There was no suggestion of any disbelief on their part. If this had been a jury, Hays would have been confident he had its attention. His voice was soothing and relaxing, almost that of a hypnotist, but the concepts he placed in the minds of his listeners were anything but that. They must see themselves as the epic hero of old, the man who fights and, perhaps, perishes in the defense of his homeland. He was preparing them for war.

"We have identified several of Britain's' principal agents in the United States. During these next several months, besides the joint sessions we will have together, I will be meeting with squads of you, some of which will be assigned the duty of trailing these allies everywhere, investigating whom they are meeting and the like. Britain is going to act through these agents and we need to know everything about them, especially their friends – our enemies – here in the United States.

This is going to be a full time job for a while so, as each of you already know, you are going to have to have stories as to why you will be away from home a lot. I plan to take a leave of absence from my firm in San Francisco. General Washington personally set aside a fund to finance this effort. It has grown considerably over the years so those of you who require income for home will have it. Some of you, I know, have enough money or businesses that will generate income, even if you are not there. You might want to take only your expenses. You are all honorable men and I respect any decision you make. The married men can tell your wives the details necessary. Remember Britain's not knowing of our existence is to our advantage, do not jeopardize it.

Some of you have sons who you think are old enough to enlist. If they are, then we will sign them up. Many of our ancestors were teenagers when they enlisted. There are some daughters, including two that have ranches named after them and a third one I met at a library in Dripping Springs whose daddies think them likely candidates for our corps, also. There were no women rangers in our great, great grand daddy's days, so this is a decision we are going to have to make ourselves in the usual democratic way, by vote. Except that I make the rule that any changes be unanimous. We don't want squabbling later as to whose idea it was to include or exclude them."

"Does any one oppose letting daughters of Rangers be Rangers?"

No voice, nor hand, was raised and Captain Jack marked the historic moment with a smile and a chuckle: "You fixing to build another bunk house for our recruits, Sam?"

The two weeks at the *Lucky Linda* passed quickly, everyone excited at the adventure and not yet frightened at the enormity of the task facing them or of its possible consequences. Hays marveled at the *esprit de corps* which developed among men working together as warriors. He had seen it in athletics and even on trial teams at his law firm. It was something descended, he imagined, from the male hunting and raiding parties of tribal man. Happy, not bothered by women and the demands of business, the Rangers laughed and joked good-naturedly among themselves as they trained. They had their own unspoken rules, violation of which could result in ridicule, shunning or expulsion, terrible punishments for most men. Hays did not witness even a single instance of selfishness. In fact, acts of kindness and altruism abounded among the Rangers. This was, Hays concluded, what, these days, they call bonding. Were the warriors of ancient Sparta any different, Hays wondered.

New Jersey Frontier

April 3, 1779

By Persons of Credit lately arrived from the Enemy's Country, we learn that Mohawk Chief Joseph Brant, had sent a flag into Sussex county, in New Jersey, to inform the inhabitants of his having been apprized that many of them, who last year had pretended Friendship and Attachment to the Cause for which he had taken Hostilities, had since taken up Arms; he now gave them Notice that no longer any Regard for Professions of that Kind would be attended to, for that every Man that did not join him upon his approach to their Country, should be deemed and treated by him as an Enemy and that he should soon lay the Country waste as low as Mushankunk. His troops had been again at Wyoming, drove off all the Cattle and every Thing else without the Fort that was moveable, where several of the Rebels had been killed and taken Prisoners.

Erik Ackermann was a pompous fellow, very pleased with himself and entirely confident that his position as publisher of a media empire was of his own doing. It was not. It began with his grandfather, Jacob Ackermann, a young German Jewish immigrant whose brilliance and survival ability had vaulted him from New York's Lower East side to the Harvard Commons. He had married the daughter of a newspaper publisher. Learning the newspaper business from copy boy to reporter, from editor to publisher, Jacob made the journal one of world renown. His son, Franklin, also Harvard educated and skilled in both finance and administration, but not journalism, had brought the paper to worldwide prominence.

Many long time readers thought the quality of the paper had begun to decline when grandson Erik Ackermann took it over. He had not been content, as his father had been, to permit the paper to continue without any major tinkering. Instead, Erik had recruited a lot of the fellows with whom he had gone to Harvard to replace some of those crusty, insubordinate old men whom his father inexplicably had tolerated .There were also some other things about the paper that Erik knew he had to change. For example, the papers' lack of social conscience appalled him. AIDS was scourging the gay population, women were being mutilated in the Far East and whales were being hunted to extinction.

Lately, Erik had been spending a lot of time on the Continent, especially in London. The British were so genteel, unlike many Americans whom Erik found to be crude. He was convinced that America's destiny was to join the world community, sharing its wealth with the less fortunate in the world. "After all, we are all people!" He would often exclaim in an exacerbated way with a plaintive look of appeal upon his face – a posture he had long practiced before his bedroom mirror. The friends Erik had made in London, some of them from families that could trace their lineage to William the Conqueror, would confess to Erik, after a dinner of intellectual discussion and perhaps a bit too much port, that they were aghast at what they saw was happening in America, how a white clique of "haves" was reversing over two centuries of the American Revolution. In America, the common man had been the equal to any one else in the nation. Now, America had classes, classes that grew more rigid by the year. The minorities were being cut off and crushed: gays, women, the poor, the disabled, the aged, immigrants, – all the children of the great multicolored and multi cultured rainbow that had been America were being exterminated, like Hitler did in Germany half a century before.

Everyone in London with whom Erik had discussed the deplorable condition of America, encouraged him to do his part to stop this fascism. After all, they argued, he had the power with his paper and media dominance to make a difference. Perhaps, it was Erik's fate to save America.

Above all, Erik was a silly man and he believed all of this. His chest swelled within him as he began to picture himself as the guardian of American Liberty and the opponent of the those Old Time Americans who were destroying all those things for which America stood. Everyday his front pages became his editorial pages and instances of what he considered to be man's inhumanity to man were exposed for all the liberals to see. Opposition leaders were pictured as womanizers and drunks. The flaws of Erik's bedfellows were ignored.

One morning Erik received notes from three of the most respected publishers in England asking him to give his attention and aid to Harry Clinton, who was going to visit him. His friends from across the Pond (as Erik was fond of saying) told him that Clinton carried with him their approval on a very important subject .Erik, of course, was intrigued by it all. In truth, he was in awe of England, an eager Anglophile impressed by everything about the British, their pomp, traditions, history, and even their accents. His friends at the paper from Harvard, who had long since concluded that Erik was a *dilettante*, quick to assume any affectation that he thought made him appear more attractive, now snickered to see that he had gone so far as to adopt some of the British phraseology. Erik now referred to "blokes" and "chaps" and promised to "ring you up".

Clinton had been watching Erik for several years. In the 21st century the media could be as powerful as a dozen armies. Clinton could not hope to carry off the coup or later manage the country without the press and media as his allies. He knew Erik's political sentiments and his vulnerabilities. Like any aristocrat, born to the position, Clinton also assumed correctly that the root nerve of Erik's personality was in his insecurity and his longing to be accepted by the titled Upper Class.

On the appointed day, Erik and Harry Clinton had lunch together in the private dining room, next to Erik's office at the paper. Clinton subtlety guided the conversation to known positions taken by Erik, with all of which, oddly enough, Clinton professed complete agreement. Similarly, the course of the seemingly casual conversation frequently touched upon mutual friends of the two for whom both claimed great respect. After the table had been cleared and they sat sipping coffee, Clinton began

"Erik" – they were already on a first name basis seeing how much they discovered they had in common – "that was delicious. How can you keep such a good chef?"

"I pay well." Erik smirked back, always eager to display the power that his grandfather's money had bestowed upon him.

"Evidently, it is just one more thing that you do well and that brings me to the reason for my visit. I come, you know, at the urging of many of Britain's finest men to express a concern I know has been expressed to you before. What in God's name is happening to this country? Are you becoming a police state here! In America today, if you are not white and Christian, you are second-class. And the gap is widening every day, with every new act of legislation that they pass that takes away the rights of more minorities." In Britain – Buckingham Palace, the House of Lords and even in the House of Commons – was the growing concern that America's actions could trigger worldwide repression. What could even the UN do in the Third World, if the world's strongest nation was committing worse atrocities in its own homeland? How could the rights of women, the poor, convict labor in China, the environment be protected, when the United States, for two centuries the model for the Revolution that had swept the world, was now a place where women were abused because of their gender and the poor and aged left to starvation and crimes, worse than any ever depicted by Dickens. Profits were more important that preserving the prairie. Profits were certainly more important than the rights of dissenters, immigrants, the gay, or even the old people. What had happened here?"

Clinton knew that Erik could not answer the question, nor did he care to hear his attempt at one. He moved right on. "I have been asked by Her Majesty if you and your media ventures could assist her and the British Government to bring some sanity back to the Administration in America, and, thereby, we hope, across the entire planet. We are working on a bold expression of Britain's concern, to be made directly to the American people. It is all very hush, hush and you should treat it so. I cannot speak of its details, yet. Indeed, I am not privy to them. But I do know that, in order to maximize the message, we need the media help and that is why we are reaching out to you as that profession's American leader. We know you are a responsible citizen.

Erik nodded, Solomon like. "My assistance is yours. Your civilization I greatly admire, while the one here frightens me considerably."

"I shall relay your reply in *haec verba* to Her Majesty. Were that your response, which she hoped it would be, she had asked me to inquire of you as to whether you would be loathe to accept a knighthood at some time in the future."

"Knighthood? I am stunned. Of course, thank you."

"I shall communicate that to Her Majesty as well."

The purpose of their luncheon achieved, Clinton refused the offer of a third cup of coffee, with the excuse that he needed to be on his way. He promised to be back in touch when he knew some more but that he felt very comfortable that, in Erik, the Crown had the best comrade possible in spreading its word that the world is a single community and that, as Erik had himself so eloquently said several times during lunch: "After all, we are all people!"

New York City,

Lower Manhattan

February 19, 2006

"It's Mr. Walsh on the phone, Mr. Dayton. Do you want to take it here or in your office?

Elias, who had been leaving for a meeting on another floor in the same building, turned around, saying: "I'll get it inside, thanks."

Back at his desk, he picked up the receiver, and, out of years of habit, a pencil and yellow pad. "Hello, Bill?" Walsh was an old friend. "What do you know?"

"That fellow you wanted to know about who is in town, just had a long lunch with Eric Ackermann, the publisher of . . ."

Elias cut in. "I know who he is. Hear anything?"

"No, it was upstairs and private, but Clinton looked like the proverbial cat who had swallowed the canary when he left. I've followed him back to his hotel. He upstairs now and I'm in the lobby."

"O.K. Stay in touch".

After he had hung up, Elias Dayton stared down at the yellow pad where he had written a big question mark. What would Clinton want with that affectacious fool, Ackermann?

Lucky Linda Ranch
February 19, 2006

Jack Hays walked down by the empty branding corral after lunch. They had almost completed their first week of training at the *Lucky Linda* ranch and there was still so much to do to launch the first phase of America's defense to the British threat.

Turning the corner of the barn, he was surprised to see the Reverend Jim McCullough, S.J., his pudgy body perched on the bottom rail of the corral fence. He had been reading something, which he had put in his back pocket, startled at his commanding officer's approach .Padre, as all called him, had been instantly liked by all his fellows, even by a few of the Rangers of the Baptist and Church of Christ persuasions who had never met a Catholic priest before, but had heard a lot of terrible things about them. His ever-present smile and gentleness disarmed them all with a few days.

"What you reading, Padre?" Hays asked.

"Pulp western fiction, Captain. Louis L'Amour. Are you familiar with him?" he replied holding out the paperback book for Hays to see.

"*Chick Bowderie, Texas Ranger*" Hays read the title out loud. Then answering Father's question, he added: "Of course, but I don't recall this one. Any good?"

"I'm just starting it, but it seems typical of its genre. I have been a fan of L'Amour's for years. Someday, I'd like to be left alone for a few months, with all of the Louis L'Amour books on one desk, and, on another, all of Ronald Reagan's speeches before he became president, especially those in the early 60's, when he was beginning the process that several years later would make the governor of California. He was a big Louis L'Amour fan, you know, and I bet you I can find, especially in those days when he was still discovering his own political philosophy, a significant correlation between what Reagan had read in the L'Amour books and what he had said in his speeches. Both Reagan and L'Amour were attracted to the same image of the

American. Their American was not a colonial figure, like a Washington, although he had his roots that far back. Their image of the American hero was that of the strong, resolute frontiersman, west of the Mississippi. He was the front line of man's continual westward movement. John Coffee Hays, for whom you were named, illustrates the type of man both L'Amour and, I submit, his student Reagan, thought was the epitome of an American."

Father McCullough, glancing at Hays, hesitated for a few seconds, as if in debate with himself. A victor emerged and the Jesuit, gesturing to the fence on which he had been perched a few moments before, said:

"Have a seat, Captain. Sunshine in February is too dear a gift to waste. Besides, I have a lecture to give, if you have the time .It's about the larger stage upon which we play, I believe that it might be applicable to our current situation – in a very broad way, of course. I shall begin at the beginning, as they say, so it might take my point a few minutes to be identifiable. It has to do with you as leader and what is expected of you. Please, be patient."

Father McCullough became the professor, Hays the student, neither particularly noticing the transformation or, if either had, seemingly not bothered by it.

"Thousands of years before Christ, the Caucasian population and the strange language they spoke among themselves emerged from central Asia and spread westward across Europe. They were the ancestors of the white race, which, of course, itself was a recent experimental offshoot of the human race of *homo sapiens sapiens*. Their jabber among themselves – Indo-European – became the mother tongue of all western European languages. The best of the gods they were to worship, the religions they were to espouse, the philosophers they were to follow, the playwrights they were to applaud became over the centuries the basis of western philosophy, which has governed the thinking of all those of our tradition, including classical America.

"There was always individuals in this new population that sought out the dangers and opportunities of the unknown, wild, westernmost frontiers. They were explorers and risk takers. They were needed to conquer the wilderness. The majority, however, the less aggressive, more dependable members of the general population, slowly followed behind these adventurers, planting farms, building villages, enacting laws and enforcing them. These first adventurers were warriors and poets, not farmers or trades men. But, by the seventeenth century, there was not much further west they could go."

"Then, the New World was discovered and the frontier gene within some of the members of these now amalgamated tribes again compelled thousands of them to migrate westward across the ocean to the wilds of America. They fought and won the Revolution against England, and then they tamed the continent, a generation at a time. First, were the Jerseys, Virginia, and the Carolinas; then, Pennsylvania and the Appalachians. Texas was big and wild enough of a frontier to take them a couple of generations to subdue and plant. California and the rest of the west gave the adventurer his last chance at a frontier."

"Of course, it had to end sometime. There was no more frontier. There was no place left to go. The settlers had come behind the frontiersmen, civilizing the land to such a degree that the talents and traits of the ruffian who had tamed the west, were now no welcome among polite society. It could only be celebrated by boys and immature men in western novels and movies. Louis L'Amour is a classic of that genre .Wonderful tales, surprisingly, containing much collective wisdom and truth within them. L'Amour portrayed a west, where law and order were threatened by anarchy, in violent clashes between idealized heroes and villains. There was always a tension between the need to express individual impulses and the need for restrictions by society. Here. Read this for example, Captain. Don't worry about the plot. It's always *good against evil*, as L'Amour saw those extremes. Focus on what is being said and the selfishness sincerity with which it is uttered."

Hays took the paper back book that the priest pushed in his direction and followed his finger to a point in the text, which began:

"You know, there's a clause in the Constitution that says the right of an American to keep and bear arms shall not be abridged. The man who put that clause there had just completed a

123

war that they had won simply because seven out of every ten Americans had their own rifles and knew how to use them. They wanted a man to always be armed to defend his home and country.

Right now there's a man in this area who is trying to take away the liberty and freedom from some men. When a man starts that, and when there's no law to help, a man has to fight. I've killed men, Jack, and it's a bad thing, but I never killed a man unless he forced me in a corner where it was me or him.

This country is big enough for all of us, but some men become greedy for money or power and come to believe that because they have the money and the power, whatever they do is right. Whenever, a brave man dies for what he believes, he wins more than he loses. Maybe not for him, but for men like him who wish to live honestly and decently."

"You are that type of man, Captain, as was your ancestors. Of course, you are "civilized" now and can restrain those more primitive, survival reactions that slumber in your genes. But, in the events ahead of us that are so crucial for liberty, will you be able to remain so civilized? And should you be? As we train, these are questions, you must ask yourself. As a leader, you may have to be decisive, ruthless, unrelenting in ways of which others might not approve. The settlers that followed Captain Jack could afford to be more forgiving and less violent than he had to be. However, he would not have survived, had he been equally as loving. No, it might well be that you, like he, must be confident in your training, in your values and in own ability to do whatever it is that has to be done. You cannot hesitate to do the things a leader must do for his people, even if you are shunned or blamed for it afterwards."

Hays remembered the news article that had reported that his great grandfather had summarily executed some confessed Mexican horse thieves rather than suffer the danger of bringing them back through Indian country to civilization. Ever since he had been a child, when he play-acted all the tales about his ancestor's daring of a century before, he had asked himself that same question. Could he have just shot a person like that? The damned Jesuit had put his finger right on it. Hays looked at the priest and said with a smile. "Down here, Padre, they'd say you have just gone from apreaching to ameddling."

McCullough smiled back. "Nonsense, I'm the Chaplain. That's my job, to help prepare you in your soul for what is ahead. But, we have talked about you long enough. What are your plans for me?"

Hays laughed and rose from the railing on which he had been seated. Giving the book back to Father McCullough, he remarked. "Class over, I see. Okay, let's walk a bit. We can talk as we go."

After a few steps, they had walked a bit before Hays spoke again: "Like you said, Padre, you are the chaplain. I thought we agreed upon that. Do you want another in your role in this Company." Hays knew something of the Socratic method as well.

"Of course not. Being chaplain is my first job. But when we are not in session here, what should I do, follow the guys around, checking up on them?" Father McCollough, answering Hays question, with a question of his own. But Hays broke the chain by not rising to the bait and responding to it. Saying nothing, the priest had to answer his own question. "I need another job. I don't have to go back to school until Father Provincial's patience runs out, which will not be soon. He was a teacher of mine at the Novitiate and he told me to do what I had to do. So, I'm free for any assignment."

"You know, Padre, I had wondered from whom you had to ask for permission to do this. Can you just come and go that way?"

"Captain, I reminded you once before that I was a Jesuit. We love intrigue. Father Provincial was very influential in the revolutions and insurrections in the Philippines after World War II. He knows that I'm up to something like that here and whole heartedly approves."

"Even though he doesn't know what side, you are on?"

"What difference would that make? He knows absolute truth and righteousness can claimed to be found on either side, Captain."

"I'm going to have to think about that last one, Padre, but what would additional assignment do you want?

McCollough did not hesitate. "You said in one of our sessions that there are some Canadian Indians that are suspected allies of England. I want to go among them and spy. Do you know anything about the Jesuit Martyrs of North America?"

Hays shook his head no and McCollough went on. "Eight of them, who were missionaries among the Huron, were tortured and murdered by the Hurons' enemies, the Iroquois. This was in the 1640's. We go back a long way in America too, Captain. Anyway that's the part of the "range" I want to ride for the Rangers."

Hays thought a while before answering. "I think that can be arranged."

The phone at headquarters at the *Lucky Linda* did not ring often. When it did that afternoon, it was Hays' commanding officer, Elias Dayton from New York, on the other end.

"Jack, good afternoon. You boys doing alright?"

"Sure are, Colonel. It's coming along real well. What can I do for you?" Hays replied.

"Got some movement that I am going to need some help on. Clinton's back in the country. He and that fellow Brownspriggs – you know, the Black fisherman from Cape Breton he met with on the earlier trip – went to Chicago to visit Ben Whitecuff the day before yesterday."

"The Black Nationalist fellow that split off from the Farrakhan people?"

"The same. It has been their *modus operandi* in the past, to make alliances with other groups like the Hessians or the Mohawks, with whom they had allegiance. This is the first time he's met a new group. I am going to need some Rangers to keep a pretty close watch on both Brownspriggs and Whitecuff and figure out what they are up to. Our advantage is that they do not know we are watching or that we know their goal. Your men have to keep out of the way but, at the same time, we need some specifics as to enemy strategy. Any questions?"

Hays replied that he understood, so Dayton continued:

"Okay, same thing with the Indians. Clinton has met with Joseph Brant, chief of the Mohawks, Britain's ally in a couple of other prior attempts. I am sure that they were not just renewing acquaintances for old time's sake. They are in the mix too and we need to know more there too." Before hanging up, Dayton provided Hays with more details – descriptions, home and business addresses of those that needed to be tailed.

Afterwards, Hays considered whom he should assign to these scout teams. The Indians seemed obvious. He had the descendants of two Ranger scouts, named Flacco and Busted Hump. Father McCullough could work the periphery. Hays' mind was already at work with a cover they could use. The Whitecuff surveillance plan would be more difficult. He had no Black rangers so infiltrating would be impossible.

Hanover, Square, New York City
July 29, 1779

James Rivington laid the two news items from his competitors' papers side by side. Together they told the story of the first phase of the War's 1779 campaign.

By May, the rested British army had begun to stir from its winter camp, although in what direction and to what end General Washington could only guess. His suspicion, supplemented by some information he had received, through Harmon Hays in Colonel Dayton's New York network, was that the British wanted to capture the American fort, located at a turn on the western bank of Hudson River, above New York City. Called West Point, it was the sentinel that stopped British ships from further sailing up the river.

In early June 1779, a number of British ships, loaded with troops, had gone up the river and had landed a great many troops on the east bank, across from West Point. One of the two news items, from the New Jersey Gazette of June 16, 1779, Rivington revealed the British purpose.

The last accounts from the Hudson River mention that the enemy are very busy fortifying at a place called Stoney Point, on the hither side of the River, near King's Ferry. It is supposed by this maneuver that they have two objects in view, the one to make a stronghold in order to enable themselves to send out detachments into Jersey to plunder and forage, the other by committing those depredations, to draw the attention of our army from covering the fort at West Point and thereby facilitating an attack against it, which, it is said, is the enemy's main object. But, in this, we flatter ourselves, they will be disappointed.

Washington was no fool. In desperate matters, the boldest stratagem was often the safest. Knowing Clinton's ultimate goal, Washington had acted swiftly. He dispatched his general "Mad" Anthony Wayne in a surprise attack that had been expertly planned and carried out. The second news item Rivington read revealed its outcome of the American assault.

Stoney Point was taken last night by surprise, by General Wayne with the light infantry of the line. The garrison, consisting of 500 men, are prisoners. We lost only four men. General Wayne is slightly wounded. The prisoners are on their march and were expected at Boon Town last night .

Rivington had heard that Sir Henry Clinton had been beside himself with rage at the unanticipated American strike that had deprived him of his imminent assault of West Point .Taking that fort had been the key to his strategy of dividing the provinces. He had been foiled so deftly here by Washington that Clinton was certain his plan had been known beforehand by his foe. Washington's spies were everywhere.

Rivington knew there had to be a scapegoat for the defeat and his money, in a wager with Townsend, was on Major Andre being made it. Gossip among the officers at the British Coffee House agreed. Someone had to be blamed. But Andre was cool and capable. He had not failed Clinton. Some spy had been to blame.

Chicago

March 11, 2006

Harry Clinton had made his North American command post at St. John's in New Brunswick. The Canadian Chapter of The United Empire Loyalists was headquartered there and it provided an ideal cover for the comings and goings of his agents. Clinton's chief North American contact, John Agnew also lived there as did many other members of the Empire of United Loyalists who had pledged their allegiance to Agnew in a mission the purpose of which was still unknown to them. Moreover, Clinton felt that New Brunswick, settled by those who fled the American Revolution, would be both a strategic as well as a symbolic site from which to launch the recapture of America.

Except for the winter cold, Chicago, where Clinton now found himself, was a far different place than St. John's. The noise of the Chicago's city traffic was audible whenever anyone let it in by opening the door that lead to the conference room in the back of the ground floor storefront. But, with the door closed, the city disappeared.

There were two men in the room besides Clinton. One of them was Richard Brownsprigg from Nova Scotia, the fisherman descendant of a loyalist slave. He ranked just below Agnew in Clinton's American command. The other fellow, also black, had been known to Clinton as Ben Whitecuff, when they had first met in London over twenty-five years before during the late 1960s. Ben had been at Oxford as a Rhodes scholar and had a note of introduction to Clinton's father from the president of the American chapter of The United Empire Loyalists. It identified him as being a descendant of a Loyalist soldier and spy of the same name. Legend had it that, captured by the Americans, he had a noose about his neck, only seconds away from Eternity, when a squad of British soldiers appeared and rescued him.

Young Ben, his descendant, was a pleasant enough fellow, Clinton recalled, but, as a student in the late 1960's, he had been radicalized by the events in Southeast Asia and the racial conflicts of the United States at the time and had vowed to devote his life

131

for justice for the African-American. But, despite having selected a path in life, unlike most of the members the United Empire Loyalists, Ben, oddly enough, kept up his association with them. One would have thought their creed was something he would have despised but, like his ancestor, he was obstinate in some things.

Ben, now known as Marcus, having rejected (reluctantly, if the truth be known), the Jewish name of Benjamin, was on the telephone and Brownspriggs using the rest room, so Clinton had full opportunity to study the room where he sat .Dominant on the wall was the photograph of Elijah Muhammad, blown up so many times as now to be more a mural than a portrait. The "Messenger of Allah", Elijah had been the leader of the Nation of Islam – the Black Muslims – for more than forty years. They were adherents of American black nationalism and Elijah preached an anti-integration message, frequently warning his congregation about "the human beast, the people or race known as the white." He called for blacks to unite themselves with their own and become self-reliant – even to separate – from the white society, physically as well as economically.

Malcolm X, Elijah's disciple, who broke with the movement in 1964, was already a martyred hero by the time Ben Whitecuff had become interested in his people. Yet, during the days of the riots in Watts and Newark and after Martin Luther King, Jr. and his gospel of non violent opposition had both been slain, Ben began reading Malcolm X's writings and speeches and he devoured their messages.

Eventually, a group attracted Ben's fervor. It preached self-reliance and self-discipline.

Brownspriggs re-entered the room at the same time as Ben had hung up the phone.

"Harry, so good to see you!" Ben exclaimed with a smile as broad as it was sincere.

"Well, it is good to see you too, Marcus," replied Clinton, stumbling a bit on the unfamiliar first name.

Ben smiled again. "Call me Ben. The other name is my stage name, but I still prefer Ben, especially among old friends. I couldn't keep Benjamin. Too Jewish sounding .Marcus Garvey and his "*back to Africa*" movement for American blacks in 1910 was more like my philosophy than anything else, so I adopted his name for symbolic purposes. Not that I want my people to go back to Africa, you understand. They are not about to abandon their investment in America and return to that starving, diseased land. We want our part of America now – here."

Ben caught himself and smiled again. "There, I go. You two are twice the number I need for an audience and I couldn't stop myself from preaching a little".

Turning to Brownspriggs with his hand outstretched, Ben said "And you, Richard, how are you? It's been a while. How's the fishing?"

Brownspriggs nodded as if to indicate that the fishing was fine, shook Ben's hand and said nothing further. They too had known each other for some years. In fact, Ben had been up to Cape Breton Island to see if he could interest Brownspriggs in the Black Nationalist movement. Quickly, both realized that the two centuries are isolation of the Brownspriggs and other Cape Breton Blacks from the rest of the world and their life among the mixture of different peoples in that harsh region had made the color of Brownspriggs skin and his sensitivity to his African heritage less important to him. There were no hard feelings .He just had not been interested.

After a few moments of chit chat, Ben expressed his surprise at the announcement that the United Empire Loyalists was going to participate in the re-enactment of the battle of Monmouth.

"Isn't that awfully dispiriting for our cause to have the world see us whipped again by those self proclaimed patriots. Independence was for white folks, not Africans. Your people had all their property taken from them by these rebel thieves and my people stayed slaves in this land of Liberty. And you are helping to celebrate that! Where's your head, man? You are worse than those Old Time Americans in Washington that are trying to enslave us again. Man, no way, I would go near that celebration except to throw a bomb. No way at all!"

It had been this especially aggressive streak in Ben Whitecuff that had compelled him and his several thousand

133

militant followers to splinter from the parent group and form battalions in every major American urban area. Their gospel was that violence speaks louder than prayer or reason. Ten per cent of the population could never get back what America owed them by casting ballots. Blacks in America had only one kind of leverage – making the whites afraid. To terrorize them. To intimidate them. From slave times, the possibility of revolts among their slaves was the white man's greatest fear. Ben saw that for himself in the 150 riots in America between 1965 and 1968, mainly against white property and symbols of white authority in the ghetto, including the ones in Watts, Harlem and Newark. The riots had brought some backlash but a whole lot of positive changes too. They had started the return to the black man of some of the money it owed him and his ancestors for enslaving them. More jobs were created. Help for those unable to work was increased. And the frightened white men passed more laws to ensure equality and even made some efforts at enforcing them .At least they did for a while, then the whites grew secure that the slave revolt had passed and the new Congress, full of Republican conservatives unwilling to reallocate any more of the riches they had stolen, started cutting back .At least this is what Ben thought and preached. It was time to scare the whites back into doing the right thing.

"I can answer your question about our participating in the Battle of Monmouth and I shall, in a moment." Clinton responded. "But first, let me follow up on something related to it that you mentioned just a few minutes ago. You said you wanted your part of America "now and here". What did you mean by that?"

Ben's face betrayed his being puzzled by Clinton's question. He did not know why Harry and Brownspriggs had come so far to see him but he was certain it had not been to argue black separatism. On the other hand, Clinton's question was not small talk. It was intended to be a gambit of sorts in a yet unrevealed match. Ben decided to treat it as an honest question and see where it led. He considered his response carefully. It was not the first time he had thought about it.

"There is only one way. Blacks must have their own nation within America. Of course, Blacks can live anywhere in the country they want to, with full equality but knowing they are not in the majority and realizing that they will be only one voice among many in any state but a Black state .But in their own state – their own homeland – they will be the majority. Minorities can live in the Black State too but they are not going to be the landlords, the storekeepers, the bosses, the teachers, the legislators any longer. The Black State is to be its own place, with its own schools, police force, courts. It will be economically on its own too. We will trade with other nations, other continents. With Africa."

Both Clinton and Brownspriggs knew that this was not a casual response by Whitecuff. Black Nationalism was his area of expertise, his obsession. He had never stopped studying it from the moment he had first discovered Malcolm X's writings. The professorial side of him – he had several advanced degrees – took over.

"Look, it is feasible. It's not just slogans like "Black Power" or "Black is Beautiful". We do ourselves a disservice when we think in clichés instead of in sentences and paragraphs. We want to revitalize black Americans by emphasizing their African origins and identity, their pride in being black and their desire to control their own communities – even to the point of establishing a black homeland in a part of the United States. This is not a new idea. I could lecture you for hours on its history. It goes back to slave days. Indeed, it's a reaction to brutal, dehumanizing slavery. Ironically, it's not unlike what the white Americans did in their Revolution. Except their's was a white revolution 220 years ago, ours a black one in the near future.

Anyway, to answer your question that is what I want, a homeland within the United States, where Black people, with Islamic or Christian ideas, can live like most white people – with pride, in strong two parented families with the male in the central role, and economically self-sufficient. That's what I want."

When Ben had stopped, Clinton pushed a note in his direction. It read: "Is it secure to speak here?"

"It' cool." Ben replied. "That plate glass window out front can repel a mortar attack. This place was specially built. We have enemies. It's sound proof and I personally debugged it before you came. Plus, I have a machine to turn on that scrambles all the sound waves for any listening device. State of the art."

Ben got up from his chair, walked to the wall and flipped a switch .Returning to the other two, he smiled as he said, "Hope it's worth the trouble."

Clinton answered and, returning the smile replied, "It will be, do not fear."

Clinton spoke for a full five minutes without any interruption from Ben. He told him that the time had come for England to re-establish her sovereignty over America and suggested that, were the black population of America to assist in America's re-entry into the British Empire, the Crown would be open to the creation of a Black Homeland of his selection for those who wanted it, plus certain economic aid to allow it to become self sufficient. He confirmed that Blacks could live elsewhere and whites could live in the Black state but that the Black state would be autonomous. It would have its own constitution, which would be designed by the African American community. In return, Clinton required Ben to provide black paramilitary groups to assist in the take over. Clinton and Brownspriggs both assured Ben that the takeover would be more or less bloodless, but that men with weapons who followed orders to the letter would be needed the day the revolution took place .Then, he explained to him about the importance of the Battle of Monmouth.

When Clinton had finished, Ben Whitecuff sat silently for some time, contemplating the enormity of what he had just heard. He had envisioned the establishment of a Black homeland, as slim a possibility as he knew it was, to be two or three decades, if not a century, away. Here, he was being offered allies in the effort to create one within the next few years and they could pick where they wanted to settle. Would he ever have an opportunity this good? He felt a rush of excitement and hope within him:

"You British sure do seem to come by and get the Whitecuff necks out of the noose just in the nick of time, don't you .I believe you can do it for my people too. Count us in."

Upstate New York
August and September, 1779

By a letter from Tioga, dated the 15th instant we learn that General Sullivan with his army arrived at that place on the 11th instant, without molestation. On his way, he burned an Indian town called New Kittanning. On the 12th at night, the whole army moved to Chemung, 12 miles distant, in order to surprise a number of Indians there, but they, having previous notice, evacuated the town, which our army destroyed, with all the corn etc. in the vicinity. While the town was on fire, a detachment of light infantry was ordered to move forward, who were fired upon by the savages, by which 6 were killed and 9 wounded. Our men bravely returned the fire, then rushed in with fixed bayonets which immediately put the enemy to flight. A party of our troops who were ordered to cut up the corn, were fired upon, by which one man was killed and five wounded. The enemy's losses in these skirmishes was not known. Our army having completed their business at Chemung, returned to Tioga.

New Jersey Gazette, August 25, 1779

General James Clinton's army, we hear, have joined Major General Sullivan at Tioga. From thence, the whole body is to move in to the midst of Indian Country in order to chastise the deluded savages and Tories, for their unprovoked, wanton and cruel depredations on our innocent and defenseless frontiers.

New Jersey Gazette, September 1, 1779

The number of Indian villages which have been destroyed by our army under the command of General Sullivan, in the Western Expedition, including those burned by General Clinton previous to the junction, amounts to 14, which, with the destruction of all their corn, beans etc. in the vicinity of those towns, will, we flatter ourselves, somewhat frustrate the savages during the remainder of the campaign in their predatory schemes against our frontier inhabitants.

The New Jersey Gazette, September 22, 1779

Since the action of the 29th of last month, the Indians have fled the approach of our army and left their settlements to our mercy. Their villages are now great heaps of ruin; besides we have burnt a number of scattering houses and destroyed as large country of corn, pumpkins, cymblines, cucumbers, watermelons, peaches and apples. This day we shall set out for Genesee and lay that country in ashes. The enemy having retreated to Niagara, we expect no opposition as we advance, but expect an attack as we return.

The New Jersey Gazette, September 29, 1779

Hanover Square, New York City

March 23, 2006

The Federal style, hip roofed, red brick building at the northeast corner of Hanover Square dated from about 1800. At one time, it had been the home of a wealthy merchant. Four stories tall, it was not very wide – perhaps 30 feet. Three times as deep, however, it extended from Pearl Street, where it fronted, through the block to Water Street on the other side, where it had still another face to show the public. Now sandwiched between two modern multi storied office buildings, it appeared out of time and place – an artifact from a New York of almost two centuries ago. From the outside, it looked somewhat forlorn, yet proud to have survived almost into the 21st Century.

The Pearl Street side of the building that faced the Square had a bar on its first floor and the Senator used a particularly hard burst of rain as an excuse to dart into it. It had not been on his agenda. In fact, the Senator had thought he would have been on the shuttle plane out of New York City, back to Washington D.C., a couple of hours ago. But, the rain and fog had shut down the airport so he had stayed behind at Fraunces Tavern for a while and had had a couple of drinks with some of the other fellows from the Battle of Monmouth Anniversary Celebration Committee that had met there that afternoon. Fraunces Tavern had been an excellent choice to hold the meeting. It had its own role to play in the Revolution. The West Indian patriot innkeeper, Samuel Fraunces, had been a friend and personal steward of General Washington. They said Washington always had a pint of beer and two glasses of wine with his dinner. Well, tonight, the Senator was well ahead of his idol.

Mellow from the drinks he had had at Fraunces', the Senator appreciated the rare chance to be by himself, without staff members or aides about. He treasured unexpected periods of solitude, like this, that forces outside his control had created. A phone call to his Chief of Staff and all the apologies and rescheduling would be attended to for him. Later, the Senator would wander out to La Guardia when the weather cleared. If it did not, then he had some places to stay in the City. No big problem. There was nothing he could do about it and he was not about to look the gift horse of solitude in the face.

Alone, his thin hair askew by the March winds and his thousand-dollar suit hidden under a drenched tan raincoat, identical to every other man's in town, the Senator knew he would not be recognized. His was hardly a household name to begin with and even fewer people would recognize his face under the best of circumstances. Those days of anonymity would end, he thought, if the re-enactment of the Battle of Monmouth still more than two years away, continued to receive as much attention as its present pace suggested it would.

The Senator was not an ambitious man. He was, however, a decisive one, blessed with an intelligence, made efficient by an excellent education. Clear for him was the course that must be taken in most situations.

"Well, Tullius," the Senator thought in silent conversation with his invisible companion, who went everywhere with the Senator since they had first met in Latin class in his third year in high-school "it appears that we shall have an unexpected chance for a nice chat. I have a good subject to start with. You know, it's been a while since we visited. Things are always so busy." The Senator stopped. The bartender was asking what he wanted to drink. He ordered a pint of Harp. He had never had Harp before but he knew it was Irish and he figured he could not go too far wrong if he drank the beer the Irish drank. The bartender brought it and the Senator dutifully pushed a twenty-dollar bill toward him for payment. Equally as dutiful, the bartender collected for the beer and pushed a pile of dollars and silver change in front of the Senator, like winnings from a game of roulette.

"Wet, out there?" he asked.

"Yup" replied the Senator.

The bartender nodded, but said nothing more, his compulsory communication completed for this beer. He went off to fill another empty glass down the bar. The Senator returned to his invisible companion.

Tullius was Marcus Tullius Cicero, the ancient Roman statesman and orator of the century before Christ .The Senator never could fathom why he and Cicero had become such firm friends. They shared some common values without a doubt. But, if one could see the two of them together --- which, of course, would be quite impossible – there would not be much doubt as to which of them was the chicken and which the egg .Cicero was the tutor, the Senator the disciple. No one knew about their friendship. If they had, they would have very quickly figured out the Senator, so much did he follow the philosophy of his mentor. For example, unlike most men of his time, Cicero had looked beyond his own self-interest, to the *res publica*, the public thing. The Senator liked to think the public good was his master too. Like Cicero, the Senator also viewed having a consistent philosophy as fundamental to life. To him, flip flopping on issues to muster votes for election was unthinkable. Not surprisingly, both the Senator and Cicero had selected

New York City

May 15, 2006

Hays had suggested that the restaurant where he had dined with Father McCullough some months before would be an appropriate spot to meet the girls. They could enter the private dining room through the secret way and avoid the off chance that they would be noticed by someone from *Women for Other Women*. There were lots of eyes in New York City and one could not be too safe. Besides, Hays had described the place to Debbie Jean back at the ranch and he wanted her to see it. Elias needed no convincing. He had had dinner there the evening before with Hays and was pleased at the prospect of a return visit so soon, the chance to taste his second choice of last night.

The three girls were ushered into the private dining salon by Joe D'Allasandro himself. Hays was astounded at the change in each of their appearances. Amelia's dark black hair was now short, like a boy's. Her attire – sharply creased slacks, a blue blazer and a bow tie – had an unmistakable mannish style to it, as did the way she stood. Linda, on the other hand, was breathtaking. Hays had never before appreciated how attractive she was. The boots and jeans were gone, left behind at the *Lucky Linda*. Now, she was stylishly and expensively attired, in an attention drawing blue suit. But of the three, it was Debbie Jean, at least in Hays' eyes, whose appearance had changed the most. She looked child like, innocent and fresh, nearer in age to 15, not 27. She wore no make up. Her long skirt and cardigan sweater that buttoned down the front were from the small town, soda shop days of the 1950's. To Hays, this timid, shy virgin image added another petal of beauty to an already beautiful rose. Hays wondered what Debbie Jean would have looked like a dozen years before.

Elias Dayton had never met any of the three girls before. As Jack made the introductions, Linda deftly slid next to the open seat next to Dayton. Amelia and Jack flanked Debbie Jean.

Margaret – apparently still without a role on Broadway – appeared to take their drink orders. She had waited on the two gentlemen the night before and knew they were colleagues of

Father McCullough, who had called to tell her and Joe that they would be needing the private room. Last night, the two men had been fun customers, witty, polite and generous with their gratuity. But, she was very perplexed as to their choice of dinner companions this evening. These ladies were a strange mixture. They were odd, not only in their number, but in their grouping. These three normally would not be friends. From her extensive experience at auditions, Margaret could sense there was some acting going on also, but she was not sure who it was that was acting.

While Margaret was getting the first round of drinks, Jack told them a little of the history of the private dining room as Father McCullough had relayed it to him, about the many famous couples and other notables who had dined here so as to be unobserved. After Margaret had returned and served everyone, Hays began with the shortest of questions:

"So?"

Debbie Jean and Amelia looked immediately to Linda. She did not need their glances of assent. They had spoken about it before. Linda would give the report.

"Everything has gone extremely well so far, according to plans. These two girls are troopers, I will tell you. When we got here, we got them an apartment together down around Soho. I needed something more *established* --- for my role, of course – so I went back to the East side where I used to have a place when I practiced law here." The latter explanation was meant for Dayton. Answering Hay's phone out at the *Lucky Linda* one day, Linda had taken one of Elias Dayton's calls. She recognized his voice instantly. And, as sure as she had been that it was Dayton on the phone, equally confident was Linda that he would not recognize her or her name tonight at dinner. Why would he? He never had acknowledged her existence several years before when they had worked together. He had been the senior partner of a legal team, representing a giant of corporate America, on a large case. She had been a very junior associate at another firm that represented a co-defendant of lesser importance. She had had a great deal of opportunity to observe him from close up. He had always seemed to her a little sad as if sometimes stabbed in the mind by a horrible thought that would not go away. Linda wondered how a man of such achievement and position could be that way.

"We had worked out a cover." Linda resumed. "Amelia and Debbie Jean were to be lovers from a small town in east Texas whose secret had been exposed. Immediately, they were outcasts, condemned from the pulpits by the preachers, shunned by their former friends of both sexes, and all but disowned by their parents. They ran away to start a life together in a place where they could be open about their love. We worked hard to make Debbie Jean a little small town young bride, an easily scared little doe, and Amelia the madly in love boy friend who would protect Debbie Jean from all the bad people of the City. I was both their protectors.

A few weeks before, I had renewed my contact with Bert Bravermann, told her I was back from Dallas, did not want to practice law any more and wanted to be more active with the Cause. I also let on that I had some money from my Daddy's oil wells that I might consider donating if some good work could be done with it. You can bet she was interested in the money part. She said they were on the verge of an unbelievable step forward, something that she said she had thought impossible to achieve in her lifetime. The excitement was all over her face. She even had to hold back saying that much, but she figured, I guess, that I was trustworthy. My interest in the Cause went way back.

Anyway, I went back to Bravermann later and told her the sad tale of this gay Romeo and Juliet couple and asked if she could get them some employment. I said I had been asked to help by a lady politician in Texas without giving any name. I know whom Bert thought I meant though, so she was open to help. Bravermann was always a status seeker and partial to women in power.

I must say she was eager to assist. Both the girls got jobs at *Women for Other Women.*

Jack looked at Debbie Jean and interrupted. How is it going?" he asked.

She replied. "It's O.K. Everyone seems to genuinely respect my relationship with Amelia. It's kind of nice actually. We get invited by them as a couple all over and we have made some nice friends. Some of the things we do are a lot of fun too, like the cowgirl country western dance nights down in the Village. They are nice people"

Seeing Jack's face drop at this remark, Debbie Jean added quickly. "They are not my type, of course, yet not bad in their own way. It's not near as terrible as I was afraid it would be."

Dayton interrupted and asked: "Amelia, what about you? The mission going alright from your perspective?"

Amelia finished her drink, and answered. "I guess so. Linda and Debbie Jean are great to work with. I like being Debbie's roommate and most of the people at *Women for Other Women* are okay and mean well. But, I'll be honest. The prejudice really gets to me. They put Debbie Jean into a good job with good pay. I get the mailroom and messenger type jobs and $4 less an hour. Talk about second class. Do you think it's because I am Mexican American?" she asked with a frown

Jack and Elias stared at her with astonishment. They did not expect this. Then, Amelia broke into a big grin and they reaameliaed she had been pulling their leg. Hays had forgotten Amelia's sense of humor, so well had she carried off her role

"Hey, I have to have a personality too. I can't just go through life being Debbie Jean's man."

Fortunately, Margaret came to take orders for a second round of drinks, just after Liz had made this remark, or else, she would have been even more confused at this assemblage. After ordering some more drinks, Dayton asked Margaret to send the waiter in for their dinner selections and the wine steward. It quickly became apparent that Elias and Linda shared an appreciation for French wines. After some spirited support by Hays for a California wine, the Texas delegation of Liz and Debbie Jean swung their support to Elias and Linda and an 89 Pomerol was selected. Margaret returned with the second round of drinks during the debate and concluded that, despite their differences, the group seemed to be getting along quite well.

When the ordering was all done and the five of them were alone again, Jack asked: "Have you discovered anything yet?"

Strangely, it was Debbie, not Linda, who fielded that question.

"We are not sure. Something is afoot that has excited them into thinking they are close to a break through of some sort. What it is, we do not know yet. We have heard reference a couple of times to a "new project" and needing to staff it with top people. Once I heard Bravermann mention to my boss something called the Molly Pitcher Project. Whether the "new project" and the "Molly Pitcher project" are the same thing and what that project entails, who knows?"

There was a brief silence and Hays asked:

"Elias, tell us about Molly Pitcher?"

Elias collected his thoughts. His mind had been going in the same direction:

"Mary Ludwig Hays. No relation to you, I am sure. She was born in Pennsylvania. Her parents were German immigrants. She married a barber by the name of John Hays too and, when he enlisted as a gunner in a Pennsylvania regiment in 1775, she went with him. She was about 30 years old at the time. It was not an uncommon practice to have women camp followers, like Mary. They washed and cooked for the men in the field and, after a battle, became nurses for the wounded. At the Battle of Monmouth in 1778, Mary was hauling water to the front lines. It was an extremely hot day. The temperatures were well above a hundred degrees and, for a few hours, the fighting had been furious. Mary's husband either was wounded or collapsed from heat exhaustion. According to the legends – which appear to contain more truth to it than not – Mary took over her husband's post in the gun crew for the rest of the battle, loading the charges into the cannons and keeping the big cannon in action."

"What a nice story" cooed Debbie Jean. Romantic."

Dayton smiled: "Actually, her contemporaries remembered Mary as foul mouthed, tobacco chewing and uncouth. But, to the patriots, she was a hero in a very important battle. She was idealized with the name Molly Pitcher, symbolic of the other women who assisted the American cause in unsung, usually even unnoticed, ways. But what has that to do with today, I don't know."

Hays wondered aloud: "Is it a coincidence that this is the second time today the subject of the Battle of Monmouth has come up. Wasn't Agnew and his Canadian Loyalists going to participate in the re-enactment of the battle?"

At that moment, the waiter came with their appetizers. Business was dropped. Elias and Linda began chatting together, she telling him about herself and he seemingly quite interested in what she had to say. Jack and Liz vied for Debbie Jean's attention.

New Jersey countryside

July 1780

The Ladies of Trenton in New Jersey, emulating the noble example of their Patriotic Sisters of Pennsylvania, and being delirious of manifesting their zeal in the glorious cause of American Liberty, having this day assembled for the purpose of promoting a subscription for the relief and encouragement of those brave Men in the Continental Army, who, stimulated by example, and regardless of danger, have repeatedly so suffered fought and bled in the cause of virtue and their oppressed country, etc.

The New Jersey Gazette, July 5, 1780

London

May 19, 2006

Harry Clinton was a creature of habit. Whenever in town, he invariably dined at the House of Lords Club. It was, of course, a private establishment, although no longer limited to the Lords of the realm. It took a bit of doing for the India House in New York to persuade the manager of The House of Lords Club to permit Elias Dayton and Jack Hays to dine there. Elias' alleged obsession with the history of the House of Lords – the Club was undeniably steeped in it – and the Manager's evident pride in his charge did the trick, however.

True to their expectation Clinton was seated only a few tables away from them. He had a companion with him – a most attractive woman – and they appeared to be finishing up their dinner. Elias was surprised to discover that he recognized the woman. It was not the type of woman one forgets. She and Clinton were speaking quietly together.

If Dayton and Hays could have heard the conversation a few tables away, however, they would have been amazed. It involved the very same subject as their own had – the re-taking of America.

"Is there any more I should know at this stage?" Pamela asked.

Clinton shook his head in the negative. "No, everything is still coming together, but it is progressing well. Our forces are organizing; some are even in training. We still have more to recruit. Their roles will be further revealed to them as time goes on and our target date comes closer. But there is no rush. We have two years to go and we do not want our allies to know too much, too soon. Some are less reliable than others."

Pamela nodded, as if she had expected such a general response .She told Harry that he had been acting like a typical male and not sharing. He preferred to keep the plot to himself. But she knew that was not their instructions from their common ancestor old Sir Henry Clinton and all their ancestors since.

"Harry," she reasoned, "if something happened to you, I have to know to take over. I realize you are not keen about that; neither am I. But, I do have to know some of the details better. Not here, but maybe we can spend the weekend in the country, at your or my place, whatever. Then you can explain it fully to me, a little at a time, so that my tiny brain does not get over loaded."

Harry did catch the sarcasm, as obvious as it was. Pamela was correct. He did not want to detail everything for her or, for that matter, for anyone. Yet, a weekend in the country with her sounded so alluring that Clinton immediately yielded.

"Splendid idea. There is so much I must tell you. I can do it the weekend after this or the second one next month, whichever suits better your pleasure."

"The weekend after this will be fine" said Pamela. "Now, if you will excuse me for a moment, it is time for the proverbial powdering of the lady's nose, and then we can be off."

Pamela rose and was passing alongside Elias' table before she saw him sitting there.

"Elias Dayton! What a delightful surprise. I knew you were in town for the Committee meeting, of course, and thought we might see each other then, but I never expected to see a colonial in such an 'native' place as this."

Elias rose to his feet and, weak voiced managed to utter "Pamela, how good to see you. You are looking quite well", an understatement, if ever there were one.

He turned to jack who, of course, had also risen to his feet in the presence of a lady, and said "Let me introduce you to a colleague of mine and a new member of the Committee, Jack Hays of Hays, Stockton & Sutter of San Francisco."

Jack stood up and shook hands with her. "Good. Another handsome Yank." she exclaimed, with a grin. "We can visit more on the morrow. At present, I need to make some emergency repairs to my face and then a friend and I are off to the theater."

She disappeared with a second smile and Hays sighed as he resumed his seat. "What an attractive lady! Who is she?"

Dayton told him her name and explained how she had

asked him, over a year ago, whether she could be on this Committee. He had just been made the new Chairman when she had telephoned. Actually, while her international experience was small, her reputation as a barrister, however, was excellent and her other attributes obvious. Hence, Dayton had not hesitated to invite her to join the Committee.

Hays said playfully. "Elias, I don't want to inflate your ego any further. Linda's flirting with you last night should be enough excitement for an older man like yourself. But, I'm sorry to admit, this gal seemed particularly thrilled to see you again. Are you on some kind of lucky streak?"

Dayton blushed and laughed. "I must be." He did not tell Hays how he himself had been taken aback by the interest that Pamela had displayed in him. Much more than made sense, even for an aggressive attorney trying to get herself known. She had definitely searched him out in order to join the committee. She had even arranged references and recommendations from mutual friends. That was peculiar because the Committee was only of minor importance in the legal community.

A few moments later they watched as Pamela returned to her table from a different direction and exchanged a few remarks with Henry. He glanced at his watch as if to say "be brief" and nodded. Together, they rose from the table and walked in the direction of Elias and Jack. They stopped as they passed their table and Pamela introduced them to Clinton as co-members of a committee she was on. Clinton was gracious and obviously proud, as any man would be who was escorting a woman as attractive as Pamela. When Elias mentioned to Clinton his interest as an historian in the Club, Clinton beamed.

"It is an old Club to be sure. My family had had the same table since the late 1700's. If these walls, could talk!"

After the exchange of a few more pleasa tries,   Clinton invited Dayton to lunch with him at the Club at some unspecified time in the future, when there would be more time to look around. Then they parted, Pamela and Clinton off to the theater and Elias and Jack to their dinner, the appetizers of which having just made their appearance.

In the lift down, Clinton asked Pamela. "What were their names again?"

She replied. "The older one was Elias Dayton from New York. The other, I believe, was named Jack Hays from San Francisco."

Clinton hummed a bit to himself as he often unconsciously did when he was thinking. "Those are both familiar sounding names but from where? I've heard them before, long ago."

Back at the table, Dayton and Hays looked at each other, smiled and then laughed. "Wow, we were so close, we could have petted him on the nose. You even got invited to lunch by the enemy" said Hays.

"Really" agreed Dayton "Maybe, we got too close. He's heard our names and that was more than he knew a few moments ago. I don't like that. Nor do I like the coincidence that this Pamela who has been sucking up to me is a friend of our nemesis. If it is not a coincidence, what does that mean? Does she know about us?" They ate their dinners without comment. It was a frightening thought that Clinton maybe already knew about them.

West Point, New York
September and October 1780

   On Monday last his Excellency General Washington
passed through this town on his way from Hartford, and his arrival
at West Point was announced by the discharge of thirteen cannon
about eleven o'clock the same day.

   About the time of his Excellency's arrival at the fort, a
most horrid plot was discovered, the infamous General Arnold at
the head of it, who, it is supposed, has been corrupted by the
influence of British gold, having agreed to deliver up the fort at
West Point, for which purpose he drew up a plan of all the works
at West Point and gave it to a spy, Major John Andre, Adjutant
General of the British Army and First Aid to Sir Henry Clinton.
   New Jersey Gazette, October 4, 1780

   Andre was taken by three young men of the militia of
Westchester County, Messrs. Pawling, Deane, and VanWeert. He
offered them for his liberty his gold watch, one thousand guineas
and as large a quantity of goods as they could bring from New
York, which, with republican virtue, they refused, informing Andre
that they were American and were not to be purchased.
   New Jersey Gazette, October 11, 1780

Lucky Linda Ranch
December 23, 2006

"Merry Christmas, Elias. I was just fixing to give you a holler." Jack Hays had been in Texas for some ten months now and his accent and vocabulary had begun developing a Texas twang to it.

"Merry Christmas to you too. What's new out there?" replied Dayton.

"Nothing. Everyone, who is not out in the field, has two weeks leave and has gone home. I am heading west later today to San Francisco, and spend Christmas with my mother and sister's family. Anything happening there?"

"Yeah, one good thing, one bad. The good is that the girls are doing fine. I have bumped into Linda a few times and she keeps me updated. The four of us had dinner last night at D'Allasandro's. I swear we looked like two couples together." Hays heard what Dayton had said and put it away to think about later. It contained too much to dwell on right now. What did Dayton mean that he and Linda had bumped into each other a few times? Were they seeing each other? He was happy to hear that Debbie Jean was okay, but he was disturbed in hearing Elias refer to Debbie and Amelia as looking like a couple. But, most of all, Hays wanted to concentrate on the bad news coming. The good could wait for a celebration later.

Meanwhile, Elias had went on: "The bad news has to do with another visit Harry Clinton made. He met John Sparrow in New York City yesterday."

"John Sparrow, the President's Chief of Staff?"

"Yes"

"Is the President involved?"

"Sparrow and the President have been cronies for too many years for us to safely assume otherwise."

"Wow! That changes everything. Whom do we run to for help, if it gets bigger than we can handle? If the President is on their side, – and, I agree, we must assume for the time being that he is –

we'd be running right into the tiger's mouth."

"Give it some thought, Jack. We have a gigantic problem if the country's desk sergeant is in on the plot. There will probably come a time that we will need official help or recognition from the Government. We can't go to him for it."

Elias chuckled. "We'll figure it out . Hey, Jack, Merry Christmas!"

"To you too and your sons." replied Jack, adding "And thanks for the gift to take home to think about."

New York City

February 21, 2007

They met in the private dining room at D'Allasandro's even though there was no need to hide their presence together – two men, in business suits, on different sides of 40, and a third man, some twenty years older than either of the others, dressed in a black suit with a Roman collar. They could have been former students and their teacher, nephews and their uncle, or three members of some committee organizing a charity fund raiser. They could have been there for any number of reasons. The least likely possibility would have been that these three unremarkable looking men were the re-incarnations of super heroes, engaged in attempting to save their unsuspecting nation from capture by an enemy poised to attack any moment. But, that was exactly what they were. Each of them was burdened by an obligation, passed on to him by his forefathers, to preserve, even at the cost of his own life, what had been won for America in its War of Independence. An attack by the foe was anticipated soon, but its form and direction unknown.

"Jennifer, where is Margaret?" Father McCullough asked immediately of her as she entered the room. The girl had a beautiful, disarming smile.

"She got a role, Father! Not a big one, but her picture's in the Playbill they give you at the theater, so it's a big enough part for that. Mr. D'Allasandro and I went to see her last week. She was good. I have the Playbill back at the bar. Everyone wants to see it. I'll bring it back for you."

"Splendid. I knew she would do it. Gentlemen, this calls for champagne, don't you think?"

They both readily agreed, although Dayton knew that Father McCullough, who had taken the vow of poverty, had not the wherewithal with which to pay for the champagne celebration. He had been up at the St. Regis Indian Reservation for several months now and obviously was happy to be back in

New York City. The dinner bill would just be a little bigger.

Jack asked, after Jennifer had left with their order: "Is she another student of yours, Padre?"

"Why, yes, come to think of it. Wants to be a writer and this is a good job for that. Quite honestly, I don't think she will have the success that Margaret appears to have enjoyed – at least, not right away. I'm supposed to marry her and young Leo Mullarney this coming June. Then, it will be babies. Maybe she'll write later in life. That's a distinct possibility .Or maybe she will recognize the gift in a child and help foster it. It really isn't important, you know. Life is a *continuum*. You are the beneficiary of someone's good deeds of generations before you and your own good works will be enjoyed by someone generations after you, whom you will not know and who will not know you. Jennifer will contribute in that way, I think."

Jennifer came back with the Playbill and the champagne. She and Father McCullough chatted about the wedding plans. Leo was an assistant district attorney in the Bronx, learning to be a trial lawyer. It would be a good match. Maybe, they will get an author out of the next generation. Or, maybe, an aspirant to become a Jesuit.

They made Jennifer join in the toast to Margaret's success, and, after she had left, they toasted a second time, this to each other's good health.

"Well, Padre. Happy to be back in civilization?"

"Really" answered the priest. "I always thought I lacked the fortitude for the foreign missions, the inedible food, the lack of even the necessities of life, the fear of the jungle and the people tough enough to survive there. But, after a year now of eating that chuck wagon grub at the *Lucky Linda* and the last few months living among the poor up at the St. Regis Reservation, I am beginning to think that I am not as unsuited to the foreign mission life as I had envisioned. It's a big difference, I tell you, from teaching philosophy at a university, discussing Aristotle's Unmoved Mover with students who, you hope, will recall, in later years, the concept as one remembers the faint aroma of something pleasurable from his youth."

"But, it's been productive so far. There is a Jesuit mission near the Reservation and I volunteered there to help with some of the pastoral duties. I told them that I was on sabbatical from the university to write a book and I wanted the solitude of that area. Buffalo Hump and Flacco were near by. They merged in with the local Indians very well. They share a trailer. Flacco's knowledge of casinos was tapped right away." Turning his head toward Hays, Father McCullough said, almost as an aside, "Captain. It was a good plan you had. The Indians see casinos on their reservations as the best way of getting back a share of America. A continent for a casino. About the same rate of exchange as the $24 Peter Stuyvesant paid them for Manhattan, I'd say. I digress. Sorry. Flacco has used his experience with the Lipan Apaches and casinos in the southwest to great advantage. He has met with Chief Joseph Brant himself about it a dozen times and has gotten pretty high up in the tribal structure.

Buffalo Hump is working another part of town. He began at the gun shows to meet the weapons enthusiasts of the area. He knew a lot about it already from his military background and he had learned a lot more at the *Lucky Linda* before we went up there. He's playing the Comanche chief role to the hilt, claiming that the Comanches and the Mohawks were the best warriors in America. They saw Buffalo Hump on horseback and could not believe their eyes. The Comanches have always been excellent horsemen and Buffalo Hump had been well taught. Truth is the Mohawks did not know any more about horses than a pig knows about Sunday." McCullough looked to Dayton and explained. "I learned that phrase in Texas. Anyway, what really made Buffalo Hump's stock soar among the Mohawks was his affinity to his steed. They had given him the toughest horse they could find after he had bragged to them one night about his horsemanship. It was a big, ugly cranky horse that seemed to revel in being contrary. They called him *Diablo* – the Devil. Buffalo Hump walked right up to that horse, put his head next to its, spoke to it for a moment and then the critter became as docile as a lamb. Flacco told me the story and said Buffalo Hump used the old Comanche trick of blowing in the horse's nose to pacify it. It was how they broke horses.

"Both Flacco and Buffalo Hump have reached high up in different segments of the tribe. Neither one minds criticizing the U.S. government at every opportunity, saying, for example, the Indian still has to fight for anything he is going to get from the white society. Buffalo Hump especially has made a lot of bad friends, which, I guess, in our situation is good."

Dayton asked: "Have you learned anything yet about what those bad friends are up to?"

The Padre replied: "Are they on the proverbial war path? Clearly, yes. The Mohawks are a matriarchal tribe. Women rule the home and tribal affairs. Men are warriors. There has been little chance to practice the warrior craft for the last two centuries. But, from what I have learned from Flacco and Buffalo Hump – and seen first hand from my work at the Mission – there is a renaissance underway for the men. The orders to dust off the men's organizations – the remnants of the warring and hunting parties of past ages – comes directly from Chief Joseph Brant and only within the last year. For those Indian men who don't know all the tribal customs regarding the warrior and his obligations to the others of his party as well as to the women, children and old people of the village, old tales of life before the white man have been resurrected and told to gatherings of males. Like the morality plays of Europe of the same era, these tales tell the men what is expected of them in battle. Buffalo Hump has gone to some of these meetings and he reports that they are clearly martial in nature. No targets announced yet except "them" which Buffalo interprets to mean anyone non-Native American.

Now, there is one thing specific happening that we would be foolish to ignore, even though I do not know how it fits together. Maybe, you have some other pieces of the puzzle and can make better sense out of it .A "war party" – that is how they refer to it themselves – has been formed, led by Chief Joseph Brant, to participate in the re-enactment of the Battle of Monmouth at the end of June, 1998. It's getting plenty of publicity on the reservation. The Canadian Government plans to send over a thousand Indian braves to it, all dressed in the garb of the time, armed with bows and arrows, guns, tomahawks and everything authentic to the period. They are not taking their role lightly. Brant and the other tribal elders are recruiting warriors now .They train twice a week. I do not know much about this Battle of Monmouth thing, maybe you know or can find out more about it. From what I have read, it is something the U.S. Government is sponsoring to pat America on its back. That is the criticism of it on the Reservation at least, but Brant is behind it full force and the Brants have been chiefs of the Mohawks since the American Revolution and they will stifle the radicals who oppose being "Uncle Tom" Indians as they call it.

McCullough studied the faces of Hays and Dayton for any reaction to his report. The two had glanced at each other and then Hays filled everyone's champagne glass as if to occupy the time until his superior could elect a course of action.

"Well, Padre, you were correct. That is an important piece of the puzzle that you have brought. This is the third reference we have had either to the Battle of Monmouth re-enactment or to something associated with it. Agnew and the Loyalists in Canada are forming brigades of loyalist descendants to represent their ancestors at the battle of Monmouth. You tell us that Brant and the Indians are doing likewise. *Women for Other Women* have a hush, hush Molly Pitcher Project, a pretty obvious reference to the battle.

We must find out more about this re-enactment. It's building up to be a huge event, I am told. Our enemies intend to be there, apparently very well armed. Virtually all American leaders will be present – the President, his Cabinet, hundreds of Senators and Representatives, Justices of the Supreme Court, our top military men."

"Sounds like Guy Fawkes and the Gun Powder plot, doesn't it?" asked the priest.

Met with blank expressions, McCullough first chided them, then explained. "Gentlemen, did you not study history? In 1605, Guy Fawkes tried to blow up all of the civil, military and ecclesiastical authorities in England at one time at the opening session of Parliament. King James I, his son, Crown Prince Charles, both houses of the English Parliament as well as all the chiefs of State, Bishops of the Church of England and the generals and admirals all were there. Fawkes was in the employ of the Spanish, who wanted to restore the Monarchy to the Catholic branch of the Stuart line. Fawkes stowed barrels of gunpowder in a vault in the House of Lords, where they were meeting. It was discovered at the last moment and the English government was spared. How the course of history might have been different had that fuse been lit and all of English authority blown to kingdom come. The British know how close they came and Guy Fawkes Day is still a celebrated national holiday in England, you know. Anyway, may not a form of the Gun Powder plot be happening at the Battle of Monmouth? All of our leaders will be there. Our enemies armed and under cover of friendship, will be there. A coup would be possible, if not, likely. I realize that once the British captured our leaders that would not mean they would control the country, any more than the British controlling Boston, New York, Philadelphia, or Charleston during the Revolution ever meant they had controlled America. But, they have undoubtedly have a plan for that too."

There was a period of silence as each of the three men pondered the puzzle and the possibility that the Padre had raised. Even if these commando types, commissioned by Britain could capture the government, how could they control the countryside?

Dayton asked: "Were any Jesuits involved in the Gun Powder Plot, Father?"

"Father Gallivan was beheaded for allegedly having master minded it but I am sure he was an innocent scapegoat." answered Father McCullough, a trace of a smile on his lips.

The bottle of champagne was emptied the same moment that the waiter had come in to take their dinner orders. Wine was ordered and brought and a range of small talk touched upon until they were alone again. Then Father McCullough asked: "Correct me if I am wrong, but isn't this getting too serious for us to handle alone. Deranged zealots with weapons are going to be in tomahawk range of all of our unarmed American leaders in an effort to overthrow the government of the United States. Back in the beginning, Captain Jack had indicated that there was a way

161

to go all the way up to the President to get his help, if it became bigger than us. I think we are approaching that point. Maybe, its time to go to the President and blow the whistle on all of this."

His suggestion brought no direct response from either Hays or Dayton. Instead Dayton said:

"Maybe, we need a Jesuit in on this since intrigue seems to be right up their alley."

"I am flattered at your trust, Major," the priest replied.

"We have reason to believe the President's Chief of Staff, John Sparrow, has been compromised by Clinton. That may make it possible, perhaps even likely, given the long and close relationship between the president and his Chief of Staff, that the President is similarly compromised. If he is, then we give up our only advantage if we approach him – Clinton's not knowing that we know his goal. Without the element of surprise at the right time, we cannot pull this off .We cannot take the risk of losing that advantage by letting them know that we know."

"And, yet," countered the priest "you cannot afford the other risk, the one to the government and people of our nation, if you do not stop this plan. Who or what is in charge of the re-enactment event? If we are going to prevent this, we need to know a lot more about the details of the event. It would be nice to make some friends among the organizers too."

Dayton said: "As I said, I do not know much. We have a lot of research to do about it now that the clues are beginning to point in its direction. I've followed the whole re-enactment thing generally. Elias Dayton had fought with General Washington at Monmouth and, over years, as a hobby, I have studied the battle. I visit the battlefield every so often. So, I've been interested in the re-enactment from an entirely different perspective. The person in charge of the re-enactment is the Chairman of that new Joint Committee on the Renewal of American Values."

"Frank Moriarity, the Republican from Ohio?" Hays volunteered.

"That's the one," said Dayton "He's in charge. I don't know a single thing about him. Do either of you?"

Hays replied that he did not but Father McCullough asked: "Is his full name Francis X. Moriarity, Jr.? And is he about 50 years of age, from the Cleveland area, and been in the Senate for almost 12 years, if not more?"

Dayton and Hays looked at each other and Hays shrugged. "The name sounds right, now that you say it. He's from Ohio, but I don't know where. The age sounds in the ballpark too and he has been in the Senate for a while. Do you know him?"

Father McCullough smiled. "Know him? I taught him. I was a Jesuit scholastic at St. Ignatius Prep School in Cleveland. Francis Xavier Moriarity was a student of mine for all three years I was here, in the early sixties."

"What about him? Is he approachable? Will he remember you? Could he be reached by Clinton?" were among the barrage of questions hurled at McCullough by the other two men. The appearance of the waiter with dinner spared the priest from close examination by two expert attorneys. McCullough used the time during which the dinner was brought, more wine opened, and the food tasted, to get off the witness chair. When the waiter vanished, McCullough went first.

"Let me see how many of your first round of questions I can answer and then you can follow with a second round if I omit any thing. Does that sound fair?"

McCullough's being a member of the clergy, a university professor and older, somehow outranked Dayton's being a colonel or Hays a captain ."I am aghast that you would think that any one of my students could ever forget me. I have stayed in loose contact with Moriarity over the years. A dinner, a drink, Christmas parties. We have been on several Boards together. Approachable. Certainly. I believe he would do anything reasonable I requested. Could Clinton get to him? Never. He is smart, honest and dedicated to the *res publica*. I should know. I taught him Cicero in his junior year. In fact, I was sort of his mentor. He called me Tullius. Yes, I know Frank Moriarity very well." Father McCullough had to stop himself from adding: "I should know him. I programmed him and was his confessor." They needn't know that.

New York City

February 8, 1781

Sir Henry Clinton read the dispatch for a second time and then angrily threw it onto the table. With Arnold's exposure and Andre's capture and execution, Clinton had again failed in his first mission, to take the strategic American fort at West Point and the Hudson River it controlled. Now, his second mission seemed in jeopardy and he was absolutely powerless to do anything about it. The expedition to subdue the South was faltering after the initial successes at Augusta, Savannah, Charleston and Camden. Those English victories had not extinguished the flames of rebellion. Bands of rebel guerrilla fighters had made pacification of the backcountry all but impossible.

Clinton had a feeling it would get worse. His intelligence sources told him that the American plan was to keep Cornwallis and his larger army, off balance, and eventually run it ragged, by a series of rapid troop movements through unfamiliar terrain, while the British flanks were constantly harassed by the guerrilla forces. Clinton had sent two warnings to Cornwallis about this strategy. Each was ignored as Clinton knew it would be. The dispatch he had just read reported a stinging defeat for the British at some Godforsaken place called Cowpens. Cornwallis was now pursuing the Americans through the mountains of North Carolina, like a stupid dog chasing its own tail.

Cornwallis was Clinton's problem .Clinton had never liked him, either as a man or as a soldier. Sir Henry Clinton also knew that there was nothing he could do about the situation that was developing. His second in command, Lord Cornwallis, had more power at the Royal Court than he had and, Clinton knew, he had it all directed against him.

Clinton also was aware of the dormant commission that Cornwallis held that allowed him to take command of the forces in America, should Clinton become incapacitated. As a practical matter, Lord Germain – Cornwallis' ally, Clinton's enemy -

easily could classify Clinton as incapacitated with the signing of his name to a proclamation to that effect. Cornwallis would be his automatic successor.

Clinton had no choice but to offer his resignation to Lord Germain. He had done it several times before and it had been refused, as, he had no doubt, it would be refused this time again. The American War had proven to be a disaster. It could have only been won at the outset and, then, only temporarily. The voices against the war were rising in England. Someone had to be a scapegoat and Lord Germaine was not about to permit Clinton to avoid that role. Clinton was in command, but not control, as the final scene was playing out in the south. It was not an enviable position in which to be.

Butler Trading Ltd. Lear Jet

Over Saskatchewan, Canada

April 19, 2007

Each of the twins was dressed differently, Walter in a sports jacket, John, a sweater. Their hairstyles differed also, Walter's longer than his brother's and with some gray showing up near the temple – and he the younger of the two by a full two minutes!

The twins had remained virtually identical as they matured. In fact, an uninformed observer, upon seeing the brothers alone on separate occasions, would conclude that it had been the same man, clad and styled differently on different days, so close the resemblance had continued for their almost 43 years of life. It was only the two of them in the cabin of Butler Trading, Ltd.'s private jet as it headed west toward Vancouver, in Canada's Provinces of British Columbia.

"Do you believe them?" Walter asked.

"I think so," replied his brother. "It does not cost them anything to do what we ask and the lesser intelligent among them will actually believe that waiting will increase their options. Getting a piece of the American economy is pretty tempting to Quebec. It needs more markets and the capital we promised, if it could hope to survive as an independent nation as the secessionists want. Of course, the smarter ones will figure out, as the plot is revealed to them, that the Queen does not lightly suffer the loss of her colonies. They will realize that, if the United States can be retaken, the long-term likelihood of their independence is minimal. However, the chance to make a substantial fortune themselves and their progeny by going along with their dumber comrades should win over the smarter ones at that point. They will sell out the others for the proverbial 40 pieces of silver."

"Brother, I must congratulate you once again on your strategy. It is truly a work of genius."

"Don't be silly, Walter, it was your idea as much as it was

mine. I just uttered it first. It could have been you but you were eating a pistachio nut at the time, as I recall." What he said was true. The twin's minds operated almost simultaneously and in tandem.

"Whatever – it was brilliant. Harry Clinton will tell us the day the Guy Fawkes Project is to go off .When that day arrives, we will be long the euro and short the dollar with all the major American, European, Asian and Arab banks. Come the retaking of America, the dollar will tumble, the euro will soar. We will cripple the American financial institutions and take a healthy junk from our competitor nations. Each of us personally will quadruple what we have now, much more if we go on margin .So will our companies, Canada herself, and all of our associates, including, our friends in Quebec who have promised to keep their people in line during the transition. Giving them a piece of the action, incidentally, was your idea, John and brilliant. Using some of the profits made in the foreign exchange swap with the Arabs or Japs to pay the Quebec men their bribes. Absolutely brilliant."

John smiled at his brother's praise. He respected his brother a great deal and was pleased that he had noticed his contributions. "Yes, the two best parts are that it will cripple the United States and Canada's emerging the big winner. The Toronto Exchange will become Wall Street; Canadian banks will replace the insolvent American banks; our insurance companies will take over theirs; our economy, with Britain and German help, will overlay theirs."

"And that is only part of it", his brother chimed in. "We have the ultimate inside information and we will be poised to use it. Imagine the American stock market. The stock prices will fall to a fraction of what they are trading at now. We will have the cash and we will buy, and buy, and buy. We will end up owning IBM. We will end up owning GE. We will own them all – or at least enough of them for control purposes .And, we can make a killing on the commodities markets in the same way. Gold will go sky high and American governmental obligations will plummet. The wealth of America will suddenly shift from its institutions, pension funds, and little old ladies and into Canadian hands. Then, we will re-build America the way we want it – with us and the members of the network we are putting together on top this time. It is overdue. It will have taken us over 230 years to get back what the rebels took from our ancestors, but we will – with interest!"

Lucky Linda Ranch

May 23, 2007

"Elias, I have the report from our boys tracking the Butler brothers. I'm sending it along to you by the regular channels, but I thought you would like to hear the high points first over the phone."

"Please" replied Dayton. "Maybe, some of the puzzle pieces will be there."

"If they are, I'm missing them. Our scouts here are Rip Ford and Nelson Lee. Rip is an accountant, a certified one. His firm in Dallas specializes in the securities and financial markets. In fact, Rip worked for the Securities and Exchange Commission, up in Washington D.C., for a few years after school. Nelson is an attorney, out of one of the big Houston law firms. Family has millions from oil. Also can fly a jet himself and that has come in handy since the Butlers get up and fly off with almost no notice. The two of them know the financial markets and that is where the Butler Trading Ltd.'s operate most these days.

Anyway, Ford and Lee have been dogging the Butler brothers for the last few months, following them in a jet, as they criss cross Canada in their Lear Jet. Whenever the twins visit with someone, then the boys do some research on their contact and then add him to the list to be further watched and studied. So far, the two Butlers have had well over a dozen high level meetings, in secluded spots, usually with a single person at a time, but sometimes with two or three. We haven't been able to get close enough to eavesdrop on the conversations. It's been tough enough just to keep up. But, our fellows have come up with two things that may be clues.

First, judging by backgrounds of those with whom they met, our agents have concluded that the talk has to do with money and other financial matters. The people with whom they have been meeting have been the presidents of Canada's biggest banks, pension funds, insurance companies, investment bankers, money managers and other institutions with great clout in the financial market place. Our boys, who, you will remember, have some experience in these matters themselves, both liken it to corporate takeover preparations. A group is being formed to do something involving big dollars and it is doing it in secret. These are big, very big players.

Secondly, our people note that all these people with whom the Butlers have been meeting in private, with one exception, are all members of the United Loyalist Empire Association. Names like Atherton, Browne, Fanning, Humphreys, Mason, Peters, Robinson, Skinner and Winslow. There are no late arrivals to Canada in this group. No Jews, no Italians, no Orientals – even though there are a number of these equally prominent in the Canadian financial markets. Everyone whom the Butlers are meeting can trace his ancestors to the British who fled the American provinces during the Revolution. The exception I mentioned involves the ones they met from Quebec. Their ancestry in Canada goes back even further to the French settlers and fur trappers, who, unwillingly, came under British control when France ceded Canada to England in 1763. They are also among the leaders of the Quebec movement to secede from the rest of Canada. Maybe, that plays a part but I do not know. But the men from Quebec were important men of finance, like the others. They each also have a long history of friendly dealings with Butler Trading Ltd., extending sometimes, through their ancestors, back to the fur trading days."

Dayton did not say anything right away. The conclusion appeared inescapable and that made it all the more important not to jump at it. Instead, he reasoned out loud, with Hays on the other end, capable of objecting to anything for which a proper foundation did not lie.

"Obviously, it is not a coincidence that all these individuals are ancestors of Loyalists. Since the Loyalists are our proven foe, then these people must be viewed with some suspicion. Since they are consorting with the Butlers, whom we know are in league in some fashion with Harry Clinton, whom we know to be our principal enemy, the degree of suspicion must be even higher. Whatever it is that these Loyalists are up to with the Butlers, we must view it as being inimical to our interests. Agreed?"

Hays spoke his agreement into his end of the phone and Dayton continued his line of reasoning.

"The next question then must be 'What are they doing?' The boys are right. It has to involve money. That is the common thread in this group, that and their loyalist origins. Agnew and his thousand Loyalists are busy drilling and training as soldiers, under the guise of appearing at the re-enactment of the Battle of Monmouth. Butlers' Loyalists are also drilling and training at what they do best – controlling the financial side. They are going to use finance like a weapon, but how and when? The latter question is the easier of the two. If both Agnew and Butler Loyalists are regiments in the same army opposing us, it is reasonable to consider they will attack in some concerted fashion. Logic tells us must happen about the same time as the re-enactment of the Battle of Monmouth, since we know Agnew's regiment will definitely be there. How exactly will they attack, the second question, cannot be answered from the information we have available. Most likely, the attack will be an economic one and the battlefield being some sort of financial market. But that is as far as my reasoning will take me. Do you see anything that does not follow?"

Hays answered, "No, the Padre would have been impressed by your logic. We know more now than we did before, but it is still not enough."

"Speaking of the Padre, has he had his meeting yet with Senator Moriarity?"

"It's happening today. I had suggested that I go along but the Padre thought it would be a mistake and complicate things. He knows the Senator and, more importantly, claims to know how the Senator thinks, which makes sense since the Padre had helped educate him. He's stopping in the City on his way back from D.C. to the Reservation." Dayton responded, "I'll let you know what he tells me and we can ponder where it puts us."

"Okay, fair enough. Things do seem to be happening. Keep in touch.

Arlington National Cemetery

May 21, 2007

"Peekaboo, I see you. I'm over here, Francis. It is I, Tullius."

Senator Moriarity turned around just in time to see the portly, crew-cutted figure of Father McCullough, waving at him. Dressed in a black suit with a Roman collar the only evidence of white, the priest jumped from behind a large monument erected to the dead of the Spanish American War.

The Senator sighed, shaking his head back and forth as if this type of greeting from his former teacher were nothing new, maybe even to be expected. He called out as the two walked toward each other with hands extended. "Father, you are too much! What are you doing? And why are we meeting here in Arlington National Cemetery. The taxpayers provide me with a perfectly good office, where we could have met, had coffee, and visited a while about old times." Senator Moriarity was very fond of his first mentor, respected and admired him and still found his various eccentricities to be amusing.

"Nonsense." replied the priest. "On Capitol Hill the phone would ring a hundred times, the office could be bugged, people could overhear. I can think of a score or two of reasons why this is a better place to do what we have to do."

"And what may that be, Father?" asked the Chairman "You told me it was quite important and that you would tell me about it when we met."

"In good time, Francis, in good time. And only if you pass the test, Francis. You may not be the one to help. In fact, you may be the enemy."

Father McCullough paused, seeing his former pupils' eyes widen at this last remark. He smiled understandingly and gently said. "Francis, I am not doubting you but I do come on a serious matter, extremely serious. And before I divulge my mission, I must first determine whether you are the right person to assist us in these unusual and perilous circumstances. We need not be somber about

173

it, however. Let's go back to the good old days!"

The Senator, perplexed, did not respond. Father McCullough diverted from the path, scampered across a small patch of manicured lawn and plopped himself down on a long, flat grave monument of an admiral from the late 1800's.

"Master Moriarity, you stick, you stone, you worth than senseless thing, it is your honor to perform for the class this morning and show us all how well you have learned your lessons, please rise."

Moriarity grinned nervously upon hearing the familiar opening. He had last heard it over forty years before at high school in Ohio. The speaker of the command at that time had been a young Jesuit Scholastic, named McCullough who was not fifteen years older than 16 year old Francis and the rest of the junior class. Despite the passage of time, despite the changing of roles and locale, the Senator, feeling slightly silly, nevertheless became the obedient student once again. He stood up and meekly acknowledged his good fortune to have been selected, just as he had done countless times as a student so many years before.

"Thank you, Father. With Jesus' help, perhaps, I will not make too great of a fool of myself."

"Master Moriarity, you are familiar with Cicero's Catalian Conspiracy?"

"Yes, Tullius."

The priest smiled. The Senator had called him Tullius. That was a favorable sign that the careful implanting of a set of values in this high school student forty years before had taken root and grown. Some might call it brainwashing or programming. It was not. Every man has a free will and can choose his fate. But, the Senator's recollection of the mantra word Tullius was reassuring.

"*O tempora, o mores*! You are familiar with the phrase, Master Moriarity?"

"Yes, Tullius."

"Then, enlighten your classmates who have squandered their study time foolishly on other things. Translate it for the class and describe for us the context it which it was uttered and its significance to us seekers of wisdom two thousand years later."

The Chairman answered like the schoolboy into which he had been transformed. "Translated, the phrase is 'Oh, times that we live in, oh, customs that we hold dear!' It was exclaimed in despair by Cicero to the Roman Senate during the Cataline conspiracy."

"Provide us with some of the background, please."

"Yes, Father. In 63 B.C., Cicero had been elected Consul of Rome by the Roman Senate. It was the highest office in the Republic of Rome. The consul was one of two who, for a year at a time, jointly governed the Republic of Rome, instead of a King. It was during Cicero's tenure as Consul that the Catalian conspiracy arose. Cataline was a Roman soldier and politician, who had turned to demagoguery to build popular support. He promised the disadvantaged the abolition of debts and urged the redistribution of property. He also was plotting to seize control of the Government by force. Cicero learned of the plot and denounced Cataline in the Senate and the coup was thwarted. The question O *tempora o mores* asked of the Senate by Cicero, roughly translated for today would be "What's happened to us? What has happened to our old time values that this scoundrel, Cataline, could try to seize the Republic right from under our nose? It's significance today, I suspect, is the same as it was then. The foundations upon which the Republic of the United States were formed are being altered just as those of Rome were in Cicero's day. Old time values and strengths that purchased independence and liberty, that tamed the west and then which spread across the planet are in danger of being extinguished in America by newcomers and naive liberals who want to re-make the country the way they want it to look, often based on some half accurate picture they have of utopia, not unlike the abolition of debt and the redistribution of wealth of Cataline's promise."

Father McCullough nodded his approval and asked a second question.

"*Cui bono?*"

The Chairman did not hesitate giving his response. "To whose benefit? The question Cicero asked and that all public servants must always ask when administering the public good, the *res publica*. Who benefits? Is it the state and the people or is it the rich, the corrupt, the powerful? Cicero did not profit from his acts in saving the Republic. In fact, he was exiled for it. Years later, he made the supreme sacrifice and suffered martyrdom at the hands of the Republic's enemies. "

Again, the Jesuit nodded his satisfaction at the answer. "One final phrase for you to identify Senatus *consultum ultimum.*"

The Senator smiled. The end of the test was at hand and he knew the last answer. "It means the 'extreme decree of the Senate'. Cicero had the Catalian conspirators summarily executed. No trial, no public forum for their cause. Execution. It would be the reason Cicero was later exiled. But Cicero knew that some actions are necessary to save the Republic, even though they would appear cruel and ruthless and would be criticized afterwards."

"Bravo!" exclaimed the priest, jumping up from his gravestone seat, clapping his approval at the same time. "You have pleased an old teacher. But do you still believe what you just said, about the good of the Republic coming before all else?" McCullough's voice dropped during the last part of the question, asking it softly like a whispered prayer.

"Very much so, Father. It is my life."

"Francis, you have passed the quiz with flying colors. Let us sit down at some quiet bench and I will tell you what the Republic needs of you."

The Senator remained quiet for the hour it took the priest to tell him the complete story, beginning over two centuries before and the American Revolution. He concluded it, saying:

"So, you see, the Republic is once again in jeopardy – perhaps, by a combination of promises and force as in Cicero's time. We do not know yet. We do believe, however, that the re-enactment of the Battle of Monmouth will most likely be the time and place selected for the coup. We must prevent it but we cannot approach the President for assistance because we cannot be certain that he is not involved also. It was fortuitous that your Committee is managing the event – that is, of course, if you elect to help us. Will you?"

"Your first question, Father, should have been do I believe this crazy story you are telling me. But the answer would have been 'yes, I do believe it'. I have been very troubled by the groups who are getting involved in the pageant. They don't fit. They should be protesting it or disrupting it. Now, of course, it begins to make sense. They are wolves in sheep's' clothing, to borrow a phrase.

And let me tell you another thing. You may well be right about the President. The White House has been sponsoring group after group to be parts of the re-enactment. He's even talking to the Queen directly about it. I've always thought the President to be a decent man, with good values, but ill advised and weak. I would trust him very little under the present circumstances. His Chief of Staff, John Sparrow, is a bastard, a Benedict Arnold, if I've ever seen one."

The Chairman rose from the bench on which they had been sitting. For several moments, he looked across the hundreds of acres of graves of American warriors who had served the nation in battle, many perishing in the act. His voice cracked as he said: "Tell your people, Tullius, that I will cooperate. The Republic must be preserved."

Harry Clinton and the four others, all very senior government officials and members also of the venerable House of Lords, waited until the Queen had taken her seat and the imperial nod given, before they took their own seats at the old table. They were taken aback to see she was accompanies by her son, the Crown Prince.

"Gentlemen, I have read your report and I must say the Guy Fawkes Project seems to be moving along rather nicely. I am quite impressed, Mr. Clinton, at the alliances you have fashioned with so many varied groups. Some of them reach quite high, do they not?

"My son has a few questions, if you do not mind. Your Queen is not getting any younger, is she?"

The message was unmistakable. Her son, no matter what they though of him, which she guessed was not much, was now involved in the Project. "Of course not, Your Highness."

The Prince read from a piece of paper. It might have been a list.

"Do you think you will be able to orchestrate them all into one force at the proper time?"

Having risen to his feet, Clinton answered. "I believe so, Your Excellency. It has to be done delicately, of course. Each group has a distinct defined use and is provided only enough information as to our true plans to permit it to perform its function, nothing more. One does not want the help to know too much. It will only confuse them."

"I am curious as to how the Blacks fit in. Can you elaborate on their role? Perhaps, it will give me a better appreciation of the details of the operation. The report does not provide much of that."

"Certainly, Your Excellency. Indeed, the role of the

178

Blacks in the re-acquisition of Britain's colonies of America is an excellent illustration of how the plan is to work.

Actually, we have two black groups involved. One led by Richard Brownspriggs, a Cape Breton fisherman descended from American slaves liberated during the War in America. They call themselves the Black Pioneers and will form a unit of the Loyalist troops at the Battle of Monmouth re-enactment. They will also contribute members to portray soldiers and camp followers from the horde of loyalists civilians that followed the army from the abandoned Philadelphia to New York in 1778. The Black Pioneers will have various assignments on the Day. They will take into custody certain American government leaders and other personnel not already committed, for example.

The other Black group calls itself The Ethiopian Regiment. That had been the name of a force of ex-slaves that fought against the Rebels in the insurrection. This group is a radical one. They are led by another descendant of an American Black in the revolution – Ben Whitecuff, now going by the name Marcus. His group has bases in every major American city and is well accepted by the community. They want a black nation in America and we are prepared to oblige them, not just for their support of the Day, but for their long-term cooperation. They will not be at the re-enactment, but will have two uses. First, their armed members will make certain that no counter groups rise up in any of these cities in opposition to the re-acquisition. Secondly, they will lead the American Black community in immediately supporting the new regime. We will let them announce their "alliance" with Great Britain and it will serve as prototype for arrangements with more of the minorities. It will not take long to have amass such a plurality of votes so that the re-acquisition can be confirmed constitutionally, by the vote of the people in its approval."

The Prince smiled and said. "Well thought out, Mr. Clinton. Your report mentioned an alliance with the Orientals. What did you have to promise for their aid?"

It was Clinton's turn to smile and he wondered, as he did so, whether smiling in the Sovereign's Presence constituted some breach of royal manners.

179

"All they wanted was a promise not to permit any more immigration into America from the Pacific Rim countries, including their own. They do not want America to become Asian. They fear becoming lost again among the masses. They certainly do not want their own state within America. They want to become American. They just do not want America to become Asian."

"Nor do we" said the Prince, at the same time raising his eyebrows to display that he, too, was perplexed by the oriental mind. Then, he asked:

"Do the Americans suspect anything?"

"I am certain that they do not have any inkling of their fate whatsoever," Clinton replied confidently. "After all, it has been 230 years since the War. They could not possibly anticipate a counter attack after so many years. It is exactly because of that element of surprise that the Guy Fawkes Project seemed so feasible."

"I suppose you are correct" spoke the Queen for the first time after her son took over. "Well, I am satisfied that the Project should move forward. We shall meet again in another three months. The "Day" is less than a year away, is it not? Does anyone have anything to add?"

Hearing nothing, Her Highness rose, smiled and exited, with her son at her side, through the door into her private quarters in the Palace.

New York City, Midtown
August 22, 2007

Erik Ackermann re-read the single sheet for the tenth time without pause. Although he was Publisher of the paper and personally approved each editorial, he rarely became involved in conceiving or drafting them. Sometimes, he suggested topics for the editorial page, like the government's failure to find a cure for AIDS or the horrid fighting in the Sudan. But he had far too many responsibilities to spend the time necessary in front of a word processor to write the editorial himself. The staff actually authored them. This one, however, he was writing himself, from scratch to final copy. In fact, virtually no one else at the paper had even seen it. They would read it in the paper tomorrow on their way to work .Erik thought the idea such a brilliant one that he did not want it tarnished and cheapened by staff discussions as to proper phraseology, effective placement and other such shop talk .Erik thought himself a pretty good wordsmith – he was Editor of the paper, as well as Publisher – and he did not need others to tinker with his language. He liked it. It had come out splendidly. Eric read it aloud to his empty office:

Is it time to look even farther backwood?

Proclaimers of Old Time values insist we look to Protestant, male dominated, slave owning colonial America to find the blue print for the American of today. Well, if "old" is "good", then why not look back even farther, to Britain, for guidance? Has it dawned on anyone that, as much as our Constitution, especially its First Amendment with its rights of free speech and an unfettered press, is a wonderful expression for the period, the idea behind it came from something deeper and older? I refer, of course, to the Magna Carta, the Common Law and the wonderful British balance of power among the Monarchy, the House of Lords and the House of Commons. Maybe in separating from England, the colonists threw out the baby with the bath water.

181

No one can deny that Britain has many excellent institutions that exceed their American counterparts. I need only refer to their equal quality medical care for all people, to their loving understanding of their elderly, to an enlightened and respected legal system that permits police control without weapons, to the way they embrace their immigrant cousins from Africa and India with a human warmth unknown on this side of the Atlantic. The British practice what the Editor of this paper always preaches: "We are all people!"

Maybe some of our rough and ready leaders in Washington, who like to "play king of the hill" as long as only they can win, should be more like the British and cede power to the other lads for them to have a go at it for a while. So much more civilized. It may be heresy to some whose bread is buttered in the American way, but should we not take a second look at what we kept and what we threw away of the British system over two centuries ago? Should we not invite more British leaders of industry, government, medicine, the arts to America and learn from them a more mature and civilized approach to life, an approach our ancestors perhaps too hastily had discarded?

This would get some attention, Eric concluded. Perhaps, it would spark a movement that will lead to love and brotherhood around the world. "Sir Eric Ackermann awarded Nobel Prize for Peace." Now, that would be a headline!

With the most unbounded pleasure, we can assure the public, that dispatches have the moment arrived, giving an account of the unconditional surrender of Lord Cornwallis, on the 17th instant, to our great and magnanimous General Washington."

The New Jersey Gazette, October 24, 1781

On board *HMS London*

October 1781

Sir Henry Clinton seemed resigned to what would now happen. His and his country's fates were sealed, even though the final day was still some time off. A sip of wine almost missed his lips as the *London* lurched in heavy seas in the Chesapeake Bay, off Virginia. The British commander in chief was grateful in having Cornwallis as a scapegoat. The man had ignored all of Clinton's orders, never directly, but always effectively. He had chased the Americans across the South, without catching up to them. In the process, he depleted his own army's strength and number. Finally, Cornwallis erected a base at the port of Yorktown in Virginia to rest .Clinton immediately recognized that his arrogant general had made himself vulnerable to a land-and-sea blockade ordered him to return to New York. Stubbornly, Cornwallis refused to leave, foolishly believing his position to be a beach head in the American South, when, in reality, he had painted himself in a corner from which he could not escape.

Washington saw his opportunity. He raced his 7000-man army south, taking with a like number of French troops of Count Rochambeau who were in Rhode Island and began a siege of Yorktown. Soon, a French fleet under the Comte de Grasse formed off the coast, preventing either a British escape or rescue by sea. Then, began almost two weeks of intense bombardment. Clinton had received a dispatch from Cornwallis. It was obvious from it that Cornwallis was crushed and about ready to capitulate. Clinton immediately ordered a fleet, with 7,000 of his troops aboard under his own command, to assist the besieged Cornwallis. As they neared Virginia, however, they picked up a pilot, who told them it was already over. Cornwallis had surrendered on October 19th.

Clinton decided to send one of his vessels with a dispatch to Lord George Germaine in London, advising him of the probable capture of Cornwallis and his some 8,000 British troops and that Clinton was returning with his forces to New York. Let Germaine explain to Lord North and His Highness how his favorite Cornwallis had ignored all orders and lost the war. In a painfully embarrassing strategic blunder, Cornwallis had lost a great portion of the British army in America.

Clinton knew that he would be replaced as commander in chief and that the war was effectively over. Parliament was already criticizing the six years of failure where the mighty British army had been able to capture only a few cities along the coast but nothing more. It was highly unlikely that, in these financially difficult times, another effort would be launched.

Draining his glass of wine, Clinton sat at his desk in his cramped quarters aboard the *London* and began writing his report to Lord Germaine. Captain Melcombe and the *His Majesty's Sloop Rattlesnake* would be sent to London with it. Clinton wished he could be present when, four weeks or so from now, his Lordship read the report and realized all was lost.

"Agreeable to the information which I had the honor to give Your Lordship in my last dispatch, the Fleet under the command of Rear Admiral Graves, sailed from Sandy Hook on the 16th instant and arrived off Cape Charles on the 24th, when we had the mortification to hear that Lord Cornwallis had proposed terms of capitulation to the enemy on the 17th. This intelligence was brought to us by the pilot of the Charon who came off from the shore and said that he had made his escape from Yorktown on the 18th and had not heard any shooting since the day before. The Nymph frigate, also arriving the next day from New York, brought me a letter from his Lordship, dated the 15th, the desponding tenor of which gives me the most alarming apprehension of its truth .Since then, we have been plying off the coast with variable and hard gusts of wind to the present hour without being able to procure any additional information, except from two men taken in a canoe, whose report exactly corresponds with the former.

Comparing, therefore, the intelligence received from these people and from others since come in, we cannot entertain the least doubt of his Lordship's having capitulated and that we are unfortunately too late to relieve him, which having been the only object of the expedition, the Admiral has determined to return with his fleet to Sandy Hook."

"Boy!" Clinton cried out when he had finished his writing and had blotted the sheet.

From nowhere, young Hays appeared.

"Bring this to Mr. Hopkins to write out in that handsome hand of his and then tell him that I want Captain Melcombe to personally deliver it to Lord Germaine. If he can, I want him to observe his Lordship's reactions and report them to me. Meanwhile, bring me another bottle of port and ask the captain of the *London* to see me. We are returning to New York and, unless I miss my guess, soon back to England. The war is lost, Mr. Hays, and that fool Cornwallis is the blame. A chapter of our lives is about to close and another will open. We shall not give up what is ours. Now, go and do as I say."

When the boy had brought the bottle, opened it and poured a glass for Sir Henry, he left. As soon as he was gone, Clinton allowed himself to slump in his chair. He had many things to consider. He would submit his resignation and he was confident that this time it would be accepted – that is, if he were not relieved of command first. Then, he would return to England and the family manor. Mary liked England, even though she was snubbed by many for her common American birth and their lack of formal wedding vows. He would take up his seat in Parliament and ally himself with his cousin and protector, the Duke of Gloucester. From there, he would await the next war. There would always be another one.

But, this war was over – at least, this stage of it. The British occupied only New York City, Charleston and Savannah, little to show for six years' investment in men and money. But, Clinton knew the struggle for America was far from finished. He remembered his discussions with the King and his ministers when he was last in London. Britain would never surrender America. There would be a try at retaking it and, if necessary, another and another, until England was restored to her rightful lands. This was an orderly retreat, not a surrender.

Robert Townsend entered the offices of the *Royal Gazette* with a dark, hard look on his face. He glanced about the room, but seeing only his friend and partner, editor Rivington about, his face lightened, his mouth softening almost to a smile.

"Well, Jeremy, I imagine that piece you did in your last paper that Lord Cornwallis had repelled Washington at Yorktown had been an error."

Rivington grinned back: "Poor information. It sometimes happens in war."

"Well, your error has become the subject of some perfectly putrid poetry in the *New Jersey Gazette*. Would you like to see it?"

"Of, course," responded Rivington. "The readers are my audience and, perhaps perversely, the more I irritate them, the better I view my performance as being. Strange, but again, it happens in war."

Mr. Collins,

In your next issue, please to inform Jemmy Rivington that, although he tells us that two ships of Count De Grasse's squadron, attempting to force a passage up the York river, above Gloucester Point and York-town, were obliged to return defeated, we hear that our illustrious General Washington is returning north-eastward, crowned with laurels plucked from the brow of Lord Cornwallis, victorious.

"When British glory once begins to fade,

Jemmy no more pursues his wonted trade,

Nor post nor pay can now bring out a word,

E'en the Gazette royal submits to the sword;

Tho' brib'd to print, his coward heart misgives,

Invention fails him – vainly he strives

To forge a falsehood but the authentic tale,

Of hosts subdued, terrifies the pale

Frightened Rivington, whose well told story

Trusts not honest Whig nor hapless Tory.

Cornwallis taken! – 'tis no more nor less --

Alas! 'tis true – What think you now of Congress?"

"Robert, my friend. You were too kind when you styled it 'putrid'. It is even more decayed than that. But accurate. With this battle, the war is over – or soon will be. The King, Parliament, the merchants of London, even the people, are tired of the war. They will not begin anew with a fresh army. I am afraid, partner of mine, that our thriving British Coffee House business will be finished. This newspaper too will lose its readers with the end of the war."

Townsend shook his head. "Jeremy, we – you especially – will be fortunate, if the next mob is not successful in hanging us. Once the British abandon New York, we are dead men."

"So sweet of you to care, Robert, but I shall be fine and so will you. Indeed, I expect we shall be rewarded for my efforts to irritate the Americans into frenzy. You will see."

BY HIS EXCELLENCY

W i l l i a m L i v i n g s t o n

*Governor, Captain General and Commander in Chief in and over
the State of New Jersey and the territories thereunto belonging,
Chancellor and Ordinary in the fame*

PROCLAMATION

      *WHEREAS it has pleased Almighty God, Father of
Mercies, remarkably to assist and support the United States of
America in their important struggle for liberty against the long
continued efforts of a powerful nation, it is the duty of all ranks to
observe and thankfully acknowledge the intercession of his
providence on their behalf. Through the whole of the contest, from
its first rise to this time, the influence of Divine Providence may be
clearly perceived in many signal instances, of which we mention
but a few: in revealing the councils of our enemies, when the
discoveries were seasonable and important and the means
seemingly inadequate and fortuitous; in preserving and even
improving the union of the several states, on the breach of which
our enemies placed their greatest dependence; in increasing the
number of and increasing the zeal of and attachment of the friends
of liberty; in granting us remarkable deliverance and blessing us
with the most signal successes, when affairs seemed to have the
most discouraging appearance; in raising up for a most powerful
and generous ally, in one of the first of the European powers; in
confounding the counsels of our enemies and suffering them to
pursue such measures as most have directly contributed to
frustrate their own desires and expectations and --- above all, in
making their extreme cruelty to the inhabitants of these states,
when in their power, and their savage devastation of property, the
very means of cementing our union and adding vigour to every*

190

effort in opposition to them.

And as we cannot help leading the good people of these states to a retrospect of the events which have taken place since the beginning of the war, so we recommend, in a particular manner, to their observation, the Goodness of God in the year now drawing to a conclusion, in which the confederation of the United States has been completed; in which there have been so many instances of prowess and success in our armies, particularly in the southern states where, notwithstanding the difficulties with which they had to struggle, they have recovered the whole country which the enemy had overrun, leaving I HAVE THEREFORE thought fit, by and with the advice of the Privy Council and from a deep sense of our indispensable duty to celebrate with united hearts, in social worship, throughout the whole continent, the praises of the Great Disposer of all events, who has so often and so conspicuously during the present war displayed His Omnipotent Arm for our deliverance, to appoint the said THIRTEENTH DAY of DECEMBER next to be observed in this state as a day of THANKSGIVING and PRAISE, hereby recommending to the Ministers of the Gospel of every denomination therein, to perform the Divine Service and to the people committed to their charge to attend on publick worship on that day and to abstain from servile labour and all recreations inconsistent with the solemnity of the festival.

WILLIAM LIVINGSTON

G O D S A V E T H E PEOPLE

Lucky Linda Ranch

August 25, 2007

Elias Dayton had arrived at the *Lucky Linda* a day before the other two. He had wanted to visit with Jack Hays for a while to determine how much they should trust Senator Moriarity. Father McCullough said he was safe, but then again how much wiser was it to trust the Jesuit?

Although they argued strenuously between themselves, each alternatively playing the Devil's Advocate with the other, it was evident that both men were ready to leap at the chance of enlisting the Senator to the defense, sight unseen. There was no alternative. To foil Clinton's plan, they needed access to the planning of the re-enactment event, where the coup seemed likely to take place. What better way to gain entrance than through its Chairman, an influential, well respected Senator with his heart supposedly in the right place? There was always a risk going to an outsider, but this one seemed minimal and unavoidable.

Sam Luckie brought the Padre and the Senator out to the ranch in his pick up. As they approached the *Lucky Linda* on a scorching hot dusty afternoon at the end of August, the Senator, squeezed between Sam and the priest in the front seat, wondered to himself what kind of fate it was that had brought him, with his boyhood mentor, thirty-five years later, to this spot in west Texas. He believed Father McCullough's story, but looked forward to meeting Dayton and Hays so as to better comprehend the likelihood of this incredible attempt actually being made. He had checked out both men and their ancestors. Their pedigrees were matters of historical record. The rest of the priest's tale had checked out as well. It was all-plausible, but could it be true, much less imminent?

Sam had spent the latter part of the ride from town taking advantage of the fact that he had a United States Senator in his pick-up. To him, a captive in a manner of speaking, Sam related his theory that too much beef was being raised in the United States and Mexico to command high enough prices come market time to insure a profit and that foreign beef should be barred .The pick up passed the empty cattle pens .Sam had been proven right. Prices were low and he had decided to wait another season before restocking this ranch with a young herd.

Elias and Hays emerged from the ranch house upon hearing the sound of the truck outside. Father McCullough made the introductions – the Senator insisted on being called Frank – as they walked in the main house. Sam left them at this time, saying he had some chores to attend to and would drop off the Senator's bags at the bunkhouse on the way.

The small talk did not last long, not even all the way through the lunch of soup and sandwiches. These were all men of action and a challenge lay before them that needed immediate and full attention. Dayton began with a comprehensive narrative as to how the British plot had been hatched two and a quarter centuries before, how it had been detected, past attempts and past defenses and, finally, what they had amassed about the upcoming attempt. He summed up the last part:

"This is Britain's first attempt in more than a century. They have no choice. This is their last hurrah .They have their back up against it. The Monarchy is openly mocked. Now it is only a member of the common market and its influence as a world power diminishes daily. South Africa is gone. Australia and Canada have grown apart. The British must reverse the downward spiral or soon they will be a Portugal - with a wonderful past, but no future in the 21st century.

We believe the re-enactment of the Battle of Monmouth at the end of June, 20088 will be the time and place of their attempt to take back America. We do not know their plan but know that they have allies – foreign and American, some we know, some we don't – who will also be participating in the re-enactment. We also know that all our senior government and military leaders will also be there, in one spot, easily captured or slaughtered. What we do not know is how they can expect to control a nation of 300 million people just because they kill or take prisoners some two or three thousand or so of its leaders. That's the question that has tortured Jack and me. How could they possibly hope to get away with it afterwards? We think there is only one way for them to keep power after the coup. Look at the allies they have enlisted here – the minorities and radical groups purporting to speak for the poor, the disadvantaged, the second-class citizens. It might start as an armed takeover by a foreign power but it will quickly be transformed into a political coup. High-ranking political leaders within our own country-- demagogues really – must also be in on it. At the end, a whole political party – the conservative Old Time American types – will be eliminated in one swoop .So, probably will be their wealth. In other words, Britain is helping our minorities take over America in some mutually satisfactory arrangement, the terms of which we can only guess. But we are out numbered big time.

We have one weapon. We know about them – or at least, some of them, – but they do not know anything about us. We may not be able to prevent the explosion but perhaps we can pick the time and place of the detonation and render it ineffective in that fashion. Your assistance as the Chairman of the Re-enactment Committee will greatly enhance our ability to control this monster."

All three men looked at the Senator's expression as if to get an inkling as to whether he understood or believed this fantastic tale. The Chairman said nothing for a moment, looked quizzically towards Father McCullough and asked.

"Lucius Sergius Catilina?"

His former teacher nodded. "Remarkably the same." Then, realizing that neither Dayton nor Hays was following the conversation, the priest interpreted the reference for them.

"Lucius Sergius Catilina, known popularly as Catiline. He had been a soldier and public servant of Rome, praetor in 68 B.C. and governor of Africa in 67 B.C. When he returned to Rome, he was charged with abuse of power and prohibited from running for consul, the top position in Rome and one that Cataline coveted. Frustrated, he turned to demagoguery, promising the people anything they wanted in exchange for their support. He promised abolition of debts and redistribution of property to enlist the poor as followers. At the same time, he plotted to seize control of the Senate by force, end the Republic and to make himself Emperor."

"Marcus Tullius Cicero – a friend of the Senator and mine

from way back --" Father McCullough continued with a smile, "learned from his spies of what was afoot and denounced the traitor Cataline in front of the Senate. The plot was foiled. Catiline escaped by fleeing to Etruria. Acting pursuant to *Senatus consultum ultimum*, – 'the extreme decree of the Senate'-- Cicero had the other conspirators summarily executed. No trial, no public forum for their cause. Execution."

When Father McCullough had finished his explanation, the Senator assured Dayton and Hays that he understood the predicament and answered that he would help them in any way he could.

"I am all yours. Everyone in Washington D.C. has either gone back home or to the Maryland or Delaware shores for the next ten days until Labor Day."

"Excellent" responded Dayton. "We can begin right away, if that suits you."

"Senator, as I mentioned, all the signals point toward the coup's being sprung during the re-enactment of the Battle of Monmouth. We, of course, know the general scope of the event but the specifics published regarding it so far have been few and not very informative. Can you give us an overall picture how it's supposed to work? Then Jack and I – Father also – will have some questions to ask you based on bits and pieces we have picked up in our investigations. Can you do that?"

"Of course" answered the Senator. "The Battle of Monmouth was the largest, longest and last battle between the main armies of the two protagonists. It took place in central New Jersey, in western Monmouth County, near the town of Freehold. It was all farmland then and the area, though built up some now, is still rural. More than that, a couple of thousands of acres that comprised the battlefield were purchased and made into a National Park. There is more than enough land to re-enact the entire battle as it in fact happened, only slightly scaled back. Believe me, this is no little task seeing as among the British, Hessians, their camp followers, the Continental Army, the New Jersey militia who rushed to the battle and the citizens of the surrounding farms, there were over 20,000 participants back in 1778. We can accommodate less than 25% of that number, but that will still mean about 5,000 involved in the event, as spectators, performers, and dignitaries.

The "battle" will begin at about 10:00 a.m. and, speeded up, will be over at 3:30 in the afternoon. Then the ceremonies and speeches will begin. That will last a little less than two hours. The celebration follows that. Champagne, fireworks, bands. Of course, all of this will all be covered by the press, broadcast live from the battlefield. The days are long at the end of June and we will use every bit of daylight we can get.

As far as the notables attending the event, we presently expect the President, the Vice President, Speaker of the House, the entire Supreme Court, joint chiefs of staff and well more than a thousand senators, representatives, military men, bureaucrats etc. Virtually, all American leaders will attend. So will the Queen of England, the Prime Minister, the president of France, the Chancellor of the United German Republic, among foreign dignitaries.

England, Germany and Canada will supply approximately 2,000 soldiers. Another thousand will be auxiliary troops, --- civilian Loyalists, Indians, slaves who fought for the British in exchange for freedom. There will also be the camp followers. So many there were in 1778 – wives and girlfriends, servants, peddlers and the like – that they made a train a dozen miles long. These people will be from Canada and England also.

On the American side we are going to have an equal number of troops. We will also have townspeople and other locals. We will even have a Molly Pitcher brigade to illustrate the role that women played in the battle and the War for Independence. Few of our troops will be actually military types. Too great an honor, I guess, to squander on mere soldiers. Invitations to play a role in the re-enactment as an American soldier or civilian are "hot tickets" as they say .The Republicans and Democrats have the same number. I dispense ours. The President's Chief of Staff has the others.

I have brought with me some maps and other things that may help you better visualize the battlefield and how we plan to organize the day's activities. Ben took them to the bunkhouse. I can get them if you want."

"No, they will be very helpful but they will keep for the moment," said Elias. "Let me ask a question or two. What about the pyrotechnics. There wouldn't be any live ammunition?"

"Of course not. The muskets and artillery pieces will fire blank cartridges only."

Dayton asked. "My second questions follows from the first – i.e., how do you know that everyone is shooting blanks and, for that matter, what exactly are the security arrangements in general regarding the event?"

Senator Moriarity nodded as if he understood not only the question but the direction in which Elias was headed in his examination. " The answer is the same. The White House and the Secret Service are in charge of security. It is expressly out of my Committee's responsibility. As far as I am aware – and as Senator I am well advised on the event's plans – the foreign participants will provide their own replicas of weapons and no inspection is planned of their armaments. An inspection had been considered under the heading of safety, not security, but the decision was made that it would run counter to the sense of international brotherhood and the burying of animosities among the participants which the event is supposed to foster. The American participants will for the most part be supplied their replica weapons by the Government. The plan – quite confidentially – is that the cost will be underwritten by a major soft drink manufacturer and then presented afterwards to the participants as a memento. Details aren't complete yet but the hope is that much of the cost of the event will be borne by corporate America. In exchange, a lot of business executives will be among those to play soldiers that day, I suspect .

"Mr. Senator" Jack asked. "Do you know – or can you find out – the identities of the enemy forces? Take the Indians you mentioned before. We believe that members of the Mohawk Nation may be part of the plot, just as they had been part of England's forces in the American Revolution. We know some names. If we can match them on your list, we will have people to watch. We think we can name some Germans too as well as some other groups."

"No, Jack. I don't have any names yet but I do have rough breakdowns as to how many Indians there will be, how many women will be part of the Molly Pitcher brigade that I mentioned, how many Hessians etc .I have that also with my other materials in the bunkhouse. Also, I should be able to find out more with a little looking.

Elias replied. "That would be good. We will work out a way for you to pass along what you find without compromising yourself. But, there is another area in which we need your assistance, Senator, in addition to helping prevent the coup at the re-enactment. It is a very delicate assignment. We need a core group of Senators advised as to what is going on. We do not need them to do anything before the attempted coup but we need their support after we thwart it. With the event's being televised, there is bound to be an immediate public reaction to the coup attempt and our preventing it. A statement from a credible body of American leaders will have to be made and an explanation given as to what the American public had just witnessed. We cannot go around soliciting support after the fact. We may all be in jail."

Father McCullough interrupted "Tullius, remember how Cicero persuaded his fellow Senators of Cataline's conspiracy and the danger it posed to the Republic. You must do likewise, not in a public forum of the Senate, but quietly, among those senators whose honesty, integrity and patriotism are beyond reproach. You must tell them about the threat. They must see it unfold on the day of the re-enactment and they must stand up afterwards and identify to the American public what had happened. And, if we fail to prevent the takeover, they, knowing the full story as to how America was re-taken, must be the ones who ferment opposition among the citizens."

"But, Senator," joined in Dayton "you must be certain of the ones to whom you speak. The enemy's not knowing that we are on the alert is our major weapon. We know Clinton is recruiting allies among the same ranks. You must be absolutely sure of your confidants."

The Senator nodded his head, understanding the rationale behind those instructions. That was not what was concerning him.

"I know the ones to whom I would speak. I have been in the Senate with them for many years and I know who have values and who are merely opportunists, motivated by concerns other than the good of the Republic, the *res publica*." Looking at his former teacher, he added, "I see now, Father, the reason why you asked me about Cataline and whether I remembered what *cui bono* meant. No, I know the ones to ask. What I worry about is convincing them. There isn't a 'Father McCullough' we can use for each of them who can get away with such an outlandish tale."

Elias nodded. "We anticipated that. More accurately, General Washington anticipated that more than two centuries ago. He gave my great, great, great grandfather Colonel Elias Dayton a letter to be delivered to those, in his words, 'who have heard the message of Thomas Paine and who value the Republic of the United States and her independence.' You can show that to them and we can provide you and them other indicia of the message's authenticity. General Washington was the ultimate spymaster. He provided for many things."

The Senator replied. "I see. Well, it is fortunate we have such a protector from so long ago. Of course, I will begin speaking with them when I return. I assume during the next ten days, you will fill me with all the details I will need."

There was a silence. They had accomplished a great deal for their first visit. The Senator had to be at a point where he could absorb no more. Father McCullough knew when his class was tired but he had one final point to make before class was recessed. Speaking to his former student, he said.

"Frank. You don't know this but I am the chaplain to Captain Jack Hays Ranger Company. Now that is a low profile position because there are only a few Catholics among them. But, you just mentioned 'our protector of a long time ago', referring to George Washington. I needn't remind any of you of another Protector we have from even longer ago, from the Beginning. Perhaps, it would be appropriate if we remember and seek His Assistance in the enormous task we have before us."

Elias immediately said "Padre, perhaps you can lead us in a prayer for that help."

Father McCullough nodded, lowered his eyes, bowed his head and began:

"Let us pray. Dear Lord, You once displayed your affection for America in aiding her people to overthrow a cruel ruler. America became your Land where liberty and love lived in the hearts of her citizens.

We are in difficulty again. Perhaps, it is not our fault, but, in our charity, we have become overwhelmed by our own altruism. Or maybe, it is our fault. In our affluence, we may have sadly become blind to the needs of our neighbors. Our people are fragmented and there is sincere confusion among them. Many citizens are now at odds with their fellows. That is neither new nor unnatural. With your grace and inspiration, these people will again, as they have often in the last two centuries, blend together and adjust the mix of differences that is America. Your blessed land will grow even stronger from its assimilations of other peoples and cultures. America will continue to be a beacon to the unfortunate and an example to the democratic urges of people across the world.

However, in our confusion and squabbling, our ancient enemy has returned and the demon has struck a deal for the souls of some of our citizens. Because of it, our Nation is at great risk and it appears that for Your own reasons, Lord, you have chosen the four of us to rescue it. We do not question your plan, nor wish to avoid being Your servants, but, please give the four of us and our comrades in the field as well as all those who must battle the enemy, the wisdom of your good counsel and the courage to fight, even unto death. Give each of us the strength, at the moment it is needed, to submit to the will of our ancestors, who through your infinite power, have directed us to this time and place, and to do the inexpressible.

Grant us this through Our Lord, Jesus Christ".

To which, all three answered "*amen*", even though none of them understood the final phrase, "to do the inexpressible."

New York City

December 12, 1781

The London fleet will sail from New York in about eight days. Lord Cornwallis goes home on the Robust, and the traitor General Benedict Arnold and his family on the Edward, a twenty-gun ship.

The New Jersey Gazette, December 12, 1781

*   *   *   *

Headquarters at Fishkill. December 6. We hear from New York that the Hessians and other German troops are called home by their respective princes .

New Jersey Gazette, December 12, 1781

London

December 31, 2007

It had been Pamela who had suggested an early, quiet dinner on New Year's Eve, at a small restaurant off Kensington Square. Harry Clinton had been very pleasantly surprised at her initiative. He hoped it indicated some feeling for him that transcended the peculiar relationship which their common ancestor, Sir Henry Clinton, over two centuries before, had forced upon his first-born male and female heirs of every generation. They had enjoyed two pleasant weekends together at the Clinton ancestral home in the countryside and had dined together around London a score of times, if not more, the past couple of years. It had been primarily in discharge of the obligations they had inherited. Yet, working in tandem seemed natural and easy for both and the spare moments together, away from the tasks at hand, were the most enjoyable Clinton had ever remembered spending with a member of the gentler sex. Pamela was intelligent, witty and strikingly beautiful. Even though their ancestors had once been siblings, Clinton did not consider Pamela in any sisterly fashion. He knew, however, that, without question, the present was an inappropriate time to foster anything beyond their present arms length relationship. Duty to Britain took precedence over all.

Pamela was especially chatty at dinner, telling her cousin, many times removed, about her visit with her brother and his family this Christmas. She was godmother as well as spoiling aunt to his twin boys and it was evident that they brought out the maternal, softer side of the feared barrister. Clinton, in turn, told her how he had spent his holiday in London at his sister's flat. He did not like his brother-in-law, an insurance man, and he stayed only as long as politeness dictated.

"He reduces everything to statistical probability. It drives me crazy, even small talk. For example, I say to him 'Do you think it will snow this week?' He will answer: 'Historically, during the month of December, we average 3.2 inches of precipitation and 45 degrees temperature, although freezing or below temperatures can be anticipated some 30% of the time. Adjusting for the greater potential for cold weather when the wind is out of the northwest, which it is fully half the month of December, and multiplying it out according to a formula the Weather Service employs, I believe we have between a 22% and 26% chance of snow this week, slightly higher as we approach its end.'"

Pamela laughed at Clinton's mimicking his brother-in-law. "I know. I could never be so precise and exact in my thinking. I sometimes act more out of intuition than I do measurement. There is an element of unpredictability about every situation, the more complicated it is, the more likely the number and variety of the 'unexpected' to be expected, if you know what I mean."

"Indeed, I do. Take our upcoming event, for example." Clinton instinctively stopped for a moment, looked about the restaurant and lowered his voice. "We have so many threads that have to come together in the proper pattern that we must anticipate that some things will not go as planned. But, we can keep those things to a minimum by constant practice and rehearsals. During the next four months, all of our units will be drilled intensively for the big day. They will not be told the full story yet, of course.

They do not know about the *grand finale* that is planned, much less how world changing it will be. But, they have been selected by their leaders as reliable, able to pull the triggers when necessary. We will tell them the full mission shortly before it is to occur. Each unit will have someone assigned to quietly dispose of any who get cold feet. Mother has given her approval to move to the next stage of the project."

"We are getting close, aren't we" said Pamela.

Clinton sipped his wine, nodded and said:"D Day minus 180 days, I believe. Almost half a year away. Not long at all when you consider we have been planning it now for the better of three years."

"And eagerly awaiting it since 1776." joined in Pamela. There was a pause and she continued. "Am I still going to be there for the kill?"

Clinton did not hesitate. "Of course, I promised you. I need you – there." the last word being added as an afterthought to avoid an unintended, but accurate, *double entendre*. "The 'unexpected', about which we were just speaking, can happen to me as well. You must be there to take command, if I fall. There is no one who knows all the plans or whom I trust as well as you."

Pamela blushed, pleased at Clinton's respect and reliance on her. He really was not as unimaginative and dull as she had once thought him to be, when they would meet on occasion growing up in the London scene. "Well, thank you", she said sincerely. "I do need to make arrangements with the Courts if I am to be away for an extended period. Can you give me any idea of when I should go?"

Clinton hesitated. He wanted her there, but not as a co-commander or even as a second in command. He wanted her there because he had fallen in love with her. He wanted her to be there to witness his greatest victory and to fall in his arms, the start of a romantic relationship about which he could not stop thinking. "The first of June would not be too early. We may hop around a bit on the North American continent for a week or two making certain all our forces are on the ready. They will start assembling in the States the third week of June and from then to D-Day will be so hectic that you will wish you were back in Old Bailey", he finished with a laugh.

"Don't wager on that. It sounds so exciting." she replied. "Can I ask you something?"

"Of course" he answered.

"I am going to the States in three days. Can I lease an auto and drive out and see the battlefield?"

"Why are you going?" Clinton asked suspiciously.

"Oh, an international legal committee of which I am a member. Last time, they met here. Now, New York and next Tokyo." she answered without any apparent recognition that Clinton was concerned. She sensed he was, however, and had picked her words carefully.

"Did not we meet some of those people once before, perhaps when they were in London for the last meeting?"

"What a remarkable memory." she praised him. "Yes, I recall we met two of them at the House of Lords Club. You and I were off to the theater and did not visit very long."

"Yes, yes. I seem to remember. One of them was interested in the history of the Club, was he not? He was to call me for a tour of the old place, but he never did. What were their names, do you remember?" Clinton asked as smoothly as he could. Did Pamela have a romantic interest in either of them was the real question he wanted to ask, but he could not reveal such jealously.

"I do not recall the name of that good looking California lawyer. He's a recent addition to the Committee. The older fellow is its Chairman. Name of Dayton. Christian name Elliot or Elias, I believe."

"Yes, and I thought at the time that I had recognized the name. It still sounds familiar but from where I do not know. It will come to me, I daresay. Not important" He was relieved. She did not even know the name of the handsome one and she thought the other fellow was old. He better watch this urge of his to be possessive and jealous. It could ruin their relationship, even before it began.

"About visiting the battlefield, I am afraid that it is not open during the winter. In fact, it may well be under snow this time of year. Try the theater instead and see what the Yankees have been stealing from us of late."

Indian Point, Maryland

January 11, 1998

The two men eyed each other nervously. The Senator, as much as he had tried, had been unable to find an easy way to begin. Senator Signori, already apprehensive at having been asked by his old friend to come alone and in secret to this place on the Potomac, fifty miles south from Washington DC, cut to the bone: "Goddamn it, Frank what is this about? Is something wrong? Your family? What?"

His friend shook his head and smiled reassuringly. Signori reacted to it: "Thank God. I was afraid you were going to tell me you had AIDS or cancer or something like that."

"No, no, nothing like that. But, as you can guess, it is a matter of extreme importance but I do not know how to begin. We are about the same age and educated alike. We have been in the Senate about the same length of time, and have been on the same side of most issues over the years. But what I really want to visit with you about is Cicero."

Signori had been following the Senator up to this point. In fact, he thought he knew where he was headed – looking for support for a Presidential bid in 2008 or 2012. Wasn't everyone? But the reference to Cicero had derailed him.

"Cicero, like in *O Temora o mores* Cicero?"

"Exactly! The same Cicero who put the good of the *res publica* and the preservation of the republican virtues above his own selfish interest. Now, you know George Wickersham, don't you?"

"If you mean, the man who is the curator of The Smithsonian, the answer is 'yes'."

"Fine. I want you carefully to read this letter from him." The Senator handed Senator Signori a letter on Smithsonian stationary that was addressed "To whom it may concern". He read the body of the letter:

Senator Francis X. Moriarity, Jr., Chairman of the Joint Senate and House Committee on the Identification and Renewal of American Values, has asked me and several professionals at the Smithsonian with the appropriate expertise in certain disciplines to examine a letter, dated April 28, 1791 purportedly written and signed by President George Washington. Before beginning our physical examination of the letter, we did a computer search of all known Washington correspondence in public and private hands. We made private inquiry to the leading Washington collectors. There is no previous record of a letter of the sustance and date of this one. If it is authentic, it is a new item.

We have been cautioned by Senator Moriarity that this was a matter of extreme national importance and that the contents of the letter must be protected from disclosure and that only I could read its contents in their entirety. Operating under this restriction, we analyzed exact copies of the handwriting of particular words, not necessarily in their original order. In any instance of doubt, the original letter and the words under scrutiny, with the remainder of the text suitably masked, were made available to the examiner. In addition, the parchment itself, the ink and the integrity of the document – that it was a product of having been cut and pasted together – were all tested by leading experts in these disciplines.

Moreover, an experimental, but fascinating, examination of the documents was made for fingerprints. Dr. Rusk of Yale has pioneered a method of searching objects that have been touched at one time by famous people and to try to lift from them ancient old fingerprints. First, he concentrates on objects which were personal to the dead man and, therefore, more often held sacred by those who honor his memory. This means the items are locked up, rarely touched and generally protected from the atmosphere. Ideally, he takes them from widely distant collections to minimize the possibility of recurring fingerprints that might come from, for example, a Washington scholar who may have examined a number of the originals. Then, he takes the fingerprints of anyone known to have handled the object so as to identify his prints among those collected and exclude them. Finally, all unidentified fingerprints are run through Government archives that contain hundreds of million of prints. If they are found there, they are culled out also. The fingerprints remaining that are found on more than one item are "possible", those unidentified prints found on more than a half a dozen items are deemed "probables".

Our conclusion from the above examinations is that this entire letter is in the script of George Washington, that it was written on parchment and with ink from that period and that it bears the same fingerprints as Dr. Rusk's extensive files believes are George Washington's. Dr. Rusk has also advised that the fingerprints of John Adams, Thomas Jefferson, James Madison, and Andrew Jackson appear also on the document.

The letter was signed by Wickersham and had a handwritten P.S. to it *"Senator Signori --There is no doubt that the letter is authentic. You come to see me and I will show you the results of every test and let you examine every witness. These are George Washington's words."*

Signori read the letter a couple of times. The first reading was for meaning, the second for understanding.

"Okay, I have read it. The part about the fingerprints is remarkable but that is not why you gave me this. You have a letter from George Washington for me to read?"

"No," the Senator laughed, seeing an opening to make a point. "*You* have a letter from George Washington to read. I have the same letter. So do a few others. Here."

With that, the Senator handed Senator Signori a flat envelope." This is the original. Wickersham has placed a translucent cover on the pages to protect the document and the fingerprints. But, let me give you some background before you start."

Senator Signori nodded, slipping the sheets back into the envelope. He had been anxious to read the mysterious letter, but he could restrain himself a while longer.

The Senator began. He spoke slowly and deliberately, but like one telling a story. "Back in 1790, George Washington asked the first Congress under the newly enacted Constitution for a contingency fund for him to use to hire spies and covert operators. Washington was an extraordinary spymaster during the Revolution, you know, and probably won the war as well there as he did on the battlefields.

The threat of foreign invasion did not end with the Revolution. Washington knew that and, since there was no CIA or FBI around to whom to delegate the task, he took charge of espionage again, just as he had during the war. And it was not just he who did this. Every President, down to Grant, I believe, ran the nation's intelligence operations.

This letter you are going to read comes from that period, when President Washington resumed being spymaster. Those to whom the letter was given were Washington's most trusted aides and agents during the Revolution. The letter speaks about a plot which they know was in the works by Britain to retake the United States and to establish the country's defense to it. An organization was set up, funded by cash and public lands, today of enormous value, to assure that there would be men on watch. As I mentioned, President Washington headed the team, his former agents were his lieutenants. When Washington left office and public life, he decided to confide in his successor John Adams regarding the on going danger from the British. But there was no easy chain of succession for his lieutenants. When they aged, their first-born sons were to be entrusted with the duty to be vigilant for the redcoats return. And so it was for many years, until one President did not trust his successor and the chain was broken. Fortunately, it remained intact among the other members, the descendants of Washington's associates, and it continues to this day. It was good that it did, because, three times at least, Britain has tried to regain part of what it felt was wrongfully taken from it after the Revolution – the War of 1812, the attempt to buy California and annex Texas in the 1840's and its support of the Confederacy in the Civil War in the hope of an alliance between the two afterwards. There were some other episodes. Like all I am telling you, everything, with the exception of the counter espionage group Washington fashioned, is a matter of historical fact, subject to your verification, if you want.

This letter was given to me by one of those descendants of Washington's lieutenants. A member of their team is well known to me and I trust him explicitly so I agree to give the help that has been solicited. Another attempt by Britain to take America is imminent. There will be some force, but mostly, it will be a coup. A number of American leaders are thought to be in conspiracy with the British. I think you may be too. Are you?"

Senator Moriarity made the accusation and asked the question abruptly and harshly. Poor Signori looked at his friend with his mouth agape and his eyes big. He had all he could to assimilate what he had just been told about the British and the last bit about his being part of the plot was beyond his comprehension. His befuddlement saved his life. Moriarity had been watching Signori's face carefully to see if he gave away, in either his expression or some bit of body language, an advance knowledge of the British plan. If he had, Moriarity was prepared to kill him on the spot with the pistol he had been nervously fingering in his jacket pocket. Back at the *Lucky Linda*, Captain Jack Hays had given him and Father McCullough some lessons in the use of firearms. They could not afford to lose the element of surprise and, if the Senator had guessed wrong about Signori's virtues – or even suspected that he had – then Signori would have to be removed and Senator Moriarity would have to do it. That is one of the reasons he had selected this place, far enough away where he would not likely be recognized, were a body to later turn up.

"Am I what?" asked Signori, the Senator's question finally sinking in. "Am I in league with the British to take America? You got to be crazy. Is this some kind of joke – an initiation or some thing?"

"No. The letter from Wickersham is real and it says unequivocally that the letter from Washington was real. The letter is addressed to you and me and some more like us. Our help is needed. Read it. I wish I were crazy, then the nation would not be at such terrible risk. But, I am not crazy. We are on the verge of a political coup that will place the British and an alliance of American minorities in control of the United States, under some bizarre form of government. Read."

This time Senator Signori finished extracting the sheets from the envelope. The handwriting was still dark and bold, despite the years. It took a little effort, like walking across a stony beach, but he could make out the handwriting:

We do not know when our foe will shed its sheepsclothes and again seek to rip our throats asunder and feed upon our carcass. We know from one of our most trusted agents who has seen and heard first hand the formation of the plans against us, that a perpetual oath has been sworn by some in London, among them the Evil George, his Ministers North and Germain and General Clinton, to resume their assault upon America upon the first and best opportunity, even if that were to take a century or longer.

We shall be sentinels, alert to this threatened peril. However, since the threat is perpetual and our days on this orb numbered, we must provide for others to stand sentry after we are gone. General Dayton is my second in command. He will set our strategies and lines of defense. Congress has provided for funds and properties that will permit us to keep this watch as long as our foe is a risk. That too will be under the General's command.

General Dayton, his designee or successor, likely will have to recruit others into the company. It is for those that I have prepared this letter, so that they might know not only General Dayton's authority from me but my expectations of them as Americans to assist again in repulsing the enemy. I read Thomas Paine's words to the troops the Christmas night we marched to Trenton and turned the tide of war.

"These are the times that try men's souls. The summer soldier and the sunshine patriot will, in this crisis, shrink from the service of his country, but he that stands it now deserves the love and thanks of man and woman".

It is more appropriate here. You have tasted liberty and independence. You will know what you and your children will lose upon any return tyrants like the monarch and ministers of Great Britain."

"O, Good Lord" Senator Signori uttered.

*   *   *   *

Jack Hays had arrived a half-hour earlier at D'Allassandro's than did the others. He spent the extra moments over a glass of beer and in snatches of pleasant conversation with Sherrie, the newest hostess. First, they spoke of her two predecessors, Margaret's now flourishing career on Broadway and Jennifer' as an expectant mom. Then, she hinted at some of the joys and sorrows of her own life, as if daring Jack to ask a little deeper. Then, it was the weather and finally an exchange begun with a question by her.

"That partner of yours is some ladies man! Is he going to be here too, tonight?"

Jack asked whom she meant and she described Elias Dayton. Then, he asked what she meant by the "ladies' man" remark.

"Well, he's here often with that very pretty dark haired, very stylish lady. I think she's from Texas originally. You know her."

Jack nodded. He did. She was referring to Linda of the *Lucky Linda*, the outside contact with Debbie Jean and Liz. He knew she and Elias had become friends. Sherrie went on:

"Well, last night he came in with a knockout and I mean knockout. She spoke with a British accent and was stunning. I served them in the back. I think she was a lawyer, but she could have been a starlet, a Miss Universe, even a princess. She was something else, I tell you."

A party of four came in and Sherrie took them to their table. That ended the topic and gave Jack a quiet few moments to consider what Sherrie had just said. Hays thought he knew who this second woman was too. The combination her being British, a lawyer and "stunning" most likely mean it was the lady barrister Pamela from London. She would be in town. There was a meeting of the Committee this week. In fact, that was the excuse Hays himself was using for being in New York. There was no reason why Dayton and Pamela should not have dinner together. It was peculiar, perhaps, that they had dined in the private, soundproof room and that Dayton had never mentioned it to Hays, although they had been together most of the day. It became extremely peculiar when one added to the mix the fact that she was Harry Clinton's girlfriend, their arch enemy. Also puzzling, as the flattered Dayton himself had earlier admitted, was that the extremely attractive woman had been sucking up to Dayton for more than the last year. She even angled to get on the Committee. Could it be of a business nature? A romantic interest? Could she be recruiting him? That would mean that they knew about us. Was he trying to enlist her? More likely, although Jack was, at first, a little offended for not being let in on it. But, he knew right away that was silly. Dayton was the Commander. Washington had alliances with operatives about no one knows to this day. Witness the members of their own group. It was the right – perhaps, sometimes, the duty – of the Executive to keep some things to himself.

Sherrie returned and whispered a little too loudly: "I just let in one of your party – a tall, gray haired man – to the room in back, if you want to join him. Two more are coming? Will they be coming in this way, do you know?"

Jack answered:" Yes. Father McCullough and that ladies man you were talking about. Do me a favor. Don't mention to him what you told me about his date last night. I don't want him to think I'm prying into his personal life. Okay?"

"Of course, what do you think I am anyway? A blabber mouth?"

Hays smiled rather than replying and he walked through the restaurant to the private room where Senator Moriarity was already waiting. Within minutes, they were joined by the other two, had ordered a round of drinks and were soon in deep discussion.

The Senator had brought with him updates of the lists of the American and foreign groups participating in the June 28th Battle of Monmouth Re-enactment, the day's schedule of events, dignitaries attending and the like which Dayton and Hays had requested. The two of them would spend the next few days poring over bits of information, trying to find first the pieces that belonged to the puzzle and then trying to fit them together. They simply had to learn all there was to learn about the enemy's battle plan.

Senator Moriarity also reported that he had met with three of his comrades in the Senate and advised them what was transpiring. Each eventually believed and will cooperate. He said: "It was remarkable. The letter from Washington made each of them feel as if they were standing before God and that God was speaking to them, which, I guess, Father, maybe he was. After it sunk in and they understood broadly what had appeared to them, their faces looked as if they had seen the Beatific Vision. None gave any suggestion of having already been compromised by the other side. I have several more lined up during the next several weeks, remaining that I will report on next meeting."

Dayton nodded and again reminded everyone – being unknown was their strength.

Father McCullough had a long report to give. He had spent the last several weeks in Canada with Flacco and Buffalo Hump. Both of them had infiltrated Chief Brant's inner circles. In fact, Flacco had become one of Brant's most trusted advisors. Because of his prowess on horseback, skill with a rifle and his apparent bravery, Buffalo Hump had become a "war chief", the leader of the Indian horse company that was to go with Brant as part of the British Auxiliary Forces to the Battle of Monmouth re-enactment. His braves had been training on almost a daily basis. Essentially it was one maneuver, they were practicing – an attack on American troops with war whoops and rifles blasting. All of Brant's war party were warriors. There were no grandfathers or honorary chiefs among them. They were, to a man, hard and dangerous, with a hatred for America and the white man. They were eager for the day to come.

Flacco, a chief himself among the Lipan Apaches, had a different role than did Buffalo Hump. He had become Brant's envoy to a number of American tribes to build a network with the Indians of Canada, to their mutual benefit and political strength. He was to identify and recruit into a loose alliance the leaders of each tribe who would be willing to fight – and here he was very vague as to how – for a return of some of the lands of the continent to the Native Americans.

"We are getting similar reports from our people up in Nova Scotia. The Black Pioneer organization, made up of the descendants of the freed slaves who went to the British side during the Revolution, have been in training too .What's frightening here is that only some of them will be part of the British Auxiliary Forces and wearing uniforms. The others will be part of a train of civilian camp followers that traveled with the British army. All of them training with weapons and hand-to-hand combat! They are not coming here for any re-enactment. We can be certain of that."

Butler Trading Ltd. Lear Jet

Over Hudson Bay

January 27, 2008

The phone buzzed on the Butler brothers airplane. They were deep in the Hudson Bay region of Canada, some 20,000 feet above its arctic waters. "I bet that is Harry" said John, at the exact moment his twin brother Walter reached for the phone.

"Hello, there" spoke the other side "Is Romulus there?"

"No, Scylla lives here", said Walter.

"Excellent, this is Harry."

"Hello. Wait a moment, if you will. John is getting on another instrument so we can all chat. There, how is everything proceeding?"

Again, Clinton responded "Excellent. It is why I am calling" an odd thing, perhaps, to be saying seeing that the call had been pre-arranged days earlier. It was no coincidence that the Butlers were near the North Pole and Clinton himself was aboard a British military plane, not so very far south of Iceland in the north Atlantic. "Everything is on schedule. Value date is 6/30."

"Value date 6/30 confirmed" both brothers said, first to each other and then into the phone.

"Cheerio" rang off Clinton. The risk of detection was remote but there was no reason to increase it by meaningless babble on the phone. The key information had been passed and the Butler twins did not have to discuss it to know its meaning and import. June 30, 2008 – 6/30 – was the date for all their financial transactions to mature – the value date. The dollar would be crushed by then, the American stock markets crashed, its banks failed. Then, the frenzy of Canada's, England and Germany's feeding on the carcass of American business would begin.

(From the Royal Gazette, March 9, 1782)

HOUSE OF COMMONS

Motion made by Sir James Lowther:

"That it is the opinion of the House that the war carried on in the colonies and plantations of North America, has proven ineffectual, either for the protection of his Majesty's loyal subjects in the colonies or for defeating the dangerous designs of our enemies."

Lord Northship said, in response to some of the remarks of Mr. Powers, that the war had never been a favorite of his; on the contrary, he had always considered the war a cruel necessity, but yet as a war founded on a truly British basis, a war instituted to support the just rights of the Crown and of the Parliament of Great Britain. In that point of view, and only, should the war be regarded as just in its origins and necessary, however calamitous to the country, as its events had unfortunately proved.

His Lordship went into an examination of the motion, either with regard to peace or war. The words of the seconding motion was to resolve against all future efforts to subdue the American provinces. "All efforts?" asked this Lordship. Great Britain will never covenant to cede what is now and which will still shall be forever in the future, hers! His Lordship showed that, if the present motion was acceded to, it is, in effect, tantamount to a motion for immediately withdrawing all the troops, in other words, for abandoning the American War and British rights altogether. He asked whether the gentlemen in the house were prepared to go that length. Were they ready to say that New York or its dependencies ought not to be kept, either as a post whence we might annoy the common enemy and offer assistance to our West Indies islands or with a consideration to have something in our hands to make peace with.

Mr. Burke made a very long speech in favor of the motion.

Lord North was very ably supported by his colleague in office, Lord George Germain, who replied to Mr. Burke.

The debate continued to two in the morning, when the opposition having exhausted all their force, the House divided and the motion was lost by the following numbers:

> *Against the motion 220*
> *For the motion   179*
> *Majority   41*

Indian Point, Maryland
February 13, 2008

Senator John Martinez, Democrat from Arizona, was found dead today along a hiking trail in the western part of the state. Death apparently was caused by a gunshot wound to the head. The FBI has taken over the investigation and, at this time, has not ruled out, pending an autopsy and medical examiner's report, either murder or suicide. Local authorities, however, have privately told reporters that they believe foul play was involved as there is some evidence of a second bullet entry point.

Senator Martinez, married and the father of five children, was halfway through his second term in the Senate. Considered moderate enough to be named to the important policy making Joint Senate and *House Committee on the Identification and Renewal of American Values*, Martinez had been increasingly frustrated during the last six months, especially with the new Speaker of the House's push for deportation of all undocumented aliens and severe restrictions on future immigration from Mexico.

The area where the body was found is generally deserted this time of year. An unidentified witness reports having seen two men walking together some twenty minutes before hearing gunfire. It is not known whether the Senator was one of the men.

Funeral services will be at Tempe, Arizona on Wednesday. The President and more than two score of his colleagues in the Senate are expected to attend.

New York City

February 14, 1998

Hays and Daytons' attendance record at D'Allasandro's had become almost as good as Father McCullough's had been in the good old days. But, tonight, neither the priest nor the Senator was present. It was ladies night – Linda, Debbie Sue and Amelia. This had been the first time the five of them had gotten together as a group in several months, although Jack and Debbie Sue had managed to see each other over Christmas time, as had, separately, Linda and Elias. The girls had been busy ever since they had been assigned to the elite Molly Pitcher Brigade at *Women for Other Women*. A lot of it was classroom work and Debbie Sue showed off what she had learned.

"Don't laugh. Women helped win the Revolution too. There were hundreds of women like Molly Pitcher who fought with the American army. Armies then were more than soldiers. Families went along and the women marched right alongside the men. They tended the wounded, helped make the ammunition, sewed the soldier's uniforms and a lot more. The train of families and others at the Battle of Monmouth, you know, was more than 12 miles long. Plus, when the men went off to war, who do you think had to run the farms and take care of the children? History doesn't appreciate any of that, however."

"Whoa" said Hays, sensing it was his obligation to rein her in. "No one doubts it, but what are you doing besides classroom work?"

"Martial arts and shooting mostly" she responded in a matter of factly monotone, without any elaboration.

"For what?" asked Hays patiently.

"To disable men."

"Debbie, let's try it this way. Give us a complete report as to your training session. Amelia will follow up with whatever you miss. Proceed." His voice had an edge to it. He did not know why Debbie Jean was being so difficult. Whatever the cause, this was not the time.

"The Molly Pitcher Brigade is an elite force within the *Women for Other Women* community that protects all the members of that community from any oppression, especially from males. Bert says that some day we will be needed to defend our sisters and lovers and we will be the first line of that defense, even if it means our deaths. I thought I was a good shot once. I'm better now and I can use a knife or bare hands to kill you or any other man." She said the last sentence coldly, as if any emotion of joy or horror at such a statement had been brainwashed from her. She went on. "Bert says the Battle of Monmouth is to be our first opportunity to practice. We are pretending that the scene is real and that the men there want to destroy us. We will attack them before they know it .It wouldn't be a real attack, unless, of course, they start it first but it will be a chance to practice our teamwork and love for one another."

"How do you know which men to practice against?" asked Dayton

"We will be told a little while beforehand. Bert says it's not a good idea to know too much too soon. We'll think too much about something we cannot change. It's better to react as we have been trained."

Hays looked at Amelia, who had been silent ever since Debbie Sue had begun. Amelia understood the unasked question and answered. Both Dayton and Hays noticed that she did not look in Debbie Jean's direction at all during her response: "That's a pretty good summary. One thing more. Even in practice, at the Battle of Monmouth re-enactment, for example, if we hear Bert scream "Kill all the men!" we will know it is no longer a test and we are to react as if it were a real danger. There is no doubt in my mind that we will hear that scream of "Kill all the men" at Monmouth. This is no test. It is the real thing."

Dayton then asked Linda what was new on her end. She had risen fairly high in the ranks of those trusted by Bert and prestigious board of women that directed the policies of *Women for Other Women*.

"Believe it or not, I am drafting a preliminary constitution and body of laws for a new state of women. Its code name is

Amazon. When Bert and the Board assigned the task to me, I protested that there were too many real needs around for me to waste my time in a make believe world. They assured me that this was very real, that I could be the James Madison – quickly corrected to Dolly Madison – of the Constitution of New Order. They were sincere. They believe a woman's state is imminent."

Dayton asked directly "Is there something wrong, Debbie?"

Debbie did not deny or protest. She glared at Amelia and said, "Ask her."

Elias looked in Amelia's direction and received the short response: "She's jealous."

"I am not" shot back Debbie.

"You are too" repeated Amelia, obviously not backing down.

Linda jumped in. It was fortunate that the room was soundproof, but she made no attempt to speak like a lady. Slowly, with Linda as the midwife, the story emerged. Amelia had a boyfriend that she had been sneaking out to see, according to Debbie. She had been trying to stop Liz from seeing him. She said she was worried that if Liz were spotted by anyone from *Women for other Women* at some pizza parlor, holding hands with a man at 1:30 in the morning, their cover would be blown. Amelia said that it's mostly in Debbie's imagination. The man, Tom, lives in the building. He assumes Liz is a lesbian. He's just nice to talk to and, someday, maybe something more would be possible. Debbie was jealous because she didn't get out to see her beau. Amelia did not mention Jack by name but everyone in the room knew whom she meant and immediately understood the tension that had been in the room.

Dayton verbalized it in a soothing, defusing manner: "These are difficult times. You are serving your nation to a point of suffering known only to ourselves. Our lives have been disrupted." He glanced at Linda and went on. "We face an almost hopeless task and the possibility of death. But we have only three and a half months more to go. If we succeed, we will have the rest of our lives to make up for the deprivations of today. If we fail, today's sorrows will not measure up to those of tomorrow. Let's get a nightcap. Let's toast to each other's success and the resumption of our lives – or, as the case may be --" he said, again glancing in Linda's direction "to begin new ones."

(From *The New Jersey Gazette*, May 15, 1782)

New York, May 8. Last Sunday, his Excellency Sir Guy Carleton, Knight of the Bath, Commander in Chief of his Majesty's forces, and commissioner for making peace or war in North America, arrived in this city in good health. The Ceres Man of War, Captain Hawkins, brought his Excellency and his suite in 25 days from Portsmouth.

His Excellency landed in the afternoon under a discharge of the cannon at Fort George and dined with the Honourable General Sir Henry Clinton, K.B. and Admiral Digby.

From the English newspapers brought by Ceres, we have the following advices, viz.

A Dissolution of the late Ministry

On Wednesday the 20th of March, Lord North informed the House of Commons, that his Majesties Ministers were no more. His Lordship then moved that the House should adjourn to Monday, March 23, in order to give the Crown time to form a new arrangement. The House adjourned accordingly.

Appointment of Lord North

Lord North is to be appointed Constable at Dover Castle and Warden of the Cinque Ports, for life, and also a grant of 4,000 pounds sterling a year, payable quarterly for life. Likewise, a grant of 1,000 pounds sterling for life too to John Robinson, Esq., his Lordship's Secretary.

The shoreline near Head Quarters

Fishkill, New York

April 15, 1782

Young Harmon Hays was once again in the presence of General George Washington, although this time his arms were not in the grasp of Continental soldiers. It had been almost four years since they had last met after the battle of Monmouth. But they had been in communication many times since.

"My sentries tell me you traveled through the British lines, up to Dobb's Ferry, with a pass signed by Clinton. He knows you are here?" Washington asked with a teasing smile on his face. He was happy to see the young man suddenly present himself to the pickets at the outskirts of his camp at his camp on the Hudson River. They had brought him into camp without any attention. The boy had not grown much in the interim. War is not a good time, even if one eats off the general's table.

"No, your Excellency. He believes I have gone to say goodbye to my sister who lives in Tarrytown."

"Goodbye?" Washington asked, now with a questioning smile.

"Yes, General. Sir Henry has been recalled. His replacement Sir Guy Carleton handed him the orders himself, he did. Lord North is out and the newspapers that came from London with Sir Guy are full of accounts of Lord Cornwallis having secret meeting after secret meeting with the King. Clinton feels certain that he is to be the scapegoat and he is anxious to return to defend his honor."

"And you want to go with him?"

"Most certainly not, General." replied the boy. "He has offered me the opportunity to return with his suite to London, where, he says, he will either employ me or find a suitable position for me. He is being decent and, if I turned him down to stay in America, he might start wondering where my loyalties lie and that would not do, Sir, not so late in the game and we so close to our goal."

Washington nodded his agreement with the lad's reasoning without disrupting his narrative. "I told him I would like to go with him but that first I wanted to say goodbye to my sister who lived in Tarrytown because I would never see her again, since I was never coming back to this accursed land. He says fine and he writes me out a pass on the spot. And here I am. The way I figure it, General, I await your orders. If you want me to, I go back. If not, I do not return. Sir Henry will notice my absence only because he would be inconvenienced by it, nothing more. He will sail within a week's time and my not returning will be forgotten as irrelevant."

Washington again nodded, not as much this time in understanding, but more in pondering. Should he send the boy back? They both knew about the statements that Clinton had made that England would never relinquish her right to America, despite appearances, and that some day, it would strike again.

"What about the others?" Washington, the spymaster asked.

Hays answered. "Everyone will stay in place until after the British leave the city. The old man, Blundell, has been asked by Clinton to return with him to England too and he has asked Sir Henry for a few days to think about it. He wants to stay and he asked me to make that request of you. He has not been well of late and he says he would like to finish his life in Connecticut, digging for clams, he says."

"What about his daughter?" Washington asked. They both laughed. After five years together in Clinton's household, Hays did think of Mary as old John Blundell's daughter. After all that is how they had come into Clinton's service, the older man as butler and his attractive, rounded 19 year old "daughter" as maid. Actually, the two of them only had met for the first time several days before when Dayton had paired them up as a team. Soon, she was Clinton's mistress – as planned.

"She wants to go back with him. She's pregnant again and Clinton is hoping it is a second son. She's asked me to request that she be permitted to accompany Clinton to England and set up residency there. She gives you every assurance that she remains in your service and her loyalties will always be to America."

"Let us deal with the first two requests. Tell the old man to stay. Tell him he has earned his rest. I assume Mary really wants to spend her life with Clinton and it is not wise to stand in the way of anything a woman wants. Tell her Godspeed. We will hold her to her vows.

"Has there been any more about Clinton's claim that a vow has been sworn among him, the King, Lord North and some others never to give up England's rights in America?"

"Not directly" replied the lad. "Sir Henry drinks a lot these days and he likes to hold his son on his lap and talk to him. The boy is too young to listen, so I do it for him," grinned Hays. "He talks about family honor and shame; that the boy will be a warrior and will win back what his father had lost and restore the family's honor. Sometimes, he pretends he is introducing the boy to the Court and he tells how the boy will bring to fruition their plan to re-take America."

Washington stood up from the chair on which he had been sitting. He was a giant to the short Hays lad.

"Master Hays. I do not order you to return with Clinton, but I do desire it. If there is any reality to this plot, it can only be determined from events in England, not here. If Clinton returns in dishonor, continues to drink his problems away and is out of royal favor, then we will have satisfied ourselves that the embers of whatever plot they once had, are out – at least as far as Clinton is involved. If not, if Clinton is a Phoenix and resurrects himself from the ashes, then the likelihood of the plot's being actual and gaining in strength increases. Then, we need someone in position to monitor it."

The boy grinned. "I figured it the same way General"

New Suffolk, New Brunswick

May 3, 2008

John Agnew, Clinton's commander of Loyalist and Auxiliary Forces of North America, looked over the roster of his senior officers. He had just ordered them here to New Suffolk for some final meetings before their June embarkation for Monmouth, in New Jersey. With most of them, he felt quite comfortable. He had better be. His life was at risk, if they did not perform. One in particular, however, had been forced upon him by politics and that nagged him like a bad tooth.

He had command not only of the Canadian Loyalists, but of the English Loyalists as well. Many Loyalists had returned to England after the American Revolution when they had maintained their wounded identity and vowed to recover the lives and properties that had been wrongfully taken from their ancestors. These English Loyalists were under the direct command of Charles Skinner, a direct descendant of Cortland Skinner, who had organized a unit of volunteer New Jersey Loyalists, known as Skinner's Brigade. In nighttime raids, they punished their former neighbors, the rebels who had driven them from their homes. Agnew was pleased with this generation of Skinner. He and his men were good soldiers, well trained and willing to follow the appointed leader, even if it were a colonial like Agnew. But, on the day appointed, Agnew would be only their titular commander. Skinner's men would be part of a larger force led by Henry Clinton or his designee. It would be their task to disarm and capture the "rebel" army at Monmouth. It should not be difficult. For the most part they were fat old men, the cream of corporate America enjoying the ultimate perk, being a part of history in the making, or, more accurately, as Agnew thought to himself, the remaking.

Agnew was less confident with the leadership of his own Queens Rangers.

He had two lieutenants to whom he had to allocate equal responsibility. One of them, James Moody, was capable of the entire command and would have been Agnew's choice for it. An ex-military man, Moody had been descended from a swashbuckler lieutenant of the same name in Skinner's Brigade. Agnew's problem was with a man named Ralph Heuser, a dwarf sized, gargoyle-faced miscreant. He came from an old family in Halifax, more known for depravity and ruthlessness than for virtue or courage Heuser 's ancestor had been a Loyalist of Dutch ancestry who only fled Middle Towne Point, in New Jersey, after having been caught trafficking with the British on Staten Island. This Heuser was no different. Agnew had been unable to stop his appointment. A judge who was rumored to have sold his office more than once, the bullying Heuser had been particularly irksome to Agnew throughout their training.

The Queens Rangers had been assigned two targets at the re-enactment. The first was to disarm and capture the real American military personnel, especially the Pentagon types, present among the dignitaries. These men ran the American military. Capture them and the snake's head is cut off. Give them a chance to react and mobile phones will call for help, while others heroically die in resistance. They must be silenced quickly – and, if necessary, permanently. The mission's purpose was not carnage, but all knew there would be bloodshed. Clinton had provided pictures of all the generals and admirals who were expected to attend and who customarily would be armed. Clinton had a mole somewhere who had been very helpful. Each Ranger had his own target, whom he grew to know from reading his dossier. Only Agnew was aware that some of those military men had already been won over to the new order. He did not know who they were.

The second objective that the Rangers were assigned was to confine, for an hour or so, the non-military dignitaries in attendance. The senators and congressmen, the judges, governors and the like, were to be corralled like cows until the bloodshed was finished and the coup completed. They were a less dangerous group. There was also a number of fifth columnists among them, whom England did not want injured. They would be the backbone of the new nation. Some others among them – and Agnew, not Heuser knew, who – were extremely dangerous and had been marked for removal. Heuser need not know that.

To Moody, he had assigned the first task, to eliminate the

military leaders. To Heuser went the less difficult assignment to keep the dignitaries and their wives harmlessly pinned up until the shooting outside was finished. Predictably, Judge Heuser whined that his troops were not "babysitters" but fighting men, but to no avail.

The Mohawks and affiliated tribes were also under Agnew's command and he had great confidence in them. Joseph Brant, of course, commanded them, just as every Mohawk war party had been led by a Brant since before the Great War. The Joseph Brant that led them then was angered when the Indians were put in the most exposed positions in battle, as if they were cannon fodder, less valuable than the British, Loyalist or even Hessian soldiers. Today's Joseph Brant saw it differently. He was honored that the bravery and skill of his warriors earned them a point position in the attack. In fact, a squad of their horsemen were to be in the vanguard of Clinton's forces that were to attack and capture the rebel army.

Frederick Baum and Leopold Buarmeister commanded the troops that had come from the Federated Republic of Germany. All were descended from mercenaries sent here long ago by the Princes, under contract to King George. Each also was a veteran of either the West German or the East German army. They were to be on special assignment, to disable and remove the television units and then to protect their replacement which would broadcast some less disturbing sights to the American public, until they were to be apprised of the coup. Brownspriggs and his black loyalists were disguised as civilians in the supply train that followed the British army. They too, along with the Molly Pitcher Brigade, fell under the command of Harry Clinton, who had not disclosed his plans for those forces.

The first part should be simple. The Americans were not expecting a battle and they should be subdued without much difficulty. Beyond that, Agnew did not know. He was not able to see how a victory at Monmouth could result in the capture of America. True, its leaders would all be eliminated but a thousand of near or equal worth existed throughout the nation to replace each captured man. There had to be a sizeable fifth column within the country and the remaining populace docile as cows. Agnew was certain there was a plan, higher up, to assure that, but he was not privy to it .If there were not such a plan, why make any attempt? Agnew would do his part and, if they would all do their parts, including that distasteful Heuser, then everything would be all right.

(Items from Rivington's Loyal Gazette of August 7, 1782 regarding the unhappy fates and fortunes of the Loyalists)

Sir Guy Carleton, in consequence of his instructions for discontinuing the offensive war in this country, has broken up the Board of Loyalist Refugees at New York

NOTICE TO NEW YORK LOYALISTS

The inhabitants within the British lines are requested to appoint in their several wards and districts, two or three persons from each to meet and confer on the subject of the following letter communicated by their Excellencies Sir Guy Carleton K.B. and the Honourable Admiral Digby and that the persons so appointed to be empowered to adopt such measures as shall be thought proper on the occasion. The meeting will be held at Rouba tavern, on Friday next, ten o'clock a.m.

It is earnestly recommended to the Loyalists everywhere, to suspend their opinion of the present important occasion and each, in his place, to continue firm in his professions he has made of loyalty and zeal for the re-union of the empire. The Independence of the Thirteen Colonies has indeed been proposed at a conference in Paris, held for the purpose of a general peace, but until a general peace is ratified, we cannot know what is to be the eventual outcome of this country. In the meantime, therefore we are bound, by every consideration of prudence and duty. To wait the issue, with that manly steadiness and cheerful reliance on the abilities and attentions of our commanders, which at present are our surest pledges of safety. By such a conduct, we shall preserve a claim to national regard and protection, which it would be madness to forfeit, since by giving away our suggestions of impatience, we can only disgrace ourselves in the eyes of our enemy, without a shadow of advantage.

(Copy of a letter from Sir Guy Carleton and Rear Admiral Digby to General Washington, New York, August 2, 1782 and written in consequences of direction from England)

SIR

The pacific disposition of the Parliament and People of England has already been communicated to you and resolutions of the House of Commons, the February 27th, have been placed in Your Excellency's hands and intimations given at the same time that further pacific measures were likely to follow.

We are acquainted, Sir, by authority that negotiations of a general peace have already commenced at Paris and that Mr. Grenville is invested with full powers to treat with all the parties at war and is now in Paris in the execution of his commission.

And we are further, Sir, made acquainted that His Majesty, in order to remove all obstacles to that peace that he so ardently wants to restore, has commanded his ministers to direct Mr. Grenville, that the Independency of the Thirteen Provinces, should be proposed by him in the first instance, instead of making it a condition of the general treaty, however, not without the highest confidence that the loyalists should be restored to their possessions or full compensation made them for whatever confiscations may have taken place.

We are further acquainted that transports have been prepared in England for conveying all the American prisoners to be exchanged. A proposition has already been made that all exchanges of men of the same description being exhausted, sailor and soldier shall be immediately exchanged, man for man, against each other, with this condition annexed, that your sailors shall be at liberty to serve the moment they are exchanged and the soldiers so received by us shall not serve in or against the Thirteen Provinces for one year.

We have the honor to be Your Excellency's most obedient and humble servants

Guy Carleton
R. Digby

London

May 28, 2008

The walls of this room in Buckingham Palace must have witnessed many serious events over the centuries, but none more so than the final meeting to report on the Guy Fawkes Project. Clinton, Lords North's and Germain's descendants and a few others whose ancestors had been in the plot since the beginning, had sat for more than a half hour, in silence, nervously awaiting the Sovereign's appearance. If approval were given, then the project would proceed to the final step before attack.

There was nothing formal about the Queen's appearance. She entered without fanfare and had taken her seat while the rising gentlemen were still unconsciously straightening their ties. Her son accompanied her.

"Mr. Clinton" she asked without any greeting to the assembly, as if she wanted to have this dreaded matter over and done with. At one time, it had seemed fun, like a lark. Now, it was deadly serious. A kingdom was at stake. But, it was a dwindling island kingdom with all her colonies grown and independent, like adult children. This was Britain's last chance to restore the luster of her Empire, or else she must join Portugal, Spain, Rome as of being of archaeological and historic interest only in the modern world. If it failed, England would be crushed by the United States. The Biblical advice that "when thou striketh a king, be certain to kill in one blow" kept repeating itself in her brain, like a flashing red light.

"Yes, Your Highness" was the respectful response.

"Tell me, Mr. Clinton. This is a tremendous risk we run, is it not? How can we expect this to work? Life is not a Peter Sellers movie after all. This is not *The Mouse That Roared*" she sputtered, frustrated at her inability to articulate how great the risk and the reward were.

Harry Clinton nodded and smiled briefly. It was a knowing, reassuring type smile, one that recognized the cause of the other's ailment and was confident of the cure.

"Your Highness. It is one of three questions each of us asks ourselves. Can it work? Will it work? And what if it does not work? Allow me to address each in order."

The Queen nodded. She was already feeling a little more comfortable. Clinton was a capable man.

"Can it be pulled off? Yes, indeed, it can. There are several components to victory here. The first is surprise. The Americans are expecting an embrace of brotherhood, not an attack. Secondly, all their leaders – political, military, business – to the very top will be taken in one fell swoop. Thirdly, we have a very, very strong fifth column network built up within the country. Finally, America is ripe for plucking. The American public has become divided into *haves* and *have nots*. The more the wealth of the *haves* has increased, even as their numbers dwindle in face of the swelling numbers of the deprived minorities, the more the hatred has grown against them has increased. Many do not believe it what the *haves* so piously call the 'American Dream'. These individuals are desperate to unseat the so-called Old Time Americans and to divide up their wealth among themselves. It's an age-old story and is coming to its natural fruition in America right this moment. We are midwives, helping it along by being the immediate means of the re-distribution of property and power, something that would take a century at the ballot box, assuming it were possible at all.

You all know how many different interests have agreed to give our coup their full support in exchange for their receiving their piece of America now. Minorities and special interests with whom we do not already have an arrangement, will flock to us afterward, not oppose us. They will be afraid that we will divvy of the *haves'* property without giving them any. The *have nots* will not see this as a patriotic issue. They do not think of themselves as Americans any more. They consider themselves first, Native American, African American, Gay, women or Mexican, to list but a handful of tribes who believe that America has let them down and is longer worthy of their allegiance or love. No, these individuals will see the coup as a chance to be liberated and to assume the power and wealth that the Old Time Americans had to themselves. They will not resist. They will not shed any tears at the bier of the American corpse. Once everything is in place, government by ballot will resume without much change. Things will get back to normal quickly. The only difference will be that we and the distressed minorities will have taken the place of Old Time America at the dinner table. And, we will be eating their roast beef at their expense! *Sic transit, gloria mundi.*"

The room had been silent throughout the first part of Clinton's presentation and this last bit of Latin witticism evoked some laughter. It allowed Clinton to shift to the second portion of his presentation.

"'Can it work?' 'Yes it can.' 'Will it work?' It should for the following reasons. First, we have preserved the secrecy of our plans. No one knows of it. The element of surprise is crucial. The capture at Monmouth should precede as scheduled with minimum disruption.

Secondly, our long-range artillery will pound America senseless. By this, I mean our financial institutions, in league with Canada' and Germany's, will control the American financial markets by the end of the day. The dollar will plummet; stocks and bonds will crash; banks and investment houses will fail. And, then, at the closing bell, we will own America.

Thirdly, America has many demagogues. We have recruited the most powerful of them, up to the very highest level .I will not go into it any further here. You have all had access to the reports of those in American government who have been co-opted by our agents. With their help and that of the leaders of the minorities, the transition should be relatively easy. We do not expect much resistance. Maybe some out west with those militia groups. They still have weapons. I, for one, hope that there is some resistance out there. We have some angry Indians who would love to be the calvary this time and let the whites be the 'redskins'."

This remark brought more laughter, giving Clinton time to catch his breath before moving to his closing points.

"The fourth reason why it should work is the American media. You know we have a powerful ally there in that Ackermann fellow and his fellow travelers in the media. The

American public will be told that Britain is good and that Old Time Americans are evil. It will alleve the guilt and aid the digestion of the American minorities as they gobble up Old Time America's assets."

Once more the laughter from everyone, including the Queen, gave Clinton confidence that his presentation was being well received.

" 'Can it work?' 'Yes.' 'Will it work?' 'It should.' 'What happens, if it does not work? Are we in World War III? Will the United States invade in retaliation?' Sadly, as our record in previous failed attempts proves, not only did the United States not retaliate in the past, it appears not even to have noticed what we were up to. Britain was never connected to the attempt. Nor will she be here, until, of course, it is safe, to do so .Your Highness will be held captive along with the other heads of States in attendance.

Were the attempt thwarted, it will be charged to some crazed Canadian Loyalists who used this moment of international brotherhood to make a sick statement as to their grievances against the United States on behalf of their ancestors 230 years before. It would be deplorable, like the slaughter of the Israeli athletes at the Munich Olympic, but nothing more. You can be certain our American allies will not give themselves away if the plan fails."

The Queen nodded." Thank you, Mr. Clinton. I continue to look forward to our victory. Proceed to the next point."

New York City
June 1, 2008

Erick Ackermann read what he had written a few more times. Then he read it aloud. A little tinkering with a line here or there, lead to still another reading. After some variations, he settled on a mood as well – a surly, angry James Deanish attitude against authority. His public relations people had recommended it too. There had to be a *snarl* here. The copy would run tomorrow as an editorial in his paper and then the theme would be all over the media in a multitude of ways – music, videos, movies, polls, public service announcements, articles, "staged incidents", all Hollywood and the media could provide. It would be a four-week blitz, ending, coincidentally enough, at the re-enactment of the Battle of Monmouth and the changing of the guard.

"No, Mr. Speaker, we will not lie down. Don't talk to us about Davy Crockett's birthday being a National Holiday or that he was the kind of American everyone should be. To many of us, Crockett murdered peaceful Native Americans, stole their lands and then turned around and did the same thing to the Mexican Americans of Texas .No, we do not see our America in any of your slave owning, anti-immigrant, woman abusing ancestors.

But if it is the Alamo that you want and a line drawn across the ground to see who is on the side of your brand of American liberty, go to it. There aren't many of you, are there? No, Mr. Speaker, this is not a white, Western European Christian male America any longer. You are the minority and the rest of us, united as one, are the overwhelming majority. Our picture of America is different from yours and, in the very near future, it will be our picture, not yours, that will define this nation. The change will come peacefully, in elections, or violently, in revolt, depending on how bigots like you, Mr. Speaker, accept the inevitable. The have nots are going to have their day, Mr. Speaker, and its going be on your check."

The Speaker will be Public Enemy Number One by the end of the month. Everyone in America who hasn't had his or her "happiness" will blame and hate him and the rest of the Old Time America proponents for having deprived them of it. When the time comes in four weeks for the coup, most of America will welcome Britain's return and the chance it promised to redistribute Old Time America power and wealth. The media was a wonderful thing!

New York City
June 21, 2008

It was the last time the four of them were to dine at the private room at D'Allasandro's before the re-enactment of the battle of Monmouth. That was only a week or so away. Their strategy was set and each was ready for the big day. The next morning Jack Hays and Father McCullough would rejoin the rest of the Ranger Company, except for those, like Buffalo Hump, Flacco, the girls and a handful of others who were on special assignment. They were scattered on the New Jersey shoreline, waiting for the signal to form. Senator Moriarity, of course, was in charge of the re-enactment that had drawn such great worldwide interest and participation. He had set up his headquarters in the old Sutphin house on the edge of the battlefield. It had been occupied by the British before the original battle but would house the American command in the re-enactment. Dayton would be there too. The Senator had appointed him as a special advisor – he was a recognized expert on the battle as well as being a noted descendant of one of its heroes. However, Elias would have his own operations to direct on the day of the re-enactment.

Aside for a toast to the mission's success, none of them mentioned the upcoming endeavor at dinner. Instead, there was good conversation, laughter and camaraderie among them. In truth, there really was little to say or do at this point. They had gone over the defense so many times that a final conference was meaningless. No one had any questions, except the big ones they all shared – would they thwart the British planned coup and, if they did not, what would happen to the nation whose protection had been placed in their hands by their forebears?

Coffee and after dinner drinks completed, they were about to rise from the table, shake hands, wish each other luck and go their own ways, when Father McCullough asked to say one last thing. He had selected the moment because what he had to say was important, indeed crucial. He began:

"It is not blasphemous, I think, to compare our present moment with Jesus' in the Garden of Getshame, a short time

243

before he was to begin his Passion and Crucifixion in order to fulfill the Divine Plan and redeem mankind from its sins. We, too, wish this cup could pass from our lips to some others to drink, that we need not taste its agony and torment. But we have been elected to suffer, like Our Lord, for the multitude, some who love us, some of whom hate us.

I know each of you, your strengths of character, which, ironically, might become weaknesses on the battlefield, weaknesses that not only might mean your deaths but that of America. You must steel yourself to do the unthinkable."

The Jesuit paused. He knew that they were not yet understanding .It had to be personalized for each our ancestors, whose souls dwell in ours at this moment, faced their Gesthemes and maybe they can help us face ours. Elias, think of your ancestor Jonathan Dayton, the son of General Washington's aide Elias .His whole life was dedicated to the Public Good. He was indicted for treason as part of Aaron Burr's plot to have the west secede from the Union. We know the truth, but the world does not. Jonathan had to silently bear the accusations of treason and die in disgrace in order to foil Burr's attempt, which, unknown to history, was part of a British plot to retake America. Were we to fail now, the Dayton family will be remembered in history as evil plotters and conspirators, not as valiant soldiers .Your boys, now in the flower of their youth, will be branded the sons of traitors. You must be prepared for that and fight forward regardless."

Dayton looked as if he were in a trance of sorts, in communion with a leader who had paid the price. The Jesuit turned his attention to Hays.

"Jack. You mentioned to me once about a news clipping about Captain Jack that always bothered you. It was the one that described how he had been prosecutor, judge, and jury for some Mexican bandits he had captured deep in central Texas, hundreds of miles from civilization. He knew he could not risk the safety of his company in bringing them back across Indian territory to San Antonio for a formal trial. But, he could not let them go, to continue to steal along the frontier. He did what had to be done. He executed them on the spot. Jack, are you prepared to be judge, jury and Executioner. It is not in your nature or your training to act such. Nor was it in Captain Jack's. But the situation demanded it, and Captain Jack was the leader, so he did not hesitate to do what he had to do, although it was, to many then, murder and today would be unthinkable .Jack, you must be ready to do the unthinkable and to do it without hesitation."

Like a hypnotist's subject, Jack joined Elias, lost in the images that Father McCullough had summoned up for each. They had become their ancestors or, perhaps, their ancestors had become them. In any event, they were one.

The priest then turned to his former student, the Senator.

"Tullius. Do you remember what Cicero and his cohort of loyal senators had to do to stop Cataline and his attempt against the Republic? He exercised *Senatus consultum ultimum*, the extreme decree of the Roman Senate. Death. Summary execution for all the conspirators. No trials. The preservation of the Republic was too important to risk with discussion, when action was required. Yet, afterwards, Cicero and those Senators were condemned and punished themselves for having deprived the conspirators of their rights as citizens of Rome. Tullius, spiritual son of Cicero, are you ready to act in a manner that others, far from the action and ignorant of the danger, piously will later call ruthless and banish you into an exile of some kind? The Senator looked up. His face was white .He said softly

"Father, will you hear my confession?"

New York City

November 25, 1783

At 8 o'clock on the morning of Tuesday, November 25, General George Washington saluted the tavern keeper of the Bowery's Bull Head Tavern. The man had just stood the General and his staff their first round of drinks of the day. There would be many more ahead.

Acknowledging with nods, bows and polite replies, the cheers and praises of the folk that lived on the nearby farms, Washington mounted his white steed and road out at the head of his troops, down Bowery Lane to New York City (today from 15th street, south along First Avenue to downtown) On his right, rode Brigadier General Elias Dayton, on his left, Major Benjamin Tallmadge. The three of them – Dayton, Washington and Tallmadge – had been the heart of the American spy system during the war and all three were conscious that they had one final responsibility to discharge.

The rear of the withdrawing British army was fewer than a hundred yards ahead. Washington could see the rumps of the horses of the departing dragoon guard. After seven years, the British finally were evacuating New York City, their last toehold in the United States. The negotiations in Paris had dragged on for 18 months before the definitive treaty had been signed on September 3, 1783.

The glee of General Washington and his companions was muffled by the sense of devastation all about them. Washington had not been in New York City since that fateful Sunday in September, 1776, when the American army abandoned it, after the disaster at the Battle of Long Island. He remembered looking back over his shoulder then and seeing the city burn behind him .The Americans had left as little useable as possible to their British foe.

Now, Washington and the other American arrivals looked from side to side in disbelief. New York was a much different place from the one they had fled in the war's beginning. It was an ugly place now, not the quaint Dutch seaport it once was. A village maiden had grown into a hardened bitter woman, never to be innocent again .The Americans, in hopes of defending the city, had chopped down its shade trees and orchards for barricades; trenches had been built across roads to impede invaders .Then, the fire set by the departing Americans had burned down more than a thousand residences and businesses, a third of the City. What the fire had not destroyed was then used by the British army and some 30,000 Loyalist refugees who fled into the City for protection from the rebel countryside .For six years, they lived in burned out, derelict homes, in foundations with ripped sails stretched across them for roofs, and in tents on muddy fields. Everything was scarred and old. The side streets were blocked by earth works .Abandoned defense trenches were now open sewers filled with stagnant water.

The Loyalists were all long gone now, too. It had been obvious to them that they and their property in America were going to be abandoned by Britain. Washington's agents had reported to him that, when the armistice was read from the balcony of City Hall, despair was written on every face and all that were heard were groans, hisses and bitter curses hurled at their King for having deserted them .For a period, New York had become an open-air auction ground as Loyalists sold all their possessions for "hard money" before going off into exile .As soon as they could, they left. Three thousand refugees on 14 transports sailed in a single day in June for England. On August 16, more than five thousand displaced souls sailed south to the West Indies. A month later, a record fleet left New York to go north, to the wilderness of Nova Scotia with 8,000. By the end of the year, 29,000 Americans without a country had landed in Nova Scotia including 1,200 free blacks with nowhere else to go.

The American column led by Washington, followed the last of their former foe all the way near the tavern in the old orchard where Clinton had sported .The British swung east from there, toward Murray's wharf and the East River, where they boarded England bound transports. The Continental troops marched west toward Broadway .Washington called his troops to a halt at Wall Street where it intersected with Broadway. The fire gutted stone shell and stark ruins of Trinity Church stood there as a symbol of the destruction that had visited New York. Washington spoke to General Dayton who wheeled his horse around to speak with an adjutant. Two commands later, Washington and Dayton had separated from the rest of the column and rode ahead, accompanied only by a squad of twelve dragoons, their eyes alert for Loyalist suicide snipers. They rode east on Wall Street a short distance and then south on Broad Street to Pearl Street. Civilians – there were a few that always survive and remain as armies come and go – stood silently, needing no explanation as to who Washington was. A left brought them to Hanover Square to the British Coffee House, next to the *Rivington's Loyal Royal Gazette*, which, prudently, had recently renamed itself *The New York Gazette and Universal Advertiser*.

Washington spoke to Dayton, who saluted him and dismounted. He entered the British Coffee House and, a few moments later, emerged with some dozen or more people. Among them were the owners of the Coffee House and the newspaper, Robert Townsend and the notorious Jeremy Rivington. A crowd of townspeople had formed. Some had followed Washington and gathered out of interest; others had planned to be there, to hang Jeremy Rivington and destroy his printing press, now that his British protectors had set sail without him.

Washington dismounted and approached the group with Dayton at his side. The growing crowd could not hear what was being said but they saw Dayton introduce the men and women who had come from the British Coffee House, one by one, to Washington, who chatted amiably with each. With each, Washington shook hands. The final two were Townsend and Rivington. With them, Washington was even more genial, smiling and laughing at times, at other times speaking intimately and seriously. Then, he shook each by the hand and embraced him, as he had learned to do from the French to demonstrate to the watching world that they were allies .Rivington and Townsend had performed their duties as agents well. Their information has been invaluable.

Back on their horses, the two officers saluted once again the dozen civilians in front of the Coffee House and then rode off to the park at Bowling Green, at the foot of Broadway, to witness the British flag being taken down and that of the United States being raised in its stead. Several of the dragoons remained behind, however, in the event that the mob did not comprehend the meaning of Washington's gesture.

Monmouth Battlefield

Afternoon, June 27, 2008

Today, the topography of Monmouth Battleground is little changed from June 28th, 1778 when the main armies of Britain and the newborn United States clashed there in the largest battle of the Revolution. A park today, back then, it had been the wheat and cornfields of a half a dozen farm families of Dutch and Scotch-Irish decent. On its rolling hills were pastured their horses, cattle, sheep and hogs. Orchards of all varieties dotted the landscape becoming natural boundaries between fields and neighbors. Several brooks, fringed in marsh grasses, ran through the valley. A scattering of farmhouses, barns and other outbuildings, distant from one another, completed this idyllic picture of rural, colonial America .

The working farms and their livestock are all gone now, of course. Times change. Fortunately, in the early 1960's, before suburban development could gobble up the sacred ground, a state park, now nearly 2,000 acres in size, was created to preserve and showcase this turning point in the American Revolution. Several farmhouses that had been occupied by the combatants during that day, and spared burning by the British, were also saved for posterity, and still remain, as silent witnesses to the battle.

At the entrance to the park, on the crest of Combs Hill, are several modern, single story structures that blend in unobtrusively with the wooded background. Collectively, they are the Visitors Center – the museum, Park Ranger's headquarters, first aid station and the like. For the re-enactment, these buildings would serve the several thousand dignitaries who were to witness the event-- the senators and congressmen from Washington, the judges, governors, generals and, of course, the President and Vice President of the United State and heads of foreign states, including Her Majesty, the Queen of England. Sturdy, lofty grandstands had been erected on the adjoining parking lots, further enhancing the hill's already panoramic view of the field of battle. The more elevated one's rank, the higher he or she sat on the grandstand. The highest --and, thus, the best – seats were in the "press box" on the summit of the grandstand, where the President, the Queen and the Canadian and German leaders were to watch the battle.

As their headquarters for the re-enactment, the British were given the Covenhoven house, located outside the park, nearer to the center of town. It was appropriate. It had been Sir Henry Clinton's headquarters before the battle. The Americans were assigned the Old Tennent Church near the northwestern section of the battlefield, as their headquarters. It too had participated in the original battle, converted by the American surgeons into a field hospital to treat the hundreds of wounded. The remaining participants, the soldiers of both sides and camp followers, were housed in tents out in the fields.

Entry to the event was to be extremely limited, by invitation of the President of the United States only! There was no general admission where the ordinary citizen could, with binoculars trained, catch a glimpse or two of some of the fighting, like a boy seeing a baseball game through a knothole in the fence. The American public were to be symbolically represented by the several hundred "townspeople", selected by a lottery in New Jersey to participate. Dressed as ordinary citizens of the colonial period, these lucky folks would gather on Combs Hill, becoming part of the scenery of the set for those above them in the grandstand. It was historically accurate. The citizens of Monmouth County had in fact flocked to see the original pageantry, their wagons full of food and hard cider, for sale to the soldiers, and, it being a festive occasion, for personal consumption. So numerous were the local residents of Monmouth who came to root on the Americans that they interfered, at times, with the troops rushing from skirmish to skirmish. At the re-enactment, they would be more disciplined, seen but not heard, part of the backdrop for the production.

No, the ordinary men and women of America were to see the re-enactment at home, on their television sets. Ackermann's Sentinel Media had been selected by the President's Chief of Staff, John Sparrow, to broadcast it, to all the major networks .The coverage was to be subtle and disguised, lest it lessen the historical credibility of the event .Several cameras with extraordinary range had been set up at the natural vantage points around the battlefield, and, of course, from the grandstand itself. In addition, a score of cameramen, dressed as soldiers and camp followers, were to roam throughout the battlefield, with hand held cameras, indistinguishable at a distance, from muskets.

June 28th, 1996 was a Thursday. The participants for the re enactment had begun arriving on Tuesday, the 26th, to set up camp and become familiar with the terrain. The event began officially on the afternoon of the 27th, when each camp held an open house to welcome members of other units, even those from the enemy forces. This international brotherhood and good will among the participants was to crest later that night with a huge dinner and concert under the stars.

The different units set up their camps in the area where the action would begin on the 28th. There was no guesswork involved. Historians have long studied the battle of Monmouth from all angles and are confident as to what happened that day on the battlefield. The British were camped on the southeastern section of the park and in the adjoining orchards that had been a part of the original battleground and were now privately owned and made available to the re-enactment. The Americans occupied the northwestern part, two miles distant. Between them lay a thousand acres of valley, green from a wet spring. In the middle of the valley, near Spotswood Middle Brook, where Molly Pitcher had fetched the water for the men manning the artillery above her on Perrine Farm Ridge, a huge tent had been erected. It was to be the "center" of this temporary town of men and women who had come together from all over America and Europe to participate the re-enactment of the Battle of Monmouth.

Senator Francis X. Moriarity considered the irony of it all. Three years earlier, he had looked forward to this day as a manifestation of a new, re-directed America that finally was rediscovering the virtues and values of its past. Now, he knew it was not a re-enactment that was imminent but an actual battle to the death, the enemy still only roughly defined but undeniably present and extremely dangerous. As Chairman of the Joint Senate and House Committee on the Identification and Renewal of American Values, the Senator and his staff had their own control center – two connected trailers – hidden away on the far side of the Visitors Center. Elias Dayton, Moriarity's adjunct today, stood alongside the Senator and asked:

"Do you want to take a cart over there or walk?" The motorized carts were on loan from an adjoining golf course, that had also been part of the original battlefield. It presently served as the campgrounds for the hundreds of Canadian, English and Black men and women who comprised the British supply line that had followed their army on their way from Philadelphia to New York.

"Let's walk, if you don't mind," replied the Senator. "It's a lot more hilly than I expected. Too hilly, I think, for one of those things."

The two of them walked down Combs Hill into the valley below it, across the bridge that spanned the creek and up the side of another hill, a mile and a half away. Almost a half an hour later and breathing hard from their walk across the hilly battlefield, the two arrived at the American camp. It was already festive, resembling a tailgate football party, without the automobiles, more than a military camp. Grills were everywhere. So were ice chests and kegs of beer. Hundreds of men, most of them in the 40 to 60 year age span, stood around in groups, laughing, discovering mutual backgrounds and getting to know each other better. This was the cream of America's business community. They, through the companies they owned or controlled, had underwritten most of the nation's cost for the re-enactment of the Battle and, thus, were rewarded with the corporate perk of being selected to participate, on behalf of all Americans, in a symbolic battle that had helped win independence. It was the ultimate male hunting party. Tomorrow, most were to be blue and white clad Continental soldiers. Today, golf attire, adorned with their corporate logos, was more appropriate dress.

It took the Senator and Dayton only a few minutes to find Hays and his Ranger outfit. The two flags flying before their gathering of tents-- those of the Republic of Texas and the United States – had given it away. There was no reason to hide the place of origin of most of the riders in this company. In fact, being known as the descendants of Texas Rangers gave them some identity within the camp and the few Germans and English, who so far had come by to visit, were impressed to meet real Texans.

Accepting a Styrofoam cup of, appropriately enough, *Lone Star* beer, from a keg that had been shipped up from Texas along with the horses, both the Senator and Dayton quenched the thirst from the trek over. It was not 100 + degrees, as it had been on the day of first Battle of Monmouth, but it was approaching the mid 80's and a hotter day was predicted for tomorrow.

"Where is Father McCullough?" asked the Senator about his old teacher.

The question drew some chuckles from the Rangers, standing around the keg.

"Putting up his tent. Been doing it for most of an hour now. Won't take no help, neither. Says he can do it, but he can't. He hasn't the slightest idea." the Texas twang of a Ranger responded.

Dayton, with a chuckle of his own at the image of the clumsy, inexperienced, impatient priest's efforts, said to Hays: "Tell him, we need to visit with him and then have someone put the thing up while he's with us. Maybe, he'll think it's a miracle." Hays nodded and looked over to one of the Rangers, who immediately went off in the direction of the tent colony in obedience to Hays unspoken order.

Father McCullough emerged moments later, perspiring heavily, his sweatshirt wet with it. "I want to report a defective tent", he sputtered good-naturedly.

Hays replied: "Go tell the Continental Congress"

The priest took the proffered *Lone Star* beer, nearly draining it in an effort, he explained, to replace lost body fluids. After a bit of chatter and refills all around, Dayton suggested to Hays, Father McCullough and the Senator that they take a walk around the battlefield.

"What do you think?" Dayton asked to the group as soon as they were safely out of earshot.

Hays replied: "If our premise is correct as to what Clinton's priorities are, then I think we have all the bases covered."

The Senator added: "Their prime target has to be the

grandstand. That is where all the leaders of the government and the military are. If they captured so many of such senior rank in a war, it would be an extraordinary feat. The war would probably come to an end. If here, they accomplish it at the outset, it is even more extraordinary."

"I grant you that premise, " said the Jesuit as if in debate. "But, what then? What happens next? How do they control a nation, merely by holding its government hostage."

"That's a second issue" interrupted Dayton. They had had this discussion before. "We must assume that they have additional attacks to make after this one. We know some involve wrecking our economy. That's what the Butler brothers are up to. And don't forget, Marcus and his merry men are armed in the ghettos of every major city. Clinton has recruited fifth columnists everywhere – in the Latin community, among the gays, the women and other minorities. There will be a number of Benedict Arnolds too in the grandstand tomorrow, willing to switch sides for their own gain. Maybe even the President? Or the Vice President, who is just as good, if you eliminate the President in the take over. No, tomorrow is only their first strike. It will be followed by other explosions. We must assume that. But, if we can stop them now-- 'head them off at the pass' as you cowboys say – then, we may be able to prevent this all from beginning. Let's concentrate on tomorrow. We cannot do anything beyond that anyway."

The Senator said: "We are all agreed that the grandstand will be the most important target? But, what about corporate America here? They must want them too, if they are intent in wrecking our economy. Or, maybe they would hold them for ransom or enlist them in their cause."

All four men nodded or grunted their agreement on that conclusion also. If the British wanted to capture the leaders of government, they also would want the captains of commerce.

Dayton smiled and said softly: " Jack, you and your squads of mounted Rangers will watch over Corporate America. Correct?"

Hays' answer was confident "Yup. We expect the attack to come from the Queens Rangers. Buffalo Hump will be up front.

We are going to use an old Comanche trick on them – with an Apache wrinkle. Don't worry about us. Captain Jack and his Rangers were never outgunned, no matter the odds, and we won't be either."

"Good. What about the cameras?" Sentinel Media was a subsidiary of Ackermann Media. Dayton did not want the people of America to view the re-enactment through the eyes of the enemy.

Father McCullough answered: "Jud Wallace is heading up that team. Replacement cameramen will be at Overlook Hill and the Grandstand. Overlook is their control center and we will take that first. From there, we can control the feed from the battlefield cameras that are individually manned. We have descriptions of these fellows with the field cameras. They will be eliminated and replaced with our people. The American Public's view of the spectacle hopefully will not be interrupted."

This earned a nod of approval from Dayton, who summarized the remaining part of the plan of defense: "The grandstand is my responsibility and I think I have that covered. The girls know their jobs and so do my men." Dayton had never elaborated on his plans to derail the main British attack and no one pushed him for an explanation now either.

The four walked for a few minutes more in silence, stopping on the ridge where Washington's artillery, two hundred and thirty years before, had rained canisters – tins can crammed full of grape shot which exploded with great damage – among the British infantry below. The big tent for tonight's dinner stood where the British had huddled two hundred and twenty years before.

Dayton turned to his companions and simply said "Good luck to us all, fellows."

Monmouth Battleground

Evening, June 27, 2008

Most of the participants from both armies in the next day's re-enactment were at the big tent in the middle of the valley, finishing an overwhelming feast of steaks, lobsters and corn. A country western band played loudly and everyone seemed to be having a good time. But, Dayton and Hays were too nervous to socialize. After they had eaten, they had gotten up to stretch their legs. They had their eyes out for the girls and spotted them, across the tent, seated at a large round table with a dozen or more other women from *Women for other Women*. Linda was chatting with Bert Braverman. Amelia and Debbie Jean were part of a larger, animated conversation, which was punctuated every few seconds with bursts of laughter. They too seemed to be enjoying themselves.

Dayton and Hays drifted off to the British camp on the far side of Dividing Brook. Most of them were still at dinner. Neither Dayton nor Hays expected to learn any secrets by their twilight stroll through enemy territory. It was out of curiosity more than anything. As they climbed a small hill, Hays spied a group of British soldiers on its summit, acting peculiarly. They were staring at something down below on the other side, elbowing each other and talking out of the corners of their mouths, like schoolboys afraid to be caught. Dayton reached the top of the hill a few seconds before Hays, and started right down the other side, before stopping dead in his tracks. He saw what the soldiers had been ogling: the beautiful Pamela, hair up and wearing shorts and a halter-top. Next to her, Harry Clinton was absorbed in reading a map, spread out on a table. Pamela glanced up, saw Dayton and immediately turned her head back to Clinton as if not wanting to be recognized. Hays saw Dayton do the same and then promptly turn on his heels, reverse direction and go back up the hill. He bumped into Hays who was just beginning his descent.

"Wrong way" Dayton said to Hays as he passed him going the other way. "Clinton is down there and we do not need to see him tonight, do we?"

Hays said nothing and followed Dayton away. He was very troubled by what he had just witnessed. Dayton and Pamela had made eye contact with one another and then quickly turned away. He could understand why Dayton did it, but why did she? In fact, what was she doing here at all? She was the only woman among the soldiers and she looked to be sharing Clinton's command. Why had Dayton had dinner with her at D'Allasandros six months before? Why did he did know her at all? This was too much of a coincidence to ignore. Should he confront Dayton with it? After all, Dayton was Hays' commanding officer and Dayton did not have to share his complete battle plan with him. But what if Dayton were a Benedict Arnold, prepared to betray America's defense? Then, he must stop him. Yet, if that were the case, was it not better not to reveal his fears and thereby put Dayton on guard?

At the bottom of the hill, a shaken Pamela kept her eyes fixed on Harry Clinton for a full minute, as he studied the map. Finally, she dared to look up again in the direction where she had last seen Dayton. When finally she lifted her eyes in the direction of the ridge, he was gone. She let out a sigh, unintentionally loud enough to get Clinton's attention.

"I am sorry, Pamela. Rude of me to be so obsessed. Come. We shall miss dinner if you let me tarry here any longer. You must be famished. I am."

As Clinton folded the map and gathered up his other papers, Pamela asked whether they would be returning to the tent after dinner.

"No" replied Clinton "We shall go directly to the trailers. It will be too dark to do any thing here anyway." Clinton had two large trailers assigned to him, several hundred yards from Overlook Hill and as remote. One was his living quarters which he was lending to Pamela tonight. He would sleep in the other trailer, which, tomorrow, would be his field command center. A modern day general, Clinton planned to spend the entire day there, in telephone contact with all his lieutenants across the battlefield. When he emerged from the trailer at the day's end, England will have re-taken America and the Clinton name revenged .The family had waited a long time for this day.

Monmouth Battleground

Morning, June 28, 2008

The first of the guests began arriving shortly after dawn, binoculars and cameras already around their necks. A nearby racetrack had been impressed into service as a staging area for the Dignitaries arriving by auto. There, long limousines from Washington D.C. and New York, discharged their passengers, the elite of the American power base, whom vans then ferried the rest of the way to the Battleground Park. Hospitality tents had been set up around the Visitors Center that provided breakfast. The museum was, of course, open and, in it, the guests could view some of the artifacts of the battle they were about to see re-enacted. Special exhibits were set up, as well, in the parking lots that gave the visitors a preview of what they were to observe later that morning.

The armies and other participants had been up since before dawn. Their camps had been struck and there was no sign of the huge tent in the middle that had housed last night's party. Out of sight to the visitors, behind the far hills and in the wooded acreage to the east, the armies were readying for the start of the battle, scheduled for 10:00 a.m. The Presidential party and the heads of foreign states in attendance would arrive by helicopter from Washington D.C. and the embassies in New York City precisely at 9:25. As they mounted the press box ---according to the schedule at 9:42, – the Marine Band would play *Hail to the Chief*. Then, with every one of the Dignitaries in his or her place, the Band would play the national anthems of Canada, Germany, Great Britain and the United States. Ideally, it would then be exactly 10:00 a.m.

The preparations had all been excellent and it was 10:02 as the two thousand voices proudly concluded "the land of the free and the home of the brave". The soothing voice of a well-known television news commentator, also selected by John Sparrow and partial to the Administration, was heard live through earphones provided all the guests.

"Good morning and welcome to the Monmouth Battle

Grounds. Today, you will witness, in the valley below you, the recreation of a struggle between armies of yesteryear. Today, as then, more than two centuries ago, these armies, like our nation, were made up of men and women of many colors, of many races and nations. On this battle field, the Continental soldiers of the almost two year old United States of America stood strongly against the best of British and German soldiers, against the intrepid Loyalists fighting to retain their homes, against the brave African American valiantly earning their freedom from slavery and against the unfortunate Native Americans, hopeful they could block America's migration westward into their hunting lands.

You see gathering in front of you the townspeople of Monmouth County who, 230 years ago flocked here, like yourselves, to be eyewitnesses to a battle that would change history. As you will note, they plan to picnic as they watch. Perhaps, they can be persuaded to later share some of their provisions with you. We shall see."

At this point, approximately a hundred men and women dressed in colonial costumes drifted in from behind the visitor's center. Some came in carriages, others in wagons, loaded with food and drink. A dozen or more were on horseback, but most arrived on foot. The women were bonneted, with long dresses of calico and gingham and homespun striped petticoats. All wore cloaks, invariably red or blue, that fell below the knees. The men were dressed in buckskin and linen breeches, homespun and flannel striped shirts, with shoes with brass buckles and white stockings and hats of all descriptions. Some also wore multi colored jackets, despite the heat promised as the sun climbed to its spot in the sky from where it too would watch the day's pageantry. They all assembled on the rise overlooking the valley, some fifty yards in front of the grandstand. Off to the side was another group of women, similarly dressed in clothes from the colonial era. This was the Molly Pitcher brigade. They, like their legendary namesake, would give drink to the thirsty during the battle. However, it would not be the soldiers in the battlefield who would experience their kindness, but the Dignitaries in the grandstand. Four of the most attractive of the Brigade, including Debbie Jean and Amelia, were to serve the President, the other heads of states and their parties in the press box.

"Please look to the east, that is, on your right side. You see the rear guard – the Queens Rangers – of the British forces preparing to resume their march to Navesink Hills on Sandy Hook Bay, some 25 miles distant, to board transports for New York City. The rest of the British had already begun their march.

Suddenly, from the northeast comes General Charles Lee and a large force of Americans. They plan to cut off the rear guard and engage it, while General Washington and his greater force from Valley Forge, approach from the other direction and squeeze the Queens Rangers in a pincer movement. Let's watch a bit, shall we?"

For the next twenty minutes or so, the people in the grandstand saw Lee and his men encircle the British rear guard and began their attack. They skirmished for some time and both sides drew up their artillery and began firing those bigger guns at each other. The grandstand rocked in the thunderous cannonade that erupted.

"Look to your far right." the earphones interrupted. "It is the main force of the British army returning to aid the rear guard. Lee realizes that he is about to be caught between the two British forces and he and his men race off across Rhea farm, pursued now by the British".

Still firing, the Americans withdrew toward the west. At first it was an orderly retreat, but then panic set in and the rebels ran as if they had been routed.

"Ladies and gentlemen, you are about to witness one of the bravest acts of American history, a proof of the heroism of the Father of our Country, General George Washington. On your left, you can see he and his forces arrive. He is on the white horse at the head of the column. He will intercept the retreating Lee and confront him, cursing him for his cowardice. Then, with sword upraised, General Washington will lead his own forces and even the Lee's fleeing soldiers back at the British."

The scene in the valley below formed as it had been promised in the earphones. In somewhat exaggerated fashion that held the attention of all the viewers, the man playing Washington drew his sword on high, rallied his men and led them into the teeth of the pursuing British. Rifle fire continued on end, like strings of exploding firecrackers, and the smoke from the repeated discharge of hundreds of flint lock muskets rose above the fighting, hanging over it in a cloud. Neither side budged and more soldiers on both sides fell, dead and wounded, with every volley. The artillery too kept up its attack, sending --in the original conflict --iron balls the size of grapefruits at each other as well as canisters full of jagged metal to explode and maim the enemy. After a half hour of this bitter battling, both sides dropped back and regrouped.

"In late morning on the day of the original battle, both sides rested, exhausted by the near 100 degree heat and sickened by the carnage visited upon their comrades. We too shall take an intermission. The lovely ladies of the Molly Pitcher Brigade have lunch and refreshments for you all. Enjoy it and our celebration of liberty. Please retake your seat by 12:25 as the re-enactment of the battle will resume promptly at 12:30."

The Dignitaries left the grandstand and milled around the tents that were serving the drink and food. At the insistence of John Sparrow security was minimal --two Secret Service agents. He felt that a greater presence was neither necessary nor desirable .He appeared correct. The President, her Highness the Queen and the other heads of state wandered unmolested about with the others, chatting happily about the display they had just witnessed.

American HQ

Noon, June 28, 2008

There was no time for lunch at Dayton's command headquarters. Senator Moriarity and Father McCullough were with him and they had Jack Hays on his mobile telephone.

"So far, so good. We guessed right. They didn't make their move in the first half of the battle."

"Hays replied: "Didn't think they would. There was only the center ring in action. The second half will have skirmishes all over the place, a lot more confusion where they can do whatever it is they are planning to do."

"Are the Rangers all set for the attack this afternoon?

"Yes, looking forward to it. The way it is scripted, we expect Agnew and some of his boys to get rough right near the beginning of this afternoon's show."

"The television transmission?" Dayton asked and the priest answered.

"Being taken over right as we speak .The networks are all taking a break during lunch to do background on the battle, profiles of Washington, Clinton etc. At Overlook Hill, where they are broadcasting from, Sentinel's field cameramen are returning to get their afternoon assignments. When the action goes live again at 12:30 this afternoon, it will be our people in the booth as will be the cameramen who return to the field. Everyone has silencers and Overlook Hill is isolated. There should not be any problems."

"Excellent" replied Dayton. "Senator, you better get back out there and stay close to the President. He's a principal character in this drama – good or bad, I don't know – but he has to part of the action somehow during the coup. Call me on your mobile phone the moment you see anything odd. Understand?"

Hearing no questions, Dayton simply said:"Let's do it."

British Headquarters

Noon, June 28, 2008

There was no time for lunch at Clinton's Headquarters either, although Pamela was brewing some tea, while Clinton spoke by phone to his people spread across the battlefield. He finished at the same moment as she set out the refreshments.

"All seems ready" Clinton said as he took a seat across from her. There is nothing you and I can do now, but sit back and watch. The next few hours will tell the tale. I hope Ackerman's people get some good shots this afternoon. Sparrow has the message that will be broadcast to the American public at the end of the contest, explaining the country's new allegiance with Great Britain. Some key Americans, who have come over to our side, will address their constituents extolling the benefits of the new arrangement. The helicopters are all ready to fly the American leaders out to the Canadian wilderness. This will crush American morale. Tomorrow, when the markets open, the dollar will drop to nothing and the Butler brothers and the Canadian, English and German banks will make a killing. We will own America as well as it leaders. Much of its population will see that their bread is buttered with us and come over to our side. It will work. The fear of some of the minorities and the greed of some of the others will carry the day." Clinton said confidently.

The television in the trailer was on, as it had been all morning. It was the only way Clinton and Pamela had been able to see the re-enactment, holed away as they were .Now, the TV was telling about some of the American officers at the original Battle of Monmouth. The mention of a single name amid all the others caused Clinton's brain to snap to attention. The announcer had spoken of Washington's aide, Colonel Elias Dayton.

"Elias Dayton! That is the fellow you know. The one we met in London. That's where I knew the name. From the history of this battle. He was Washington's spy. He's been infiltrating us. He knows!"

A look of the horrible realization that his plan had been betrayed crossed Clinton's face at the same time that Pamela pumped two bullets into his forehead. Mary Blundell, Sir Henry Clinton's mistress of two centuries ago, had feared this day. She had promised General Washington a lifetime allegiance to the United States, despite her returning with Clinton's and their children to London. It was a pledge she kept, passing it down her female line. Their duty was to foil, not assist, the re-capture of America. Pamela had fulfilled that vow. It was little solace to her, however, as she sobbed uncontrollably over the body of the man she had just slain.

Monmouth Battlefield

Afternoon, June 28th

"Have a nice lunch?" the earphones asked the Dignitaries who had all returned to their seats in the grandstand in advance of the 12:30 deadline. "This afternoon's re-enactment begins with the British Grenadiers and the Queens Rangers mounting a charge against the American lines and pushing them back across Dividing Brook to Spottswood Creek. The fighting was fierce in the valley as well as in the woods and along the hedgerow. I believe the battle is to resume now."

As if on cue, chorus after chorus of rifle fire filled the air and the cloud of smoke reappeared. After several minutes of intense fire, a squad of some fifty or more mounted Queens Rangers appeared from behind a hillock and charged the Americans. The several students of the battle in the grandstands were taken aback by this change in the course of the battle. There had not been attack by a squad of dragoons in the original fight. However, most noticed, at least those with their binoculars trained on the action, only that the calvary charge was led by a bare-chested, war painted Indian. He aimed his men at a place in the American lines, along the crease of the valley, mid way between Combs Hill and Perine Farm Ridge. The Americans there, where the footing was better than on the sides of the hills, had begun an offensive and were hundreds of yards in advance of their comrades. However, when these venturesome Americans saw the enemy on horseback charging towards them, they panicked and fled back towards their lines. With a war whoop audible to those in the Grandstand, the war chief urged his men faster, onward for the kill.

What was not audible to the Dignitaries watching this all unfold, were the shouts of some of the Rangers to those in their ranks who did not know that the battle was about to become real:

"Get down. Those bastards are using live ammo. God

dammit. Get down. Take cover. Don't move. They are trying to kill us. They are using real bullets. Get down." Corporate America's representatives knew how to obey and they fell behind hillocks and other protections or just fell to the ground as if dead. The remainder of the line were Hays Rangers and they did not seek shelter. They knew exactly what to do against the charging Queens Rangers, led by their comrade Buffalo Hump.

The Comanches had a prize battle maneuver that Captain Jack Hays had learned and used himself against other Indians and the Mexicans. His descendant now, a century and a half later, was going to use it against the British. The Comanche strategy was elegant in its simplicity. Charge the pale face but then recoil, as if in fear, before their counter offensive, letting the center of the Indian line continue to collapse and fall back until the pursuing soldiers discovered themselves caught between two wings of Indians. Then, the flanking warriors meet, pincer like, at the enemy's rear and they all open fire on the enemy caught in the middle, as if in a bag. Hays had improved upon this stratagem by adopting the Apache method of attacking from ambush. Hays had stationed sharpshooters in the woods and along the hedgerow. They were to pick off the leaders of the charge as they entered the trap.

The plan worked perfectly. The part of the American line that was in advance of the rest fell back against Buffalo's Hump's charge and he led the Queens rangers literally into the Valley of Death. Moody and Agnew had already been shot from their horse by the sharpshooters by the time the rest of the squad realized they were being attacked from both sides and the rear. Quickly, those who had not been hit threw down their weapons and raised their hands in surrender. A cheer rang out from the Grandstand, without the Dignitaries there realizing that, unlike this morning, real blood had just been shed.

"Wasn't that exciting?" asked the ear phones, confused by the change in script, but too much the veteran commentator to reveal in by his voice ."It appears that this squad of British dragoons has been captured and will become prisoners of war. But, wait a minute, what do we have approaching us?" The voice was relieved. The action was returning to the script. "Some more of the British forces. I can see some Hessian uniforms among them."

Again, a student of history would have been surprised by this. At the actual Battle of Monmouth, the Americans had dragged pieces of artillery to the top of Combs Hill, where the Visitors Center now sits, and fired down on the British artillery below that had been supporting the British infantry's advance. But these were not Americans who were climbing the hill, but a force of nearly a hundred British Redcoats, Loyalists and Hessians, led by the Loyalist gnome Ralph Heuser. Unbeknownst to the Dignitaries in the Grandstand, they were become participants in the drama. It would all be on camera. Dayton had planned it that way. Even if he could not stop the British, he at least wanted the American public to see the coup take place, so that loyal Americans could react before the next series of British attacks which he knew would be forthcoming.

The British forces pushed their way through the "townspeople" and lined up in front of the grandstand. They pointed their muskets at the crowd.

"Ladies and Gentlemen. These gentlemen wish that all of you, except our Special Assistants, remain seated for a few minutes, while some preparations are made. Would the Special Assistants come forward please."

Nearly a hundred men and women got up from their seats and joined the British force in front of the grandstand. There was good-natured bewilderment in the stands. This had not been in the program. It was a surprise, but judging by the number of senators and congressmen, generals and governors and other leaders that were Special Assistants, the surprise had been long in the preparation.

When all had taken their place, the voice from the earphones resumed:

"There is to be a change in the Program. Today, the British and Loyalist forces will be successful. They will be the victors at the Battle and you will be their captives. This is quite authentic, I assure you. Please do not get up. It could cost you your life."

The recently elected Speaker of the House jumped up and began to yell "who is resp – " before the gargoyle shaped Heuser fired several shots into him. Bleeding, the punctured body of the leader of America's conservatives fell onto his neighbors, who started screaming. More shots rang out from Heuser forces as they tried to keep the panicked people in their seats. Then, the two Secret Service agents assigned to watch the President began shooting down at Heuser, his men and the Special Assistants. According to the plan, those two agents were to have been eliminated by two of the Molly Pitcher Brigade dispensing lemonade. Instead, the two would be assassins stood motionless, the barrels of Debbie Jean and Amelia's revolvers in their respective backs.

"Now" shouted Dayton into the earphones and the "townspeople" opened fire on Heuser and his men .They had not expected an attack from the rear and the "townspeople' modern weapons, hidden in the wagons, chewed the British and the Special Assistants to pieces before many had a chance even to turn around and return fire. Those that did lived only a few minutes more. Father McCullough and Senator Moriarity, both armed, were among the "townspeople". The Jesuit said to the Senator:

"Remember, Tullius. *Senatus consultum ultimum.*"

Moriarity nodded as he and the others continued fire into the bodies of their foes. No prisoners. The traitors must all be executed. No trial. They all must die now.

Lake Tahoe, California

July 4, 2028

Dear Son:

I picture you having read this long story up at the Cottage, sitting on that long dock into the lake. That is where I had received the commands of my forefathers that sent me on this remarkable mission. I am sure Tahoe is as lovely now as it was when I was man alive.

Let me finish the story and then make a demand upon you.

The English plot was foiled, of course, by our actions. The television camera had captured it all – the assault, the treason of a hundred American leaders and their death in the battle that followed. Papers found on Sparrow's body included a speech which, after the coup, was to have been read to the American people by the President of "New America", announcing its entry into the Commonwealth, of almost fifty other former territories of Great Britain, located all over the world. The evolution of New America was a recognition, Sparrow explained, that the rich "*haves*" were never going to share their wealth voluntarily, and in fact would do all they good to increase their booty and secure it in their sons, for generations to come. The "*have nots*" of varying descriptions, had to, once and for all, rid society of the "*haves*" in one action, like a fire that erases a forest, thus permitting competing trees to finally reach for the sun". Sparrow's also proclaimed a temporary coalition of minority and special interests groups, directed and assisted by Commonwealth and Great Britain, to run the country until general elections could be held in November 2008 or early 2009. Taxes were to be abolished and wealth to be re-allocated among the citizens according to need. Maximum incomes and net worth of families would be set and, anything in excess would be surrendered to the government for re-distribution to those who heretofore had been deprived of their fair share of America. A new plan of Union would be proposed which would assure that power and wealth would never again be concentrated in a small part of the population. The Plan would include separate states or homelands for qualifying special interests, as well as "mixed zones" for those who were prefer a more traditional life style.

With all the traitor "Special Assistants" slain, it took some weeks of investigation before any detailed explanation was released to the American people of what it had been that they had also witnessed on the television.

The version finally released was a limited one, meant to minimize the incident. A group of bitter Canadians, descended from Loyalists exiled after the American Revolution, had attempted a coup. They were assisted by traitors within the government, the hundred Special Assistants, who had hoped that the American public would flock to them, seeing as they were promising them the assets of the rich and powerful. Sparrow's speech was not proof that Great Britain was part of the plot. Indeed, Her Highness was shocked at the speculation. There was absolutely no reason to suggest either that the president of New America, who was to read the message, was either the current president or vice president, or, for that matter, any identifiable individual.

The investigation did not go far. It was in no one's interests. Clearly, many more were involved than just the Special Assistants. Whether the President, Vice President or whoever was involved was something those who sought healing did not want to know. The voice in the earphones maintained he read the script that John Sparrow had given him and no one seriously challenged him. Nor did anyone want to investigate what minorities had been involved and what had been the true involvement of the nations of England, Canada and Germany. The threat was over. There was nothing linking them directly and it was all better left undisturbed.

Some paid a price, of course. Hundreds of the enemy died and some of our own men as well. The Butler brothers and their team of British, Canadian and German banks and financial institutions did not fare too well either. Senator Moriarity addressed the nation that afternoon from the Battlefield. He assured the nation that the President was safe, that this lunatic fringe incident was over, and that he knew the American public would understand if they ended the TV transmission earlier than scheduled as people needed to get home and the FBI begin its investigation. He did such an excellent job of calming and comforting America that the next morning did not bring a collapse of the American markets as a coup would have precipitated. In fact, the Dow was up over a hundred points and the dollar markedly stronger than the day before, having just shrugged off a coup, without any apparent consternation .It was the Butlers who were wiped out – two centuries of wealth lost. Erik Ackerman lost also. His Anglophile public relations campaign, timed to peak at the Monmouth re-enactment, was promptly viewed as collaboration with the enemy. He fled to England where he sought political asylum. The Queen denied the application and Erik ended his own life, which every one thought an appropriate resolution.

Without an investigation, the Rangers were able to drop more or less out of sight. No one ever knew how we had defended the Republic. The Secret Service got the praise and they did not turn it down as undeserved. And that was good too. Remaining unknown to the enemy is still our greatest weapon. Father McCullough went back to the Bronx to Fordham to teach philosophy. Pamela, whom I had mistrusted at the end, returned to England but was forever changed by the experience. She never married and, with Harry Clinton's death, the Clinton line from Mary Blundell died out. Amelia did marry, the fellow Tom with whom she had been flirting in the last days of her undercover work. Linda and Elias stayed together. Of course, you know about your mother and me.

As I said, no one wanted too extensive of an investigation of the incident for fear that the exposures may lead to his or her own door step. Yet, those in power knew that only the tip of the iceberg had been viewed. The groups responsible for this treason, if they could not be punished, had at least to be repressed .There was to be no more opposition to the policies that Old Time America was forcing down the throats of the minorities ceased. Any one who protested was associated with coup attempt and John Sparrow's chilling speech about the minorities taking over American and redistributing the assets of the more fortunate. As result, society grew less tolerant toward anyone not willing to conform to what he was taught were American values. Those who disagreed were culled from the ranks of future leaders, sentenced to a second-class citizenship, until they or their children better understood what it was to be an American.

      How bad has it become? If you were caught with this manuscript as to how the New Order was formed, you would be killed and the document destroyed. But, the story must be told, so that liberty and self-government someday can be restored to the people. Father McCullough is ancient but still alive. Senator Moriarity is dead but has left children. You know them and Elias' children as well as the sons and daughters of the Rangers from Texas. You must get this manuscript to them and they must circulate it to those of like mind who want to restore our Republic. They know to expect you. The story must be told. America has a new enemy now --itself --and you and they must help her rid herself of it.

                 Love,

                 Dad

Other Heritage Books by Richard B. Marrin:

Abstracts from the New London Gazette*: Covering*
Southeastern Connecticut, 1763-1769

A Glance Back in Time: Life in Colonial New Jersey (1704-1770)
As Depicted in News Accounts of the Day

Going to Court in Texas: Riding the Circuit, 1842-1861

The Paradise of Texas, Volume 1: Clarksville and Red River County, 1846-1860

Passage Point: An Amateur's Dig Into New Jersey's Colonial Past

Runaways of Colonial New Jersey: Indentured Servants, Slaves,
Deserters, and Prisoners, 1720-1781

Other Heritage Books by Richard B. Marrin and Lorna Geer Sheppard:

Abstracts from the Northern Standard *and the Red River District [Texas]:*
August 20, 1842-August 19, 1848

Abstracts from the Northern Standard *and the Red River District [Texas], Volume 2:*
August 26, 1848-December 20, 1851